Arms of  Brothers in Arms
Love
Samantha Kane

ELLORA'S CAVE
ROMANTICA®
www.EllorasCave.com

LOVE'S STRATEGY

Valentine Westridge and Kurt Schillig are lovers, and have been since the Peninsular War when lonely young officer Valentine let himself be seduced by the equally lonely Kurt. Now they're back from the war and intent on beginning the future they dreamed of together, one that includes a quiet country estate, horses, dogs, children, and each other. Their plan, however, also requires a wife. At the suggestion of a mutual friend, Valentine and Kurt believe the financial security they can offer to impoverished widow Leah Marleston will help her accept the unusual sexual relationship they are suggesting.

Leah is at her wit's end, creditors having taken everything she owns to pay off her late husband's gambling debts. She must find a way to support herself and her two children, or be forced to marry her abusive and obsessive brother-in-law. In Valentine's and Kurt's arms, Leah discovers a passion she never knew existed. Brought together by necessity, bonded by desire, these three lonely people find themselves fighting against all odds for a love that was never part of their plans.

LOVE'S SURRENDER

Lady Vanessa Carlton-Smythe is from one of England's most well-respected families and the daughter of an earl. She has lived an exemplary life—the perfect daughter, the perfect lady. Until one Christmas Eve, when she meets two men who unleash her secret desires. She can't surrender her heart, only her body, and only for the next twelve days. After Twelfth Night, their affair must end and she will return to a life that is slowly suffocating her.

Veterans Nick and Oliver have been constant companions since Waterloo. They share everything, including women and a bad reputation. When Lady Vanessa catches them in a compromising position, they are seduced by the longing in her eyes. Cool, distant, unattainable—the more she protests, the more they want her. Vanessa's desires prompt the two men to finally give in to their feelings and become lovers. When desire becomes love, can they convince Vanessa to leave her privileged life behind and surrender to them forever?

An Ellora's Cave Publication

www.ellorascave.com

Arms of Love

ARMS OF LOVE
Samantha Kane

ᔓ

LOVE'S STRATEGY
~9~

LOVE'S SURRENDER
~107~

LOVE'S STRATEGY

ഌ

Acknowledgements

∞

I would like to thank my editor Raelene Gorlinsky for discovering me, supporting me and believing in this series. She has been a true partner in bringing the brothers in arms to life.

Thanks go to all the RWA authors and organizations that helped me with Regency research. Any errors contained herein, alas, are the sole responsibility of the author.

This book, like all that have come before, could not have been written without the support of family and friends. So…

…for Will, who wishes to be known from here on out as my Smokin' Hot Big Brother (SHBB), for being a font of historical and literary knowledge, and for his interest in all aspects of writing. And of course his SHW, Kathy (sorry, ladies);

…for my sister Jeri, who finally bought an e-book reader; and

…for my ever-lovin', who cooks, cleans, does the laundry and watches the hooligans so I can live the dream. He read this book approximately five hundred times, and only complained the last hundred. For that, rest assured, dear reader, he received more than a heartfelt thanks.

Chapter One

&

"Leah, there are two gentlemen here to see you."

Leah's blood ran cold at her mother's announcement. More? Were they never to leave her alone? She slowly straightened from where she was bent over tending the roses. February had been decidedly warm this year. She put a hand to the small of her back, realizing even as she did it that it wasn't her back that was really bothering her. She was just so tired. Tired of the incessant demands of creditors, and tired of trying to make ends meet as those same creditors relieved them of everything of value.

"Mama?" Her son Sebastian also stood up where he'd been playing soldiers with his younger sister Esme. Leah's heart contracted at the concern on his face. Ten was too young to carry such worry. She made a deliberate effort to lighten her features as she smiled at him.

"It's nothing, Bastian, just my poor old back aching," she told him lightly, making a face. "You wait here with Esme while I go see what these gentlemen want."

Her mother walked across the garden to join her. At Leah's comment she put a comforting hand on her daughter's arm. "They are not here about one of Thomas' debts, Leah," she said gently, and Leah's eyes inexplicably filled with tears.

"How do you know?" Leah was alarmed at the tremor in her voice. She had held herself together this long, now was not the time to fall apart. Although really, she thought irreverently, when was a good time to fall apart?

Her mother got a very self-righteous look on her face, almost militant. "I asked."

Leah gasped in horror. "You what?"

11

"I asked them," her mother repeated, her expression mulish. "I'll not have you bothered anymore by those rude upstarts strutting through here demanding their ill-gotten gains."

Leah closed her eyes in despair. "Mother, they have every right. All those debts were legitimately incurred by Thomas before his death."

"Gambling is hardly legitimate—" her mother began, but Leah cut her off.

"They are legally binding debts according to the laws of England, Mother, and as his widow I am legally bound to make restitution."

Marjorie must have recognized the soul-deep exhaustion in Leah's voice because for once she let the subject of Leah's late husband drop. "My dear, let me get rid of these gentlemen. You go upstairs and rest and I'll watch the children for a while."

Leah smiled at her mother. She could be a trial, but under it all Leah knew she loved her unconditionally. "No, Mother, it's best I find out what they want. You stay here with the children, and I shall return as soon as possible." She started to walk away backward, wagging a finger playfully at her mother. "And no more asking strange gentlemen if they are here to collect money, understood?"

* * * * *

Valentine stood next to the empty hearth, trying not to brood. He'd never even seen the widow, for God's sake, and here he was about to ask for her hand in marriage. It was insane, and it was demoralizing that he and Kurt had to resort to taking advantage of a woman in desperate straits in order to have the life they wished for.

He looked over at Kurt. Kurt glanced up and, quirking an eyebrow, curved one corner of his lips in an amused smile. "Try not to brood, Valentine," he admonished, his German accent subtly lending a continental flavor to his upper-class British tones. He unfurled his long, lean frame from the small parlor chair in which he had been resting. "You'll scare away the poor Widow Marleybone with that expression."

"I am not brooding. And it's Marleston," Valentine corrected with exasperation, "Widow Marleston. For God's sake, if you're going to make me marry her, at least get her name right."

Kurt shrugged. "She won't have it for long, so it's a moot point."

Valentine growled in frustration. "You don't know she'll say yes."

Kurt looked at Valentine incredulously. "Surely you jest? Based on what her mother said, she's in sore need of a hero right now."

"I do not in any way resemble anyone's hero." Valentine rolled his eyes at Kurt's exaggeration. "To the widow I'll more likely resemble a villain, here to take advantage of her straitened circumstances."

Kurt let his gaze wander slowly up and down Valentine's tall, muscular frame, and Valentine felt his cheeks heat at the other man's perusal. He looked guiltily at the door, hoping the Widow Marleston didn't appear while Kurt was devouring him with his eyes.

Kurt laughed at Valentine's look. "Sooner, rather than later, the sweet widow will figure out we're lovers, Valentine. I think it's best done right away, considering I want to be her lover as well." Before Valentine could answer Kurt continued. "As for what you look like," he paused, his eyes moving over Valentine again, "you are very desirable, hero or villain."

"Kurt," was all he said in an admonishing tone. Kurt merely shrugged expansively, in that purely continental way.

Valentine sat in one of the damned uncomfortable chairs that filled the parlor. He slumped forward and ran his hand through his hair. "I don't know whether I feel like the villain or the victim, Kurt."

"Darling Valentine, even Stephen agrees. She is English, and you have a much more respectable English background than I. She will feel more comfortable marrying you. It is a simple thing really, and meaningless in the long run. She will be wife to us both."

Valentine looked up at Kurt. "And if she says no?"

Kurt shrugged expansively again. "Then there are surely other poor widows in England who are desperate."

Valentine laughed. "Desperate enough to take on the two of us? I'm not so sure."

Kurt smiled wickedly. "Ah, *liebchen*, you underestimate my powers of persuasion."

Chapter Two

&

When Leah stepped into the parlor the two men inside rose from their chairs and turned to her. They were so handsome—tall, lean, muscular, and dressed very expensively. One was dark, his hair a deep brown and his skin an olive tone. The other was quite fair with blond hair and a creamy complexion. Leah had never known men such as these—wealthy and clearly privileged. She was minor country gentry, as Thomas had been.

The dark one stepped forward. "Mrs. Marleston?"

"Yes," Leah answered, wincing at the distrust in her voice that was second nature to her now.

"I am Mr. Valentine Westridge and this is Mr. Kurt Schillig," he said, indicating the tall blond with a sweep of his hand.

"How do you do," Leah said politely, never moving from the open door. "How may I help you?"

The two men exchanged a look that Leah found hard to interpret. Mr. Westridge spoke once again. "Perhaps this letter will help," and he pulled something from his pocket. Leah looked at it with distaste. All her late husband's creditors appeared with "letters".

She sighed. "I'm sorry, gentlemen, I really haven't anything left to pay you. All my worldly goods have been sold to pay previous debts I'm afraid. This house is not mine nor are any of its furnishings. You may choose to pursue this debt in the courts, but other than finding myself in debtors' prison, I'm quite sure that very little will come of it."

The dark, enigmatic Mr. Westridge turned red, with embarrassment, Leah wondered? Then the beautiful blond Mr.

Schillig stepped forward. How delightful, Leah thought irrelevantly, that this bad news was delivered by such gorgeous specimens of manhood.

Mr. Schillig took the letter from Mr. Westridge's hand and walked over to Leah. She automatically extended her hand to receive it, and he placed it there gently.

"You misunderstand, Mrs...my dear," he said quietly. His accent was quite lovely, actually. "This is a letter of introduction from a mutual friend, Mr. Stephen Matthews."

Leah was very confused now. "The Reverend Mr. Matthews?" she asked. Mr. Schillig nodded with a small smile. Leah was shocked to feel herself responding to that smile, responding to him as a man. She had felt dead, that way, for years now, since long before Thomas's death.

She took the note and began to read.

Valentine was eternally grateful that Kurt had taken over because Valentine was struck nearly speechless by the poor Widow Marleston. She was, well, perfect. The top of her perfect head reached Kurt's shoulder. That would put her just a little taller next to him. Her hair was a glorious shade of red gold, upswept to reveal a long, graceful neck and creamy soft skin. His mouth watered with the desire to taste that neck, just there where her pulse beat so swiftly. She was very curvaceous. It was obvious she was used to carrying more weight, however. Clearly her circumstances had taken their toll in more ways than the dark circles under her eyes.

The suspicion in her voice and matter-of-fact recitation of her desperate financial situation nearly made him act the fool. He was willing to do anything for her, to protect her, to possess her. He'd almost blurted that out, hardly the sophisticated approach he'd been practicing. Why hadn't Stephen prepared them? Passably pretty, he'd said with a sly grin. Valentine had taken that to mean barely tolerable. He knew now it had been Stephen's idea of a joke.

Valentine took several slow steps back, mentally and physically. He needed that distance to get his thoughts back in order. He came to rest in his earlier position, next to the hearth. The empty hearth now represented times the lovely widow had done without, had gone cold or hungry because she couldn't afford the basic necessities for herself and her children. Never again, he vowed. She and hers would never want for anything ever again. He looked away from the dark, cold fireplace and directly into the widow's eyes.

Kurt's heart was racing. This was not what he had planned at all, not at all. He'd planned on Valentine making a pleasant connection with a woman whom he married for the purpose of having children, and who married him for financial security. A woman they would share when the mood struck but who remained a firm outsider in relation to his and Valentine's close attachment. Instead, Valentine was stricken with love at the first sight of the lovely widow. Kurt himself felt something stirring in his chest, in the place he thought was so full of Valentine no other could find room there. She was beautiful, obviously courageous, and she possessed a certain dignity and self-assurance. She was a woman with few equals. The kind of woman a man like Valentine searched his whole life for and, once found, lived his whole life for. Kurt had trouble breathing as he tried to imagine what would happen to him if Valentine were to turn him away, if the lovely Mrs. Marleston refused Valentine's initial offer, refused Kurt.

He and Valentine had been together since one fateful night during the war, when Kurt was so desperately lonely and could no longer resist the temptation of the lovely young British officer whom he'd befriended. And Valentine, equally lonely, equally desperate, had let himself be seduced by the sophisticated half-German officer. They had found in one another the tenderness and passion that the war leached out of them, filling the empty spaces that the violence and bloodshed left behind. After the war it was only natural that they stayed together. Kurt couldn't even imagine life without Valentine.

Now he had argued and coerced Valentine into doing the one thing that might tear them apart. He'd forced him to fall in love with a woman and marry. He'd thought to give Valentine the one thing missing in their lives, children and the respectability of a wife. Valentine longed for the quiet life of a country squire and Kurt was more than happy to share that life and that dream. Valentine insisted he didn't need a wife and family to make him happy, that he was happy with Kurt. But Kurt knew Valentine better than he knew himself and he had set out to give him what he needed, just as he had endeavored to give Valentine everything he needed or wanted since their first night together. Old habits die hard, Kurt thought wryly as he watched Valentine watch the widow.

Kurt turned his attention to Mrs. Marleston and he felt his cock stir. If only she would say yes the three of them together would be glorious. Not just for one night, but every night for the rest of their lives. Kurt's eyes widened in shock. Perhaps this wasn't just Valentine's dream, but his as well. A dream that had taken root, he thought, when they'd heard their old friends Jason Randall and Tony Richards had taken a wife. According to Stephen, the ceremony had included all three, with Stephen presiding, and now the three were expecting a child. If they could have it all, why not Kurt and Valentine? Kurt took a deep breath, firming his resolve. Yes, indeed, why not?

When Leah's eyes met Mr. Westridge's she was shocked by the intensity of his gaze. Stephen Matthews' letter had simply said that he'd known both Mr. Westridge and Mr. Schillig during the war on the Peninsula, and they were both trustworthy gentlemen. He urged her to listen to them with an open mind and an open heart. That was all. He gave no indication of what they wanted from her. She had befriended the young and handsome vicar upon her arrival in Ashton on the Green, and she trusted his judgment. If he said she should listen to his friends, then she would. But what could they possibly want?

"All right, I've read Mr. Matthews' letter, and I'm more than willing to listen to whatever you have to say. But I'm rather confused. Pardon my directness, but what could two gentlemen such as you require from me?" She glanced at the two men and intercepted yet another cryptic look between them. Her suspicions grew when they both hesitated to speak.

Suddenly Mr. Westridge stepped forward again, as if to speak. Leah gave him an encouraging smile, but the words seemed to die in his throat. Slightly exasperated, she turned to Mr. Schillig.

He cleared his throat with a gentle cough before speaking. "We are, um, aware of your circumstances, Mrs. Marleston, and we are here to offer you an advantageous proposition."

Leah felt the blood drain from her face as her back went stiff. "I am not so desperate as to accept that kind of offer, Mr. Schillig. Good day." She turned to the door, furious with Mr. Matthews and these so-called gentlemen.

"Oh that was marvelous, Kurt. This is surely a more disastrous misunderstanding than the one I caused." Mr. Westridge's voice was agitated, but underlying it was amusement, and Leah whirled around to give him the dressing-down he deserved. Before she could speak Mr. Westridge held up his hands as if to ward her off. "No, no, truly you misunderstood. I, we, are not offering you...you *carte blanche*, Mrs. Marleston. Far from it. You can't think Stephen would condone that, do you?"

Leah was stopped short by his behavior and his words. No, she would not like to think the kind vicar would condone that, but she'd been dealt some harsh blows of reality in the last few years.

"Well, it is *carte blanche* of a sort, Valentine," Mr. Schillig said, "of your very generous fortune, and mine as well."

Leah found her gaze divided between them again as she tried to decipher that statement. She was having a hard time deciding whether to be angry or merely confused.

"Would you give me the courtesy, Kurt, of letting me negotiate my own marriage contract?" Mr. Westridge said tightly.

Leah's reply was arrested by that one word—marriage. She took two small steps back into the room. "You had best explain yourselves better than this. I will grant you but a few more minutes to make your business plain, or I will be forced to ask you to leave."

Mr. Westridge took a step closer, and Leah could see the determination on his face. "We are here to offer you marriage, Mrs. Marleston."

Leah was dumfounded. "Both of you? You are here to court me?"

"No, we are here to ask you to marry us," Mr. Westridge said earnestly.

Leah could not control the incredulity of her expression. "Did Mr. Matthews put you up to this? Is one of you to be the sacrificial lamb? I told him I would not marry him just to solve my financial difficulties. The same applies to any of his friends."

"Not one of us, Mrs. Marleston," Mr. Schillig said smoothly, "both of us."

"No, not both of us," Mr. Westridge seemed to be stammering. "I mean yes, both of us, but you will be my wife. And not lambs. Not sacrificial lambs. You see, we want to marry you. We need to marry you."

Leah's mind was reeling. "You both need to marry me? That's impossible. What on earth do you mean?"

Mr. Westridge sighed in frustration as he ran a hand through his dark hair, leaving unruly curls behind. "This is not going according to my plan at all."

Chapter Three

ဢ

Just then Mrs. Marleston's mother and children came through the door.

"Oh I'm sorry!" Mrs. Northcott cried. "I didn't realize you were still with your guests, Leah."

Leah. Her name was Leah, Valentine thought. It was lovely and suited the woman perfectly. He looked down at the children and suddenly realized if all went as he hoped they would be his children. The boy looked to be about nine or ten, a sturdy lad with a shock of red hair and blue eyes as suspicious as his mother's. The little girl couldn't be above five, with golden curls and blue eyes that nearly filled her face. He fell in love on the spot.

"Hello," Valentine said, bending his knees so he could look them in the eye. "I'm Mr. Westridge."

"Good afternoon, sir," the boy said stiffly. The little girl moved behind her brother and stuck her thumb in her mouth as she peeked out around his legs.

Valentine suppressed a smile. "And what are your names?"

The boy looked up at Leah, and she nodded. "I am Sebastian, and my sister is Esme." Then he looked pointedly at Kurt.

Kurt laughed, and Valentine watched everyone relax. Kurt's laugh often had that effect. It was low and deep and jolly. "I am Mr. Schillig. Do you speak German?"

The boy shook his head, and the little girl quickly pulled her head back behind his legs like a little turtle.

"Well, you shall soon." Kurt looked at Leah as he said it, and she frowned back at him.

"Are you a new tutor then?" Sebastian asked eagerly.

Leah stepped forward at that point and put her hand on Sebastian's shoulder. "No, dear, Mr. Schillig is a just a nice friend of Mr. Matthews. You know we can't afford a tutor right now." The crestfallen look on the boy's face endeared him even more to Valentine. How he would enjoy a son who loved learning.

"Mother, why don't you and the children have tea and then you can supervise Bastian's studies while this little one," she tapped a finger on Esme's not so hidden nose, "takes a nap." She turned to look at her mother. "I shall be in the garden with Mr. Westridge and Mr. Schillig."

"Is everything all right, dear?" Mrs. Northcott asked.

"Yes, Mother, everything is fine. These two gentlemen are friends of Mr. Matthews. He sent a letter of introduction with them."

"Oh, well, that's nice."

Mrs. Northcott was clearly confused, but Leah did not enlighten her. Instead she turned to Valentine and Kurt. "Shall we, gentlemen?" She indicated the door, and Kurt gestured that she should precede them. Mrs. Northcott and the children moved out of their way. Valentine saw Kurt give little Esme a broad smile as he left, and the tiny tot popped her thumb out of her mouth to return it.

* * * * *

Once in the garden, Valentine made several attempts to begin the conversation. Kurt tried to let him lead in this, but despite his usual disarming charm Valentine seemed to stumble over the words.

"You see, Mrs. Marleston," Valentine began, "sometimes in war, well, men you see," he paused and coughed, "that is to say, companions can often become, um…close, you see."

Leah looked at him in confusion. "Well, of course men are drawn closer by their shared experiences, Mr. Westridge."

"Yes, yes, exactly," Valentine said happily. "And Kurt and I are, er, were, brought closer by the war."

"So you were there with Mr. Matthews?" Leah asked helpfully.

"Yes, quite right, we were." Valentine was less sure of himself here. It was obvious Leah had no idea what he was talking about.

Valentine heaved a giant sigh. "Mrs. Marleston," he began again, stopping in the path beside a small rustic bench, "Kurt and I both wish to marry you because of our relationship."

Leah and Kurt had stopped as well, and Leah looked back and forth between the men. "Because you are friends, you both wish to marry me?"

"Exactly," Valentine said, nodding his head decisively.

As Leah and Valentine stared at one another uncomprehendingly, Kurt rolled his eyes and shook his head. He stepped forward until he was next to the two of them, the three forming a loose triangle on the path.

"May I?" he asked Valentine politely.

"Oh, oh yes, please do," Valentine said, and he began to step back. Kurt stopped him with a hand on his arm.

Kurt turned to Leah, who smiled at him encouragingly. She was really quite breathtakingly lovely, Kurt thought, smiling back. And she was so sweet to poor tongue-tied Valentine.

"We," Kurt began, waving a hand between himself and Valentine, "are lovers and have been since the war. We wish to take a wife—a woman who will be wife to both of us, in and out of the bedroom. We wish to have a family. We want to have all this with you and still remain lovers."

* * * * *

The sound that escaped Leah's throat at the blunt declaration could best be described as a squeak. She stumbled back a step, suddenly lightheaded.

"Mrs. Marleston!" cried Mr. Westridge as he rushed forward to grab her arm. "Let me help you," he implored, guiding her gently to the bench directly behind her. When her knees hit the bench she sat with an undignified thump.

Mr. Schillig came up next to him with a look of concern. "I can see that I've alarmed you, and that was not my intention. I apologize."

"No, no," she said, and her voice sounded weak. She cleared her throat. "I mean, I'm...startled. This is hardly something I'm familiar with. I've heard stories, of course, but I've never met anyone who...that is...does Mr. Matthews know?"

Her face felt pale and she found it hard to look at Mr. Schillig. Mr. Westridge sat down next to her on the bench, and she thought it showed remarkable restraint that she didn't immediately throw herself off in an attempt to get away from him. These were such intimate subjects; she'd never had such a conversation before.

"Yes, Stephen knows," Mr. Westridge answered her. "He was the one who suggested we seek you out when we told him what we were planning. He said you were a sensible woman who would see the advantages in the situation."

"What advantages?" Leah asked, still reeling in shock. Mr. Matthews knew, and he apparently approved!

"You are in desperate financial straits, Leah," Mr. Westridge said gently. She knew she should chastise him for using her Christian name, but it sounded so wonderful when he said it. "I can help, we can help. We are both wealthy men. We can pay your debts, take care of you and the children properly. We can give you a fine home, and clothes, plentiful food, fires in the winter and a name to go with them—my name."

"Mr. Schillig—" she began, but he cut her off.

"Kurt, I am Kurt," he said softly, smiling at her. Her stomach flip-flopped at the thought of using his given name. Then Mr. Westridge picked up her hand and slid closer on the bench.

"And I am Valentine," he said, kissing her hand. She felt the kiss deep in her core, and the fire there surprised her. She couldn't possibly be considering this, could she?

She looked back at the tall blond man before her. What she had to ask wasn't the most pertinent question, considering all they had just told her, but it was the one uppermost in her mind. "Kurt," she tried out, speaking his name slowly. She was rewarded with another smile. "What do you hope to gain if I am to take Mr. Westridge's name?" At the slight squeeze of her hand she looked over. "Valentine, I mean Valentine." He also rewarded her with a smile.

"I will gain the same thing as Valentine, my dear, a wife and a mother for my children."

Leah's stomach clenched at his words. No, not her stomach, lower, and it was desire that caused it, not disgust. Her eyes widened as she stared at him, and she saw his brown eyes deepen with an answering desire as if he knew what she was feeling.

"This is something you would gain from also?" he asked, his accent more pronounced than it had been before.

"Perhaps," Leah said slowly. She licked her lips nervously, her agitation growing when she saw Mr. Schillig, no Kurt, watching her mouth avidly. "But you must understand this is quite shocking to me. May I...may I inquire as to why you wish to take a wife?"

"Of course, Leah. I'm sure you have a great many questions." Valentine sighed. "I know this is highly unusual—" Leah couldn't stop her snort of disbelief at the sheer magnitude of that understatement. Valentine merely arched a brow and continued, "But we hope you will at least consider our proposal." He rubbed a thumb over her knuckles, and Leah was startled to realize he still held her hand. She gently disengaged it and folded both hands in her lap. Valentine smiled a little wistfully and moved away from her slightly, clearly recognizing her need for more space. If she was to seriously consider their proposal she needed her mind unclouded by the nearness of him.

Leah waited patiently for him to answer her question. Valentine leaned forward and placed his elbows on his knees, staring at the ground between his feet. "I mentioned earlier that Kurt and I were on the Peninsula together." He looked over at Leah and she nodded.

"Yes, with Mr. Matthews."

"Yes, with Stephen and so many others. Do you know much of war, Leah?" The question was asked casually but Leah noticed Valentine's hands were fisted.

"No, Valentine," she said softly, "not about the most recent I'm afraid. My own personal struggles took precedence over the news sheets."

Valentine looked away and nodded. "That's as it should be." He sat back on the bench and looked at Kurt. "So many times we wondered, why are we here? What are we fighting for? What are our friends dying for? As young men you think it's glory, heroism. But if you are there long enough you realize it's more important things. Things such as honor and tradition, a way of life. You begin to categorize what's important to you." He looked at Leah. "Do you understand?"

Did she understand prioritizing your life? Oh yes, she understood. She'd had to do that many times over in the last few years. What was more important, the financial security of marrying an abusive bully, or shielding her children from the abuse they might suffer? And after that decision, what was more important, having new clothes to maintain a veneer of respectability and perhaps catch the eye of a potential husband, or making sure her children ate well? And on down the line, each decision altering her future until this moment. And now yet another decision stood before her. As with all her past decisions she would try to make a well-informed choice, but it would always, as in everything she did, be what was best for her children. They were the most important thing to her, their welfare her main concern. Valentine tipped his head to the side and regarded her quizzically and she realized she had not answered his question. "Yes, I understand having to choose what is most important to you."

Kurt spoke from where he had moved to lean against a tree a few feet from the bench. "Not so much choose as decide. I do not believe we were in the same situation as you, Leah."

Leah blushed as she saw the sympathetic look in his eyes. "No, Mr. Schillig. In my experience, men rarely are." Kurt merely nodded once in acceptance of this fact. Still looking at Kurt, Leah asked, "And what was important to you?"

"Valentine," was Kurt's simple reply.

Leah turned to Valentine, who was smiling wryly. "He over-simplifies. We were important to one another, the most important thing, to be accurate. But we did not just want to survive. For many who were there too long survival became the main goal. But I, we, wanted more. We wanted a future."

"Yes," Kurt whispered, and when Leah looked Kurt had turned away to stare off into the hills in the distance.

"We thought very hard about what kind of future we could have, and what kind of future we wanted. As you can imagine in our situation the two are not always the same." Valentine's voice held a bitter note.

"That is true in most cases, Valentine, not just for you and Kurt." Leah's tone was bitter as well. How well she knew the taste of future happiness turned to ashes in the ruin of what was, never to experience what could have been.

"Of course. I guess we tend to forget everyone else's troubles in light of our own. I'm sorry, Leah."

Leah smiled wryly. "Yes, well, I've been rather wrapped up in my own troubles as well. Please, go on."

Valentine sighed. "There's not much more actually. What I wanted was a simple life. I wanted a nice country life, a modest home, a pretty wife, children. I want my most pressing concern to be whether it is hunting season or racing season. I want a pack of dogs, a houseful of children, and with all that I want Kurt."

"And Kurt?" Leah asked, watching the blond man slowly turn to look at her.

"I have already told you. I want Valentine."

"I see." And truly she did. They were obviously in love with one another, a concept that should have shocked her but didn't. She understood that when your back was to the wall you could no longer lie to yourself. You found yourself doing or saying things you never would have before, but when you had nothing left to lose what did it matter? When these two men were faced with death on a daily basis they looked at one another and with perfect clarity realized this is what I want, this is what I'm fighting for. And they survived. Leah had survived for her children.

"Why me?" Leah's question wasn't vanity. While she knew she was attractive, she had almost nothing else to recommend her to a potential mate. She was worse than penniless since she had unpaid debts, she had two young children, and no familial connections. "Surely there were women in London, women with whom you were acquainted, that you could have asked?"

Kurt straightened from the tree. "We did. They would not have us."

"Oh I beg your pardon," Leah said, startled and a little embarrassed. "I just assumed I was the first woman you had approached." She smiled self-deprecatingly. "But now I understand, I am a last resort, am I not?"

Valentine looked very embarrassed but Kurt eyed her with approval. "You understand then where we are coming from, yes?" Kurt asked shrewdly.

"Why would they not have you?" Leah wanted to know if there was more objectionable about the two gentlemen than the fact that they were lovers. She surprised herself with that thought. Already, knowing them for less than an hour, the thought of their being lovers was unexceptional to Leah. Now that she understood them a little at least, she found them to be amiable and honest, so far. Coupled with their expensive attire and their assurances that they were financially able to take care of Leah and the children, these attributes far outweighed their unusual relationship.

Valentine looked uncomfortable. "They naturally objected to our relationship. We first approached a woman I knew before the war. She is now a widow and we'd hoped that being sexually knowledgeable she would understand that our being lovers was not the horrific act so many people decry. Particularly since she knew me before I met Kurt, we thought she would be tolerant. As we mentioned, we are both wealthy men and we thought that in exchange for our wealth she, or someone like her, would accept both of us."

Kurt snorted in disgust. "She swooned with horror and then shrieked for us to get out. She did not wish anyone to know that we thought she would accept such an 'unnatural', to use her word, relationship. Her vitriolic response made us more cautious. We waited months before approaching another woman. Valentine courted her singly, although I saw her and spoke to her numerous times. Only when she had softened toward Valentine and indicated she would be receptive to a proposal did we go to her and explain our situation. She didn't bother to swoon. She slapped Valentine's face and accused me of being a vile seducer of good Englishmen, and threw us out."

"But she would have taken you, Valentine? On your own? I'm sure many women would. Why didn't you pursue that avenue, marrying individually and still keeping Kurt, separate from your marriage?"

Valentine was shaking his head before she even finished speaking. "No, that is not what I want. I want Kurt. Everything else is for us, not just for me." The glance the two men exchanged made Leah catch her breath. Valentine looked back at her and sighed. "After her dismissal I confided in Stephen Matthews." He smiled at Leah. "He said he knew the perfect woman for us. I begin to believe he was right."

Kurt chuckled. "At least you have not been slapped yet."

"So merely on Mr. Matthews' recommendation you traveled all the way from London to ask me to marry you?"

"Oh no, I'm sorry. I haven't made myself clear," Valentine said, sitting up straighter with a frown. "You see, that's why I was talking to Stephen. We have purchased Cantley House, just a few miles from here. Certainly your familiarity with the area will help greatly as we settle in here."

"Cantley?" Leah asked, surprised. "I didn't know." She chewed her lip nervously. "So you will be living here then?"

Valentine smiled to take the sting out of his words. "Yes, that is our plan, to live quietly in the country as I mentioned before. Not only is Stephen Matthews a friend of ours, but the Duke of Ashland is also a friend. Since Ashford Park is just on the other side of the village, Cantley was a very good find for us."

"So my location was paramount in your decision?"

"No." It was Kurt who answered. "Your financial difficulties were. We thought that you would have too much to gain by wedding us to object to our relationship."

Leah was taken aback at his honest answer. It was rather demoralizing that her greatest asset to these handsome, wealthy war heroes was her destitution. Unfortunately they may be right. Leah thought it was time to get down to business. "I should like some particulars about the marriage settlement."

Valentine's smile grew until it lit up his entire face. "Does that mean yes?"

"I would be a fool to agree before I hear the terms."

They settled down to talk money. Leah ruthlessly crushed the sentimental part of herself that longed for romance and courtship. She wasn't a young girl anymore. She had a family to provide for. She would never leave herself open to the kind of poverty she had suffered since her first marriage. She had been young then with no father or male relation of any kind to ensure a proper marriage settlement. She was older and wiser now.

When they were done Leah was stunned. Valentine and Kurt weren't just wealthy. A friend of theirs was a genius at investing and they had a combined income that was an outrageous amount to someone in Leah's situation. They wished to settle a goodly sum on Leah. She would have the interest of that money to spend as she saw fit. They also promised her extra pin money quarterly, and a generous dowry for Esme and school fees for Bastian.

"Will you marry us, Leah?" Valentine asked as she sat there in shock.

"I…" she hesitated, unsure of how to answer him. Would the money make up for the potential ostracism she and the children might bear should Kurt and Valentine's relationship become public knowledge?

"Please, Leah," begged Valentine, "don't decide now. Take some time to think about it, please." He raised her hand and kissed it again, and Leah's eyes were pulled back to him. He kept her hand pressed lightly to his lips as he spoke. "From the first moment I saw you, I knew you were the one. We were meant to be together, Leah. Just give us a chance to prove it."

His words touched her in a way she hadn't been moved since Thomas had courted her. She felt desirable, pretty, young again. And of course, she *was* in desperate financial straits. She looked at Kurt standing there, his eyes again burning with

31

desire. "All right, Valentine," she whispered. "I will give you a chance."

* * * * *

"Then you will come for dinner tomorrow evening," Valentine said for the third or fourth time. Leah smiled. The three had walked around the cottage to where the two men had left their horses beneath a large tree. The small Northcott home had no stables or grooms.

She had agreed to think about their proposal and to meet them the following evening with an answer. "Yes, I'll come. We'd heard that someone had purchased Cantley, but I didn't know it was you."

Kurt stood in the sunshine, his blond hair gleaming. "We were friends with the late brother of the Duke of Ashland during the war, and have come to know the new Duke quite well. His companion, Mr. Haversham, is also a close friend. With Stephen here as well, it seemed the ideal place to settle down."

"So you own the estate?" Leah asked, intrigued. If she were to marry Valentine, would they live in Kurt's home? It was all so confusing to her.

"I have an investment in it," Kurt said, still smiling. "Most of my future is invested in Valentine."

Leah blushed as she was reminded of their relationship. Of course Kurt would consider Valentine's home his own. "I'm sorry, I didn't realize..."

Kurt placed his fashionable beaver hat on his head at a rakish angle. "This is all very new to you, my dear. No apologies are necessary."

Valentine drew her attention when he stepped forward. She turned and found a small frown on his face. "Leah, you must understand that Kurt is, and will always be, a major part of my life, and soon, I hope, yours. We will always live together, travel together. Kurt and I are as close as I want you and I to be someday."

Kurt came up behind Leah and raised her hand for a kiss. "As close as we will all be, soon," he said quietly. Valentine moved closer to her and turned the hand Kurt held to place a kiss upon her palm. "Yes, exactly," he whispered, looking into her eyes.

Leah felt overwhelmed by the two strong male bodies. They enclosed her in a cocoon of heat and male spice, and she couldn't stop her mind from picturing the three of them entangled in the sheets of some large bed. Her mind blanked after that, however. Exactly how did three people make love? She had never minded the marriage act with Thomas; it was nice to be close to someone that way. Kurt moved in closer and she felt his breath on her neck as Valentine touched the tip of his tongue to her palm. Good Lord, Thomas had never done that. Leah's lips parted as she found herself having trouble breathing. Her pulse was racing, and she felt hot and heavy and wet between her legs. She thought perhaps making love with Valentine and Kurt would be more than nice.

Chapter Four

ഇ

"Leah?" The male voice was harsh and Kurt's back instantly stiffened. He moved directly behind Leah protectively and when she turned toward the voice her nose was very nearly pressed into his chest. She looked up at Kurt in alarm, mixed with a little annoyance, but he merely raised an eyebrow at her and turned to look over his shoulder at the owner of the voice.

"Leah, what is going on?" The man was short and somewhere between forty and fifty. He had a portly stomach bulging out his too tight, garish coat, and the overall effect was almost comical. Kurt was not fooled, however. That voice indicated this was not a man to take lightly.

"Please, Kurt," Leah whispered, "that is my brother-in-law, Sir Horatio Marleston."

Kurt noticed that Valentine had moved to his side and was facing Sir Horatio.

"Remove yourselves from Mrs. Marleston immediately," Sir Horatio said, and it was apparent from his tone he was used to being obeyed. The look of disbelief on his face when neither Kurt nor Valentine moved made Kurt smile coldly. Leah was pushing ineffectively at his chest, and he gripped her upper arms gently to still her.

"May we help you?" Valentine asked politely, and his tone also spoke volumes. It clearly marked Leah as theirs.

"I demand you release Mrs. Marleston immediately," Sir Horatio replied.

"Oh really, gentlemen." Leah's tone was exasperated, and she gave Kurt a shove that had him stumbling back a step in surprise at her strength. "Sir Horatio is my brother-in-law."

The man reached out as if to grab her arm, but stopped at a sound from Valentine somewhere between a growl and a dangerous purr. Kurt stepped back next to Leah's side.

"Sir Horatio, may I present Mr. Valentine Westridge and Mr. Kurt Schillig," Leah said to him, indicating first Valentine and then Kurt with a graceful gesture of her hand.

"How do you do," Kurt said coldly without a smile. Valentine merely nodded once in acknowledgment.

"What is your business with Mrs. Marleston?" Sir Horatio's voice was still demanding, and the unspoken message was that he had the right to ask. Leah apparently thought differently.

"That is not your concern, Sir Horatio," she said almost as coldly as Kurt. "To what do I owe the pleasure of your visit?" It was subtle, but Kurt caught the sarcasm in her voice.

"I wished to call on you," Sir Horatio told her imperiously, "as I do several times a week." He looked pointedly at the hand Kurt had placed possessively on Leah's elbow.

"Thank you," Leah said automatically. "Mr. Westridge and Mr. Schillig were just leaving. You may go in and see the children."

"I have no desire to see the children," Sir Horatio replied unhesitatingly. "They should be in the schoolroom at this time."

Kurt's estimation of Sir Horatio dipped even lower at his quick dismissal of Bastian and Esme.

Leah sighed in exasperation. "You know I cannot afford a tutor right now, Sir Horatio, and Esme is too young. My mother is with Bastian working on his lessons right now and will not mind the interruption."

"I will wait for you," Sir Horatio said, and Kurt could practically see his feet planting themselves more firmly on the ground. Kurt turned away, dismissing Sir Horatio, and he heard the older man gasp in outrage.

35

"We shall send the carriage for you tomorrow at, shall we say seven, then?" Kurt asked Leah. He'd deliberately brought up their plans in front of Sir Horatio. The more obvious they made their claim on Leah, the better as far as he was concerned. She was theirs, by God, and he dared any man to question it.

His own possessiveness concerning her was slightly shocking to him. He could understand Valentine's immediate connection to her, he was a man of deeply felt emotions. But Kurt was usually ruled by the physical, not the emotional, except when it came to Valentine. Was he merely reacting to Valentine's desire for Leah? Or to his own newly acknowledged desire for a home and children? Or was it the woman herself? Leah answered his question before Kurt could examine his motives too closely.

"Yes, yes that would be fine," Leah said in a rush, and Kurt saw her cheeks were pink with embarrassment.

"Mrs. Marleston is already engaged for tomorrow evening," Sir Horatio interrupted harshly.

Leah's eyes flew to the older man and narrowed. "I'm sorry, Sir Horatio, but I'm afraid I do not know of a previous engagement."

"That is why I came to see you, my dear," Sir Horatio said with a tight smile. "You did not respond to my note, and I came to make sure that you were going to accompany me to dinner with the Dowager Duchess."

"I received no note," Leah said coldly. "I'm very sorry, but I am promised to dinner at Cantley tomorrow evening."

"Cantley?" Sir Horatio exclaimed, surprised. "Are you the new owner then?" he asked Kurt belligerently. "I had heard the new owner was a war veteran and a close personal friend of the young Duke." His tone indicated disbelief that Kurt could be either.

"I am the new owner of Cantley," Valentine informed him in glacial tones, "although that description does indeed fit Mr. Schillig as well."

"Welcome," Sir Horatio replied, although his tone was anything but. Kurt nearly laughed aloud. It would seem most of this conversation was being conducted in what remained unsaid.

"Sir Horatio's own small estate lies to the east of Cantley, with a portion of the Duke's land in between." Leah supplied the information in a matter-of-fact tone, but Kurt saw Sir Horatio's eyes narrow at her use of the word small. "Next to the Duke, he was the largest landowner in the area until your arrival. There are mainly small holdings here, for the most part."

"I shall have the Dowager Duchess send you an invitation to her dinner tomorrow evening," Sir Horatio told them smoothly. "I'm sure she would have invited you had she known of your arrival in our little society here."

Valentine answered. "As you are aware, we are engaged for tomorrow evening with Mrs. Marleston. Do not trouble yourself on our account."

Kurt grinned broadly at Valentine's blanket dismissal of Sir Horatio's challenge to their plans with Leah.

Sir Horatio turned to look at Leah. "This way Mrs. Marleston will not miss out on dinner at Ashton Park, a supreme privilege, I assure you." Kurt bristled at the man's tenaciousness.

"A privilege I'm sure we shall all enjoy when the Duke is in residence," Valentine smoothly countered, upping the ante in what had become almost a game.

Sir Horatio's smile became even more strained. "The Dowager Duchess would be very unhappy were Leah not to attend tomorrow night. She has taken quite an interest in her future, you know. The Duchess does not believe a young woman like Leah should remain unmarried so long after my brother's death." The unspoken implication was that the Dowager wanted Leah to marry Sir Horatio. Kurt shuddered at the thought.

Leah had clearly had enough and intervened again. She frowned at Sir Horatio. "My married state is not the concern of the Dowager Duchess." She then turned to Kurt and Valentine. "I am so pleased that you came to call today, gentlemen," she assured them firmly, "and I shall see you tomorrow evening."

Valentine looked as if he were about to argue, but Kurt laughed out loud, stopping him. "Yes, my dear Mrs. Marleston, it has indeed been a pleasure." Kurt gave a low courtly bow to her and kissed her hand lingeringly with a twinkle in his eye. Leah laughed in return, which only made Sir Horatio glare harder.

Leah turned to Valentine and held her hand out. He hesitated. "Now, Valentine," Kurt said chidingly and put his arm around Valentine's shoulders companionably. "We are being given our *conge*, my dear. Kiss the lady's hand, and we shall dream together of seeing her again tomorrow night."

Valentine obediently took Leah's hand and sighed. He held her small hand in both of his and raised it to his lips almost reverently. Barely moving away from her hand, he raised his eyes to her face. "I'm sorry, my dear. I did not mean to cause you distress. We shall take our leave. Until tomorrow then."

* * * * *

After Valentine and Kurt rode away, Leah drew a deep breath and turned to Sir Horatio. She was glad she'd had a minute or two to get herself under control after Valentine's goodbye. His eyes had burned so hot when he'd looked at her over her hand she was surprised her hair hadn't gone up in flames. Good heavens, what was wrong with her? She'd never reacted to a gentleman like this before, and today she'd behaved like a wanton with two! And it was impossible to think Sir Horatio had not noticed.

Indeed his visage was nearly purple with rage. "You behaved shamelessly, Leah, and I will not have it." His voice was trembling with his anger. "I will not have my future wife acting the slut with men such as that."

"I am not your future wife." Leah felt her own anger rising. "Men such as what, Sir Horatio? Wealthy, well-mannered, admiring? Which do you find so offensive?"

He was breathing hard he was so angry. "I saw the way the foreigner touched Mr. Westridge. You do not know of such things, Leah, and must be guided by me. They are not the sort of gentlemen who should be calling here at the cottage."

"They had a letter of introduction from Mr. Matthews, and by your own admission are close personal friends with the Duke. I hardly think that puts them beyond the pale, Sir Horatio." She allowed a little of her impatience with his attitude to show in her voice. It was a mistake, and she should have known better. His hand shot out and grabbed her arm, bruising in its grip. She gasped and he tightened his hold. She couldn't help comparing his brutal hold to Kurt's gentle one earlier.

"We have an understanding, my dear. If you wish me to take care of those mewling brats of yours, you will submit to me and be my wife."

Tears came to Leah's eyes as the pressure on her arm became excruciating. She knew from experience that he would leave bruises behind. "We do not have an understanding of any kind," Leah gasped, trying to pry his fingers off her. "You do not have the right to touch me. You have asked for my hand and I have refused you, repeatedly."

"No one else will be offering, Leah, I've made sure they all know you are mine. You have been mine since that fateful day Thomas had to beg my sufferance and moved you all into my house because of his ruin. I do not know why you fight it. Even Thomas accepted it, didn't he?" She could not get his hand off no matter how hard she tried, and he dragged her closer to him until she could feel the press of his erection against her hip as she tried desperately to turn away. "If you cannot take care of those children, I shall petition for guardianship. Do I make myself clear? Do you wish to lose them? Do you wish your mother to lose her home? With one word to the Duchess I can make all of that happen. You will send your regrets to Mr. Westridge and accompany me to Ashton Park tomorrow night, and we will announce our engagement. Do you understand?"

"Leah? Are you all right?" Her mother's voice was slightly tremulous, and Leah looked at her in relief where she stood outside the cottage door. "It is late, Sir Horatio. The children and I are waiting dinner on Leah. I'm sure your business can wait until tomorrow." Mrs. Northcott was frightened of Sir Horatio and his rages, with good reason. She'd seen Leah after several of them, when Thomas was still alive but too busy gambling to notice or care what his brother was doing to his wife. Leah knew it took a great deal of courage for her to confront him like this, and she had never loved her more.

"Yes, Mama, I'm fine. I'll be right there. Sir Horatio was just leaving." She pulled ineffectually at her arm, and after a moment of struggle Sir Horatio let go and Leah stumbled back.

"Do not forget what I said, Leah," he warned her, turning to leave. "I shall come to collect you in the carriage."

And I shall not be here, Leah thought defiantly, glaring at his back. *I will be with Valentine and Kurt, securing a future for myself and my children.*

* * * * *

That night Leah had trouble sleeping. It was hardly a surprise. She went over and over her discussion with Valentine and Kurt. She meticulously outlined, in her head of course, the advantages and disadvantages of such an alliance. In number the disadvantages were greater—ostracism, potential arrest for Valentine and Kurt if their relationship was exposed, always being wary, hiding the nature of their arrangement.

She couldn't help but dwell on the most selfish disadvantage, the fact that she would never be loved. Oh she believed that they liked her well enough, they certainly desired her. But Valentine and Kurt were in love with one another. She was merely a means to an end for them. After their meeting today she didn't think it immodest to say a pleasant means, but a means nonetheless. There was still a foolish, womanly part of her that longed to be loved. She wanted flowers and poems and declarations of undying love. She'd never had that and she wanted it so much it was an ache in her chest. Worst of all she thought she'd want it from Valentine and Kurt, and she knew she'd never have it. And there was the biggest disadvantage of all, a lifetime spent longing for what they could never give her.

While the advantages were not as numerous as the disadvantages, in importance they far outweighed them. Number one of course was the financial security marriage to them would provide. After three years of hellish poverty Leah couldn't underestimate the importance of that. The future provisions for the children were generous in the extreme and would alleviate a great burden from Leah. She also believed marriage to Valentine and Kurt would be pleasant. They were handsome, intelligent, kind and clearly heroic if one took into account their war service. No, marriage to men such as they would not be a burden. And she knew, after only a few short hours of acquaintance, that they would never abuse her or the children. Which brought her to what might be the greatest advantage — freedom from Sir Horatio.

Leah had been so young when she married. Thomas Marleston had been a pleasant enough young man, with a modest income, a sunny disposition and lively conversation. Leah had not loved him, but to her young mind marriage represented security, something that had been lacking in her life since her father's death. It took less than a year for Thomas to grow bored with his young, pregnant wife and seek his pleasure elsewhere. He did not, however, turn to another woman. Instead he turned to gambling. At first he was moderately successful, returning home with little trinkets for Leah purchased with his winnings. Most of the money was reinvested, as he called it, by paying for his next gambling venture. For the next several years it was a constant cycle of up and down, selling her jewels one day to buy new the next.

When Leah became pregnant with Esme she pleaded with Thomas to stop gambling. They had enough at that point to live modestly on the interest of what money they had, supplemented by a small allowance provided by his older brother. Sir Horatio had inherited all of their father's wealth and remained unmarried. Thomas had ignored her pleas, eventually returning home only rarely in order to avoid her censure. One year before his death Thomas had finally gone bankrupt. He'd pleaded for his brother's assistance, and Sir Horatio had allowed them all to move into his home. It was supposed to be a temporary arrangement, but Leah soon realized that Thomas had no intention of ending his gambling. Now that he didn't have to worry about providing for Leah and the children he gambled more heavily and lost just as heavily. He was never home and it didn't take long for Sir Horatio to start abusing Leah.

It started slowly, an unpleasantly firm grip on her arm if she displeased him in some way. Perhaps dinner was not to his liking, or the manor was not clean enough. He was always taking her to task for her inability to control the servants. Then he began finding fault with her person. She was too fat, too thin, too lazy. Her clothes were too tight, she was too loose, and so on. She complained to Thomas when he finally came home after the abuse had gone on for several weeks, escalating each time. His response had shocked her.

"Well, it is his household after all, Leah. You must strive to please him."

"But, Thomas, he is hurting me. Do you understand? Look, look at this bruise." She showed him her arm, which had a dark purple bruise around the wrist. When he'd twisted it she'd thought at first he was going to break it. "And last week he slapped me. Slapped me, Thomas! In front of the servants." Leah started to cry.

"Oh stop your sniveling, Leah. Many was the time my mother could hardly walk for the beatings she took from Father, and she never cried about it. She just tried harder to please him. I expect Horatio is like him, he has a very exacting nature. He expects the best from everyone. You'll simply have to adjust." He'd left the next day.

Leah's greatest fear was for the children. She almost never allowed them to leave the nursery, and took to hiding there herself when she could. Thank God Sir Horatio had little use for them and preferred they stay out of his way. Leah had no one to turn to, nowhere to go. Her mother was scared of Sir Horatio and had very little income from her father's estate. With no brothers or cousins or uncles, Leah was adrift, drowning in fear for herself and her children. Then Thomas was killed, knifed to death in an alley in a London stew.

The day after Thomas' death Sir Horatio had finally pushed Leah into running. He had casually mentioned that they would marry as soon as her period of mourning was over.

"W-what?" Leah had stammered, her heart trying to pound its way out of her chest.

She had thought Sir Horatio a devil before, but the words he spoke then chilled her to the bone. "I knew as soon as Thomas came to me with his gambling debts that it was only a matter of time before his unsavory pastimes resulted in his death, either by someone else or his own hand. I've bided my time this past year, Leah, although both you and I know you became mine as soon as you entered my house. Why else do you think I've been training you this past year? All my little corrections, my dear, were in order to prepare you to be my wife." He had reached out and touched her cheek affectionately, as if his abuse had been a sign of his esteem for her. "You are quite pretty, Leah, and I shall not be embarrassed to take you as my wife. Society will think it only proper that I care for you and my nephew and niece now that Thomas is dead. I'm sure you will strive to please me." Her mind had flashed back to that earlier conversation with Thomas, and his casual mention of his mother striving to please his father, and being beaten down for her efforts. Horatio had pulled her to him roughly and kissed her, all open, slavering mouth and Leah had wanted to retch, too frightened of him to shove him away. It was he who finally pushed her away. He was panting with lust and Leah's stomach heaved. "You have teased and provoked me for a year, Leah, but I have resisted. I took care of you and the children and Thomas' debts and now I shall have my due. As soon as your mourning is over, we shall wed. Then you will truly be mine."

Leah had managed to convince Sir Horatio that until their marriage she should stay with her mother. Now that she was a widow and he an unmarried man it was improper for her to live with him. She had gotten unexpected support in this from the Duchess of Ashland, a dragon for the proprieties and a woman on whom Sir Horatio fawned. And so Leah had escaped with the children to her mother's. For the last three years Sir Horatio had been browbeating her into marrying him. She adamantly refused. He had cut off all her funds and refused to satisfy Thomas' debts, leaving them to her. He had recently coerced most of the shopkeepers in Ashton on the Green to refuse her any more credit. Leah believed the Duchess was behind that last attempt to force her hand.

By the time Valentine and Kurt had arrived with their offer Leah was at her wit's end. She had had no idea how to support her family, no place to run, nowhere to turn for succor. Now she had them. Whether or not they realized it, they were a dream come true.

Chapter Five

ℛ

"Are you awake?"

Valentine's whisper came to Kurt in the dark, and he felt the heat of his body as Valentine rose on one arm to lean over him. He opened his eyes and saw the broad outline of Valentine's shoulders limned in moonlight.

"Yes, I'm awake." He had been. It was impossible to sleep, knowing that tomorrow their entire future could change, probably would change. There was no reason why Leah should not agree to marry them.

Valentine lay back down next to him, not touching him. "You haven't really said anything about her," he said quietly, the statement clearly meant as a question.

"Neither have you." Kurt tried to keep his tone neutral.

"I like her. I think I could love her." Valentine's tone was equally neutral.

"Good." Kurt tried not to let his tangled emotions show.

Valentine sighed. "'Good'. What does that mean?" He rolled onto his side facing Kurt. "Isn't this what you wanted? Talk to me, Kurt, tell me how you feel."

Kurt's frustration escaped when he answered. "How do I feel? How the hell am I supposed to feel, Valentine? You tell me you could love someone else. Where does that leave me?" He raised both hands and scrubbed his face impatiently. "Damn. This is not turning out at all as I had planned."

Valentine gave a mirthless bark of laughter. "I was just telling myself that," he commented wryly. "Exactly how is this not like you had planned?"

It was Kurt's turn to sigh. "I believed that you could marry a woman without having strong feelings for her. I see now that that would be impossible for you. I didn't realize that I would feel so jealous."

"Kurt," Valentine said, and Kurt felt his hand smooth over his chest. As always, Valentine's touch made Kurt's heart pound and his cock began to grow hard. "You know I love you. I will always love you. Whatever feelings I have for Leah won't change that."

Kurt put his hand over Valentine's as it ran slowly up and down his chest and skimmed over his taut stomach. "I know. I'm just confused. I want you to be happy."

"*You* make me happy," Valentine told him quietly then leaned over and kissed Kurt's shoulder. Kurt's breath hitched. "I want you," Valentine whispered.

"Yes," was all Kurt said, and Valentine rolled on top of him. Lust surged through Kurt like a bolt of lightning as soon as he felt the hot slide of Valentine's skin against his own from chest to foot. Valentine wedged himself between Kurt's thighs, spreading his legs almost as if he were a woman, and then with a subtle undulation he brought their two hard cocks together. Kurt's breath hissed out as he thrust up with his hips.

"This is where you are, Kurt," Valentine told him, his lips barely touching Kurt's as he spoke. He levered himself up on his hands, forcing their cocks even closer together, and Kurt moaned. "Here, in my bed, in my arms." Valentine began to rock his hips into Kurt, creating a heated pressure and friction of cock on cock. "You're mine and always will be."

"Yes, Valentine, yes." Kurt couldn't remember wanting Valentine this much ever before, as if he would die if Valentine didn't fuck him soon. "Kiss me, Valentine," he pleaded, and reached up a hand to clutch the back of Valentine's head and pull him down.

Valentine chuckled darkly. "You want me desperately, don't you, Kurt?" He didn't wait for an answer. Instead he swooped down and captured Kurt's mouth. The kiss was instantly hot and demanding. Valentine invaded his mouth, tasting, licking and biting. It was a kiss meant to inflame, and it did. Valentine moaned into his mouth, and Kurt knew he was as much a victim of the kiss as Kurt.

Valentine broke away from the kiss with a groan. "Christ, I think I can't want you more, and yet each time I do. I can't imagine this changing between us, Kurt. Bloody hell, I want to fuck you." Valentine ran his lips down Kurt's jaw and neck and then bit the strong tendon of his shoulder gently. Kurt groaned.

"Yes, baby, I love to hear you. Tell me what you want, Kurt." Valentine scooted down and his teeth grazed Kurt's hard nipple before his tongue began to lash it. Kurt moaned loudly, knowing how much Valentine loved to hear him during their lovemaking. The more he could make Kurt moan and groan, the more he liked it. Valentine was a very vocal lover as well. Almost every one of Kurt's moans Valentine answered with one of his own.

"I want to fuck," Kurt gasped as Valentine began to suck his nipple vigorously. "I want your cock in me tonight, Valentine. I want you to own me, to control me, to fuck me hard and fast."

Valentine moaned and gave Kurt a series of light bites across his chest to his other nipple and began to suck that one as deeply as he had the other.

"*Meine Gott*," Kurt moaned, clutching Valentine's head to him. "Yes, suck harder, darling, suck me everywhere."

"Christ," Valentine muttered after he pulled away, "yes," and he moved lower, sucking and nibbling Kurt's stomach. He licked the length of Kurt's cock, and Kurt cried out wordlessly. When Valentine took the hard, throbbing erection into his mouth, all Kurt could do was sob his name over and over. Valentine worked his mouth down to the root of Kurt's cock, not easy since he was large and wide, but Valentine had years of practice.

He savored the salty taste of Kurt's precum in his throat then he sucked deeply on Kurt's cock, and slowly pulled his mouth down and off. Kurt moaned incoherently, his head thrashing on the pillow. Valentine moved his mouth down and gently licked the soft expanse of skin between Kurt's cock and his sac, then bit it ever so softly, causing Kurt to shiver and moan yet again. God he loved that sound. It made his own cock throb and he felt it leaking. He licked again, this time lower, over Kurt's balls and then across and into the sweet, tight hole he wanted so badly. Kurt thrashed and begged, "Please, Valentine, please."

"I can't wait anymore, Kurt," Valentine growled. "I'm so hard to fuck you I ache."

He needed Kurt in a way he never had before. He needed to show him how much he loved him and wanted him. Usually it was Kurt making love to Valentine with his mouth and his hands, but tonight he had to make Kurt understand how important he was to Valentine, that there would always be a place in his life and heart for Kurt. Loving him was like breathing to Valentine. It was essential, it gave his life meaning. This is what he wanted to share with Leah too, and he knew he could, that they could.

"The next time I do this, Kurt," he told him as he climbed back up his body like a predatory cat, his voice rough, "Leah will be here. She'll be watching us." Kurt's back bowed as his hips thrust up and Kurt gave a guttural moan. "Mmm," Valentine purred, "you like the sound of that, don't you?"

Kurt was breathing heavily, his eyes shut tight when Valentine crouched above him face-to-face. "Open your eyes and see me," Valentine whispered, "really see me."

Kurt's eyelashes fluttered, and his gaze was unfocused when he first opened his eyes. Then he looked into Valentine's eyes for a long minute.

"I see you," he said quietly. "You are the same, the same man who has shared my bed for years."

"Exactly," Valentine whispered again. "The same man who loves you. You will lose nothing, Kurt, by letting Leah in. You will only gain. You will win another lover, another person who will need you and love you as I do."

"Ah, *liebchen*," Kurt sighed. "I am afraid. I am afraid of changing everything. I am afraid to love her because I think I could."

Valentine smiled and then lowered his head and kissed Kurt softly. "I'm counting on it," he told him. "Now roll over so I can fuck you."

Kurt rolled over eagerly. He loved being fucked as much as he loved to fuck. He loved everything about his physical relationship with Valentine. He couldn't help wondering if he would love to fuck Leah as much.

"On your knees, Kurt," Valentine ordered roughly, grabbing Kurt's hips and pulling him up. Kurt came easily to hands and knees and spread his legs to make room for Valentine between them. Suddenly he felt Valentine's mouth on his ass, licking at the tight bud there, first the broad flat of his tongue and then the tip teasingly dipping in. He gasped. Oh God, this was one of his favorite things, his favorite way for Valentine to prepare him to be fucked.

"Valentine," he moaned, pushing his ass back in Valentine's face. He was rewarded by a swift, hot stab of tongue delving into him. Kurt bit his lip as the pleasure coursed through him. With the next invasion of Valentine's tongue Kurt threw back his head and groaned loudly and deeply. Valentine's chuckle sent a wave of sensation into the sensitized ring of muscles he was working with his mouth, and Kurt suddenly couldn't stop shivering. He was aching with want as he was stretched to take Valentine's cock.

"I need you, Valentine," he groaned, "I need your cock so badly. Fuck me now, please."

Valentine couldn't help but smile as he heard Kurt's plea, and he knew it was a wicked smile. He loved nothing better than to reduce Kurt to begging. His cock was so hard it was resting high and long against his stomach. He could feel precum leaking from it. He couldn't resist one last thrust of his tongue deep into Kurt's channel, swirling it roughly. Kurt loved this so much Valentine had once made him come from nothing but a tongue fuck. He pulled his tongue out slowly, and Kurt groaned. He gave one or two small bites to the puckered skin there, then rose on his knees behind Kurt, his hands on Kurt's ass, spreading him wide.

Valentine looked down and very carefully pressed the tip of his leaking cock against Kurt's back entrance, spreading the precum from his cock around the lip of the hole. "Tell me what you want, Kurt."

"I want you," Kurt pleaded, "I want your cock in my ass." Without preamble Valentine thrust his thumb into Kurt. "God, Valentine! Now, fuck me now," Kurt cried.

Feeling that Kurt was ready, Valentine pulled his thumb out, making Kurt moan. "Mmmm," Valentine purred as he pressed just the tip into Kurt's ass. "It's so good, Kurt. You're so hot and tight tonight, and you want me so badly. I want to fuck you slow and deep so it lasts." His words were accompanied by his slow press deeper and deeper into Kurt, who bloomed beneath him, his ass welcoming Valentine like the familiar lover he was.

Valentine had to stop speaking as he was overwhelmed with sensation when he thrust the last few inches into Kurt. Kurt's ass was so tight and Valentine was so hard it felt like his cock was being strangled and he loved it. He groaned and thrust his hips shallowly several times, making room for his cock deep in there, stretching Kurt a little more before he began to fuck him hard and deep.

Valentine ran his hands over Kurt's ass and up his back to his shoulders. He stretched himself out against Kurt's back, spreading Kurt's legs wider and pushing him down until

Kurt's head and shoulders were on the bed, his buttocks tucked in tightly against Valentine's hips, Valentine's cock still buried to the hilt. Kurt groaned and shuddered, and Valentine felt an answering shiver race up his spine.

"I want to fuck you like this for Leah," Valentine whispered. "I want her to see how beautiful you are, how much you like it. I want you to teach her how to suck a man's cock, and how to take one in the ass."

Kurt fisted his hands against the bed and a small whimper escaped him at the same time Valentine felt his muscles tighten around his cock.

"You want her here, don't you?" He continued to whisper roughly as he rose to his knees again behind Kurt and grabbed his hips. He pulled his cock out of Kurt's ass slowly, then thrust back in hard and deep. Kurt thrust back against him moaning. "You want her to watch me fuck you. What else do you want?"

Kurt was breathing heavily, his cheek pressed against the bed, his hands opening and closing. He groaned as Valentine pulled out and thrust in again.

"I want to fuck her," Kurt gasped. "I want to fuck her while you fuck me. I want to taste her pussy first, while you lick my ass, then I want us all to fuck."

Valentine's stomach clenched at Kurt's words, and he couldn't control himself. He thrust hard and fast and deep into Kurt three, four, five times. Kurt's arms were stretched above his head, his ass meeting Valentine's hips thrust for thrust. Kurt was panting and his head was twisting back and forth against the covers. He was the picture of sexual submission as he let Valentine fuck him ruthlessly, and Valentine gloried in it.

"I want to suck your cock while she sucks mine," Valentine rasped, as he slowed his thrusts, still going deep. "I want to do it outside, in the garden, where anyone could walk by and see us. I could lie down on the bench there, and you can kneel over my face while Leah lies between my legs, and I want to taste your cum in my mouth as I come in hers."

Valentine's words made Kurt shiver and moan, and he felt his ass tighten around the long hard cock fucking him. His climax was building, his balls were high and tight and tingling with the need to come.

"Fuck me hard, Valentine," he groaned out, "I'm going to come. Fuck me hard and come with me."

Valentine complied and Kurt met him thrust for thrust, loving the feel of the hard cock going deep, the slap of hips against ass. When Valentine fucked him like this he hit a spot inside that felt so good it almost hurt. Suddenly Valentine thrust deep and stiffened behind him, holding his hips still in a bruising grip as he cried out. Then Kurt felt the hot wash of his seed inside him, and Kurt came and came, his hips jerking against Valentine's hold as he felt his own release on his thighs and stomach.

Kurt lay replete on the bed, boneless and unable to move from his kneeling position. Valentine lay curled over him, breathing heavily, his stomach and chest plastered to Kurt's back with sweat and heat. These moments were almost as sweet as the fucking to Kurt, when Valentine was so exhausted from loving him and yet wouldn't let him go.

"So you think it will be even better with Leah, yes?" Kurt asked teasingly, his voice still shallow and his breathing fast.

Valentine laughed weakly from behind him. "Better than perfect? No. Just a different kind of perfect, I think."

"Yes," Kurt slowly agreed, thinking back on the fantasies he and Valentine had just shared. "I think so too."

Chapter Six

ॐ

Leah nervously smoothed the skirt of her gown with shaking fingers as the carriage rolled to a stop in front of Cantley. She took several deep breaths, and when the footman opened the carriage door she was ready.

She had been impressed with Valentine's carriage and was equally impressed with Cantley. While not a palatial estate, the brick and stucco two-story home was obviously large, and on the outside it was well maintained. In the fading light Leah could make out both formal and informal landscape elements that even in their winter state were quite lovely. A fountain lay idle in the center of the gravel roundabout in front of the house.

She took the outstretched hand offered by the young footman. Leah had been impressed by her first encounter with some of Valentine's and Kurt's servants. They were everything that was proper in their manners and behavior. Leah was relieved. She hadn't known what to expect. This was so far out of the realm of her experience. Her stomach was in knots from excitement and trepidation.

Her perusal of the house was cut short when the front door opened to reveal not a servant but the master himself. Valentine stepped out under the portico and smiled welcomingly. "Mrs. Marleston," he said warmly, and Leah was glad he'd used her proper title and surname in front of the servants. She didn't want there to be more talk than necessary in the neighborhood.

"Mr. Westridge," Leah answered a little shyly, "it's so good of you to have me here."

Suddenly Kurt was at the door behind Valentine, grinning wickedly. "Why, Mrs. Marleston, as soon as we met we knew we must have you here as soon as possible."

Leah didn't miss the innuendo in his remark and she felt her cheeks heat.

"Kurt," Valentine admonished gently, but Leah could see the twinkle in his eye and her heart raced. "Come in," he invited, holding out his hand, and Leah stepped forward. When their hands met, Leah's gaze flew to Valentine's. Had he felt it too, she wondered, that wonderful hot slide of awareness? It felt as if the earth shifted just slightly, and Leah thought, *my life will never be the same again.* As she walked through the door and Kurt closed it behind her it all felt so right it almost frightened her.

"Leah?" Kurt asked quietly, stepping closer and laying a hand on her arm. "Are you all right?"

"Oh yes," she replied with a tremulous smile, "yes, I'm all right."

After the emotional undercurrents of her arrival, the evening progressed rather banally. They had a sherry before dinner and idly talked of the neighborhood — who was who, and who Kurt and Valentine should meet. The only thing that distinguished this dinner from any other Leah had attended was that it was just the three of them. When they went in to dinner Leah found that Valentine was sitting at the head of the table, she was sitting to his right and Kurt was directly on her right. She was a little disconcerted to be surrounded by them, but as dinner progressed with normal light conversation Leah relaxed.

"Tell us about yourself, Leah," Kurt asked after the last dish had been removed. The men opted to take their port in the dining room with her. She declined their offer of a glass and settled on another sherry. With her before-dinner drink and wine with dinner she was feeling very relaxed.

"Oh I'm very boring. My family is country bred on both sides. I grew up about thirty miles from here, in Sedgely. Our house was half the size of this one, and the grounds not nearly so impressive. My father was a kind, forgetful, playful man who adored my mother. His death in a hunting accident was a tragedy she never recovered from." Leah sighed. "I guess I haven't either."

Kurt was sitting forward, his arm leaning on the table, his chin in his hand. At her remark he reached out and brushed a stray lock of hair behind her ear and Leah shivered, her nipples puckering in awareness much to her surprise. She had never become aroused from such an innocent touch before. She immediately put down her sherry. Clearly she'd had too much already.

"I'm sorry, beautiful Leah." He smiled at her shiver. "Tell us about your marriage."

"My marriage," Leah mused. "Well, because we were alone, I think I married too young. I was only nineteen when I accepted the first offer made to me. Thomas Marleston was a good catch for a country-bred girl with very little dowry and no connections." She shrugged, not wanting to reveal the harsh and sometimes ugly aspects of her marriage. "We had two children together in a few short years. Thomas began to gamble irresponsibly, he died in rather mysterious circumstances, and I came to live with my mother."

Both men regarded her silently for a moment. In her nervousness Leah forgot her earlier decision not to drink anymore and she took a sip of her sherry.

Valentine sighed. "I think there is a great deal there that you are not telling us," he chided gently. "Why?"

"I don't know," Leah answered evasively. "My marriage was no different from hundreds, thousands, just like it."

"It was very different," Kurt argued, "because it involved you."

Leah blushed, and Kurt's fingers were suddenly there on her hot cheek, brushing the overheated skin softly. "So shy," he murmured. "Why are you here, Leah?"

She blinked rapidly several times, trying to focus on his abrupt question.

"Because you asked me?" she offered helpfully.

Valentine laughed at her response. "We did. But why did you accept?"

"I thought you wanted my answer," Leah said in confusion.

Kurt's fingers had moved from her cheek to her neck and were now smoothly brushing back and forth along her collarbone, which was exposed by the fashionably low square neckline of her pale violet gown. Leah's breath hitched in her throat.

"Tell us your answer," Kurt encouraged her, his voice a low seductive purr.

Leah cleared her throat delicately, almost overwhelmed by the desire to take Kurt's hand and press it firmly against her breast, against the hard aching nipple there, tingling with the feel of Kurt's soft caress. She looked over at Valentine, unsure of how to progress. If she was to marry Valentine, shouldn't he be the one touching her first? He was sitting back in his chair, the very picture of wealthy, self-satisfied complacence. The description made Leah smile, and Valentine tilted his head inquiringly. Leah answered before he could ask the question.

"I was thinking how self-satisfied you look, very opulent and indulgent." Valentine looked momentarily taken aback and then his laugh joined Kurt's deep chuckle.

"I look that way because that's how I feel." Valentine leaned forward, bracing both elbows on the table, and held her gaze, his face serious. Gone was the stammering lover of yesterday. "I love watching Kurt's hands on you, watching you respond to his touch. I can see your breathing getting just

56

a little ragged, your pulse quickening in your throat, and it makes me want you both."

Leah became conscious of the things Valentine described, her breathing and her heartbeat, and both increased as his words sank in and Kurt's caresses became bolder. His fingers were now running lightly over the soft swells of her breasts above her neckline. Shivers raced across her sensitized skin at the feather light brush of his fingers.

"You haven't answered us, Leah. Tell us, will you marry us?" Kurt's tone was casual, almost disinterested, but one look in his eyes dispelled that notion. His gaze was intense, pinning her to her seat.

Leah made sure to make eye contact with each man as she gave her answer. "Yes, I'll marry you."

For a moment Kurt's hand stopped caressing her and he held it tightly in a fist before relaxing it again and resuming his gentle torment. Valentine leaned back in his chair with a relieved smile.

"Thank God," Valentine said with a shaky laugh. "We weren't sure, we couldn't be sure, and the uncertainty has been killing us."

"Really?" Leah asked, proud of how calm she sounded. Inside she was a bundle of nerves over the realization that she had just committed herself to these two men for life, and she knew so little about them. "By my being here I thought you'd have figured out my answer." She glanced at Kurt and smiled. "In spite of what you might think, I don't generally let men fondle me at the dinner table."

Both men laughed, but the atmosphere had changed subtly. Kurt suddenly ran his fingers down over her breast and her tight nipple, and Leah couldn't stop a little gasp from escaping.

"You say yes without knowing what we'll ask of you." Kurt's eyes rose from her breast to meet hers. "Perhaps you should wait until you've sampled our lovemaking before making a final decision."

The thought had Leah's heart racing and her eyes went wide. "Now?" she squeaked, and winced at how panicked her voice sounded. "I mean, here?"

"Kurt—" Valentine began, but Kurt cut him off.

"Yes now, although not necessarily here in the dining room." He cut his gaze to Valentine. "It's best to find out now if she likes it, Valentine, rather than after the wedding, when it will be too late if she finds it's not to her taste."

Leah's eyes were darting back and forth between them, her mind a blank as to what she should say. If she said no, they might think she was not willing to share a bed with them both, and their offer may be rescinded. If she said yes, she was committing herself to this marriage of three, a relationship that flew in the face of everything society dictated was right and proper. For God's sake, her *husbands* would be each other's lovers, were lovers now. A day ago the idea was inconceivable. Now it was her future. And even more surprising was that the idea didn't scare her as much as it ought. In fact, it didn't scare her at all.

She'd had a marriage condoned by society, a good marriage by their standards, and it had been only tolerable at the best of times and a nightmare when Thomas had been gambling and Horatio had stepped into the void with his cruelty and possessiveness. She knew in her heart these two men were nothing like her dead husband and his brother. They would never be cruel and hurtful or neglectful.

Leah pulled her mind back to the conversation and suddenly realized Valentine was stammering in his endearing way again. Apparently he'd taken her silence as a denial. Kurt had retreated into himself, his face unreadable. Already Leah knew this was how they both responded to adversity. It was amazing how much she did know about them already, after knowing them only a day. How had she become so comfortable around them, so attuned to their feelings and desires? A sudden irrational thought brought her up short. Perhaps she'd always known. Perhaps she'd been made for these men, for this life, and she'd only been waiting for them to find her. She smiled at such a fanciful thought.

"Valentine," she said quietly, "the answer is yes, to the marriage proposal and to Kurt's suggestion. He's right, we need to find out if we are all comfortable with the arrangement before we make it permanent."

Her statement silenced both men, Valentine in shock and Kurt in assessment. "Are you always so practical?" Kurt asked her.

She had to smile. "About most things, yes, although it would seem there is very little of the practical about what you ask of me."

Valentine cleared his throat and stood. "Well then, I guess, would you like to go upstairs?"

Before Leah could answer him Kurt spoke. "I think it would be best if we went into the drawing room. The servants will talk already, but we should not give them more ammunition."

"Of course, of course," Valentine said abruptly, shaking his head at his own poor suggestion. "Not the bedroom. Of course."

Leah placed a hand on his arm. The heat and hardness of his muscled forearm beneath her palm had her sex clenching in anticipation, and Leah felt her mouth tilt in that age-old secret woman's smile. "Valentine, it's all right, relax. I'm nervous enough for us all." She took a deep breath and jumped off the precipice. "You see, I have absolutely no idea what…or…or how…" She trailed off, embarrassed again. "I know I want to, I think, but I'm not sure what I want to do." She scrunched her nose, a habit left over from a shy youth. "Does that make sense?"

At her admission Valentine's nervousness disappeared. He got up and pulled out her chair, lending a hand to help her rise. "In that case, let us go so we can show you."

Chapter Seven

∽

The walk to the drawing room was as excruciating as it was exciting. Valentine held her hand on his arm, his thumb stroking over her skin like a kiss. Kurt followed behind, a hot, imposing presence stalking them. Leah's skin felt overly sensitive, as if she could feel their eyes and their breath caressing her. It was her vivid imagination, she knew, but it was thrilling just the same. She'd never been so aroused in her life, and they'd hardly even touched her yet.

Kurt gently closed the door behind them and Leah heard the lock snick into place. She waited for the fear to come, but all she felt was excitement and arousal like a buzz in her head. Valentine brought her over to the settee. He turned her to face him, still standing, and kissed her on the cheek. The kiss spoke more of carnality than camaraderie. "What do you wish to know?" he asked her, his nose trailing softly over her hair and then down to her neck where he buried it in the curve of her shoulder. Leah felt a soft hot swipe of his tongue on her tendon there, and froze for a moment before heat sizzled along her nerve endings, straight to her sex where a dull insistent throbbing commenced.

Kurt walked over and took his place behind Leah, only this time he pressed close against her, touching from his chest against her back to the hard ridge of his cock along the top curve of her bottom. He leaned over her free shoulder and whispered in her ear.

"What do you want to learn first, Leah love? How to fuck two men at once? Or how men make love? Would you like to watch Valentine and me fuck each other?"

Leah moaned, she couldn't help it. She had never heard such talk before in her life, and definitely not directed at her. Vague, unbidden images of what he described flashed in her mind, and her body temperature rose until she felt flushed and out of breath.

"Fuck?" she whispered. "Is that what it's called?" Valentine's hands slid down from her waist and around to gently squeeze her buttocks, and Leah's legs became weak. She sagged slightly between them, and Valentine's hands tightened while Kurt's hands gripped her waist high, nearly touching the bottom curve of her breasts. She found herself wishing fervently that he would touch them, fondle them. She suddenly realized her acquiescence had little to do with practicality and everything to do with a primal kind of desire she had never felt before. She wanted them, really wanted them.

"I can see we'll have to teach you the vocabulary of love, my dear," Valentine told her in between placing light kisses on her neck and shoulders, making her tremble in pleasure. "Making love is also called fucking, although not in polite company." The last was said with more than a trace of amusement. "Did your husband never use words on you?"

"Use words on me?" Leah's voice was low and halting as she felt Kurt's hands begin a slow inexorable glide up to her breasts. He covered them, cupping and molding them in his big hands, and Leah gasped as her back arched. She'd never dreamed a man's hands there could be so exciting.

"Words to arouse you," Valentine explained. "Hearing the words can be almost as exciting as the act itself." Valentine leaned back and watched Kurt caressing her breasts, and Leah became more aroused, the act more carnal just because Valentine watched. "I love watching Kurt touch you. You have beautiful breasts. I want to see them naked, I want to suck and lick them, and watch Kurt take your nipples in his mouth, nibble them and tongue them."

"Oh dear God," Leah groaned. Valentine's words made her sex clench yet again and her breasts literally ache for what he described.

"Do you see?" Valentine whispered. "How the words can enhance your pleasure? You like them, don't you?" His voice was knowing, the question rhetorical. Leah's pleasure was obvious to all of them, her mounting desire like a wave of heat surrounding them.

Kurt's clever fingers found Leah's aching nipples and plucked them roughly, making her shudder as the sweet sting traveled directly from her breasts to her woman's entrance. "You are too desirable not to fuck, Leah," Kurt whispered from behind her, his breath hot and moist against her nape. "Your body is crying out to be taken, it wants a hard cock, doesn't it? But we'll do it your way, Leah. Whatever you want, tonight. Tell us what you want."

Leah was swamped with want, she couldn't make her mind grab onto any one thing. She had so little experience, and just a few minutes with these two incredible men had shown her there were pleasures out there she had no notion of. She leaned her head back in agitated surrender, and it lay on Kurt's shoulder as Valentine took advantage and feasted with lips and tongue on her exposed neck.

"What do you want, Leah?" Kurt's voice had become synonymous with temptation to Leah. He was the devil whispering of her fall from grace, and all she could do was follow him to her downfall.

"I don't know," she panted, her breath hitching on a sob as Valentine's kisses went lower and he licked a path across the upper slopes of her breasts. "I don't know! Thomas...it was never like this, never. He came at night, in the dark, he put it in me and he left. What is this? What are you doing to me?"

"We're making love to you, Leah, properly, the way a woman like you should have it. We're worshiping your beautiful body, loving you with words and touches. We will fuck you properly too, in the light with hot, sweaty, naked bodies straining together and cries of ecstasy. This is what we offer you. Take it, take us. Love us, Leah, and let us love you."

Kurt's impassioned promises beat against all Leah's fears, conquering them. They called to her most wicked fantasies, ones she hadn't even known she had until yesterday. "Yes, yes, please," she cried out, "that's what I want, oh God, yes, please."

At Leah's reply, Kurt stepped back and she felt him loosen her dress. He pushed it down to her hips as Valentine stepped back to give him room. Once the men's heat and hardness was no longer pressing on her Leah was able to think a little more clearly. She allowed them to take her dress off, but then she stepped to the side, away from them.

"You," she told them, her voice trembling, "I want to see you both. I've never seen a completely naked man. I want to see what I'm getting."

Valentine was taken aback by Leah's request. She'd seemed overwhelmed by their passionate lovemaking. He'd assumed she'd let them take the lead. He liked her courage, and her obvious desire for them pushed his own arousal higher, hotter. He didn't want a meek bedmate, he wanted a woman who equaled him and Kurt in passion. She appeared to be a lady who, despite her lack of experience, knew what she wanted after all.

Valentine shrugged off his coat without even answering her. Her eyes widened and she licked her lips. The shine of the moisture on her lips made Valentine's mouth water. He unbuttoned his waistcoat quickly and threw it off, uncaring where it went. Leah's breathing was ragged. Next came his neckcloth. He realized his own breathing was less than steady as he absorbed Leah enjoying his hasty undressing, her desire growing. He watched her eyes dart to Kurt and he followed her gaze.

Kurt had also begun undressing and Valentine waited until the other man caught up with him before removing anything else. When Kurt's neckcloth floated to the floor beside him the two men shared a glance. They didn't need to speak to understand one another. They would undress together now, revealing themselves to Leah at the same time.

They both took off their shirts, and Leah gasped. "Stop," she whispered. She took a step closer and then hesitated. "May I touch you?" she asked.

Kurt laughed and Valentine smiled. "Yes, *leibchen*, touch all you want," Kurt told her, his voice deep with need. He reached out and Leah placed her hand in his. Kurt guided it to his chest, and he rubbed her hand over his hard muscles, then over his nipples, already sharp with arousal. The caress had him slowly arching his neck in pleasure.

"Do you like that?" Leah asked tentatively. "When I touch you there?"

Kurt raised his head again to look at her, and Valentine didn't need to see his face to know how he looked. He'd seen Kurt aroused so many times it was an image burned in his memory. He was beautiful that way, sloe-eyed with desire, his cheeks flushed, his movements slow and deliberate.

"I want you to touch me everywhere, my Leah. My nipples, my cock, my ass," he told her, and with each word he moved her hand on him to the places he named. Leah inhaled sharply when he pushed her hand deep between his legs and onto his ass. Kurt chuckled darkly and let her pull it away. "Perhaps not all tonight, but eventually," he said with a wolfish grin.

Leah stumbled back, and Valentine stepped over to catch her, her back against his bare chest. He wrapped his arms tightly around her, grabbing her hands so that she hugged herself with him, effectively held captive. He placed his lips against her ear as he spoke. "That's how we do it, Leah. That's how a woman fucks two men, and how men fuck each other — in the ass. It feels so good, sweetheart, so hot and thick and wonderful to be fucked there. It's what we'll do to you after we're married, and what we do to each other."

"Oh my God," Leah whispered brokenly, and the slight jerk of her hips let Valentine know she was aroused by the thought rather than frightened. She watched Kurt with wide eyes, her new knowledge written on her face. Kurt slowly unbuttoned his pants and pushed them down just enough to free his swollen cock. It sprang free and bounced against his stomach. Kurt was so hard Valentine knew he must be in pain. Leah whimpered and her legs collapsed beneath her.

Valentine swept her up in his arms and carried her to the settee, laying her down there. He and Kurt quickly divested themselves of the rest of their clothes while Leah stared at them with wonder. When they were naked, Valentine hesitated. "What do you want us to do, Leah?" he asked her, hungry to please.

She looked at them and licked her lips again. It was a nervous habit that pushed Valentine to the edge. He loved a tongue on him, licking and swirling everywhere it went. At her next words, he knew exactly what he was going to do.

"Show me," Leah told them. "Show me how you both like to be touched. Show me how to please you."

Valentine turned and beckoned Kurt to him with an outstretched hand.

Kurt knew what Valentine wanted, what he always wanted— Kurt's mouth on him. Valentine loved the hot wet swirl of a tongue on his skin, and Kurt loved the taste of him. He eagerly took Valentine's hand, lowering his head to lick along Valentine's shoulder before the other man could even speak. Valentine shuddered and groaned and Kurt smiled wickedly, his eyes meeting Leah's over Valentine's shoulder. Her eyes were wide, the pupils enlarged until they nearly blotted out the pale blue.

"Valentine loves to be licked, Leah, everywhere. He loves a mouth savoring him, teasing him with lips and tongue and teeth." Kurt turned Valentine slightly so Leah had a side view and could see everything that Kurt did to him. Kurt lowered his head and slowly licked across Valentine's hard nipples with the flat of his tongue. Valentine gripped the back of his head, fisting Kurt's hair and holding him there on one nipple. Kurt bared his teeth and bit down, lightly scoring his teeth along the aroused pebble, and Valentine groaned again, louder this time.

Kurt spoke with this lips still touching Valentine. "Valentine is a vocal lover. Not just the words, which he loves to speak and hear, but the sounds of sex. He can't control himself and is given to loud moaning. He also loves to hear his lover. He is happiest when he has driven me to the edge and I can't control my own moans. I like this too, it pleases me and heightens my own desire." He turned his head and rubbed his hair along Valentine's nipple with a slight repetitive motion of his head while he looked at Leah. "I want to hear you in your passion too, Leah. I want to hear you moan and sob for us, beg us to fuck you. Never be embarrassed to express what you're feeling when we make love to you."

"Kurt." Valentine's voice was a growl. "Lick me down, and then suck my cock. Show Leah how good you are at that." Kurt's stomach clenched as he remembered similar words from Valentine last night.

Leah moaned out loud and Kurt laughed. Valentine looked at her, and Kurt could see she was as affected by the dark passion in his face as Kurt was. "Was it the words that made you moan, Leah, or the thought of what I want him to do?" Valentine asked.

"Both," Leah said breathlessly.

"What do you want right now, Leah?" Valentine's voice was harsh and his breathing erratic as Kurt licked down his stomach, paying special attention to his hips and the crease between his legs and his crotch. "Do you want to touch me, or touch yourself?"

Leah gasped and Kurt looked up at her. "Don't be embarrassed, beautiful Leah. It would give us great pleasure to watch you touch yourself."

Leah was sitting up on the settee and she had her arms wrapped around her waist. She bit her lower lip, staring at them in anguish for a minute before she spoke. "I don't know how to begin."

"Bare your breasts for us, Leah, and fondle them. Whatever gives you pleasure. Show us what you like." Kurt waited, trying not to let his impatience show. He burned for this, to see Leah rubbing her own breasts, playing with her pussy, putting her fingers in herself, coming as he sucked Valentine. It was best, he thought, this first time that she pleasure herself to their passion before they touched her. It would relax her, and she would be wet and ready for a cock then.

"Yes," Valentine groaned, "God yes, Leah, please."

She reached for the ties on her corset, and Kurt grinned in triumph.

Chapter Eight

ɞ

Leah couldn't believe she was going to do this, touch herself in front of two men. But then everything about this evening seemed like a dream. Two days ago she never would have imagined watching two men make love, and enjoying it. More than enjoying it, actually, if she were honest with herself. She hungered for it, she was devouring their passion for one another. She wanted to do the things Kurt was doing to Valentine. She wanted to do it to both of them, and the reality was she would, and that excited her beyond measure.

As she removed her clothes to bare her breasts, Leah was brutally honest with herself. She was going to touch herself not because it would give her pleasure but because it was what Valentine and Kurt wanted. She supposed for them it was like her watching them now. She really couldn't imagine getting that much pleasure from her own hands. After she was bare to the waist, Leah looked up at them.

"*Meine Gott*, you are beautiful," Kurt whispered. His face was flushed, his eyes burning bright, and Leah felt beautiful.

"Do it, Leah," Valentine whispered and she looked at him. His face was all angles, sharp and harsh with desire. "Touch your breasts. Let us see you."

She could feel her face flame in embarrassment, but she made her hands cup her breasts and squeeze them. She gasped at the sensation. It felt good, very good, and she began kneading them and running her palms over her distended nipples. She had to bite her lip to keep from crying out.

While she fondled her breasts, she continued to watch the two men. Kurt placed one hand around Valentine's muscular thigh and then wrapped the other around the base of his cock.

Keeping his eyes on Leah, watching her watch him, he leaned forward and guided Valentine's cock to his mouth. His tongue flicked out and licked the shining plum head of Valentine's very thick cock, and Leah actually moaned at the sight. Kurt smiled.

"Very good, Leah. Let me hear your pleasure. I like your moans." Kurt placed his smiling mouth against the end of Valentine's cock then, slowly opening his lips, he took the cock deep in his mouth. Leah sobbed at the desire that flamed through her, roughly squeezing her breasts. The vision before her combined with her own caresses had her sex aching and wet.

Valentine hissed as Kurt slowly pulled back along his cock, releasing it. Kurt began to lick around the thick shaft, and Leah saw Valentine shiver at the sensation. He clutched Kurt's head in his hands, fisting his hair, and turned eyes smoky with passion to her. "Show me your pussy, Leah," Valentine begged her, his voice rough with desire. "Show me how wet you are, how much you like what we're doing."

"My pussy?" Leah gasped, pinching her nipples roughly as Kurt had done earlier. The feeling was a sort of painful pleasure that she liked.

"Your sex, your mound," Valentine panted as Kurt once again swallowed his cock.

Leah blushed again but rose and took off the rest of her clothing. Kurt stopped what he was doing to look with Valentine, and Leah saw stark male appreciation in both faces. She wasn't sure what to do next until Valentine spoke again.

"Sit down again, Leah," he told her, "and spread your legs wide so we can see your sweet, wet pussy. I know you're wet for us. Do you ache to be fucked yet, Leah?"

Valentine's words made Leah sink back on the settee, her legs wide, her pussy indeed aching. "I've never felt like this before, Valentine. Is that what it is? Do I ache to be fucked? My body is a stranger to me tonight." She heard the tremor in her voice and raised her hands to her breasts again, trying to relieve some of the tension she could feel building.

Kurt spoke, still on his knees before Valentine, the other man's cock still in his fist. "Touch your pussy, Leah. Feel the heat, the wet. This is what desire really is. You were made for a cock, you want it."

His voice had the deep, mesmerizing tone that beckoned her to the forbidden, and she obeyed. She moaned at how wet she was, how sensitive. She ran her fingers up and down her crease, feeling how swollen her lips were there, how hot the aching flesh felt. She circled her weeping entrance.

"Put it in," Valentine whispered. "You know you want to, Leah. Fuck your pussy with your finger."

Leah pushed her finger into her pussy and cried out at the relief she felt at filling that empty, aching space.

"Suck me, Kurt," Valentine commanded roughly. "Suck me until I come, until you swallow all of me. Then I want to watch you fuck Leah."

"Oh God, oh God," Leah moaned, her eyes closing as she moved her finger inside of her pussy. Everything was too much, she was so full, and so confused.

"Are you going to come, Leah?" Valentine asked her, and she opened her eyes to see Kurt's head moving up and down, his mouth sliding along Valentine's cock. She felt her pussy clench her finger at the sight, and the feeling was marvelous. She moaned.

"Kurt's beautiful mouth is so hot and wet, Leah," Valentine whispered, "just like your pussy. He sucks until it's so tight, and I fuck his mouth like I want to fuck your pussy, like I fuck his ass."

Leah's cry was wild and she moved her finger harder and faster inside her pussy, trying to ease the ache.

"Yes, Leah, come for us," Valentine hissed.

"I don't know how!" Leah cried out, tears pooling in her eyes. "I don't know!"

"Sshhh, darling," Valentine whispered. "Have you never come before, love?"

Leah was shaking her head, watching Kurt suck Valentine's cock. She was shaking all over, her eyes wide, her finger working her pussy, and Valentine arched his back in pleasure as he drove his cock deep in Kurt's mouth. Kurt moaned his approval, and Valentine could feel his own climax coming. He gritted his teeth and held it off. He wanted to watch Leah come first, her first time if he guessed correctly. He tightened his fists in Kurt's hair, stopping him, Valentine's cock still buried deep between his lips.

"Press your palm against the little button at the top of your crease, Leah," Valentine panted. "Press against it while you fuck your finger in and out. It will feel so good. You'll know when you come, my love. You'll know." Leah did as he directed and her moan told him she was doing it right.

"Oh my God, Valentine, oh my God," she cried out. Her breathing was fast and erratic, and Valentine could see when she stopped watching him and Kurt and instead began concentrating on the feelings she was giving herself. It was beautiful and so bloody arousing he was ready to come that instant.

Suddenly Leah hunched her back and threw back her head, her keening cry filling the air. Valentine hungrily watched her come, her satisfaction his own. "Yes," he whispered. He glanced down and shared a look with Kurt, and he knew his lover was imagining the same thing, Leah coming with them inside her. "Soon, Kurt darling, soon," he whispered and Kurt closed his eyes and sucked hard on Valentine's cock.

Valentine moaned and let himself go. He pumped in and out of Kurt's mouth, unable to contain the sounds of his own arousal. His balls were tingling, burning with the need to come. He felt the heat travel up his cock until it seemed as if pleasure exploded from the end deep in Kurt's throat.

Valentine arched his back as the climax gripped him, crying out at the feel of Kurt swallowing around the end of his cock.

Kurt fell back, catching himself on his hands, breathless after Valentine's climax. God, he loved sucking Valentine, loved the taste and feel of him, his wild abandon when he came in Kurt's mouth. Watching and hearing first Leah and then Valentine come pushed Kurt to the edge. His cock was so hard it hurt. It felt as if he had never been this excited before, this desperate to fuck. He took a deep breath and rolled to his feet.

"My turn," he said, quickly crossing to the settee. He grabbed Leah's feet and raised them to the settee, turning her whole body in the process until she was lying down. He climbed on top of her and roughly spread her thighs wide with his knees. Only then did he look at her face. She was dazed, flushed prettily from her climax, her hair lying in wild disarray around her. She was so beautiful and desirable that Kurt's cock throbbed with the need to thrust deep within her. He met her eyes and froze.

"Leah?" he asked, hesitant. She was crying, silent tears slipping from her eyes to roll down her temples into her hair.

"What is it?" Valentine asked from where he was sitting down on the floor, still trying to catch his breath. He crawled over next to them and leaned over Leah. "My God, Leah, are you all right?"

Leah began to laugh through her tears. "Two children, and I never knew I could do that. That bastard."

"What?" Kurt asked, confused.

Leah looked at him, and wiped her eyes with the heels of her hands, like a child. "Thomas. He never told me, never took the time to let me. Come? Is that what that's called?"

Valentine grinned wolfishly from the floor. "It's called a climax, or orgasm. Or *le petite mort*, as the French say, the little death."

73

"How often can I do that?"

Kurt laughed out loud. "As often as you want. We can do that for you too. When we fuck, or when we kiss your pussy."

"Kiss my…" Leah's eyes got very wide. "You mean like you did to Valentine?"

Kurt nodded. "Yes, similar. I like to do that to women too. You smell delicious, and someday soon, I'll do that. But right now I want desperately to fuck. May I fuck you, Leah?"

Valentine laid his arms along the cushion next to Leah's head and rested his chin on his crossed hands. "May I watch?"

Leah closed her eyes briefly, and when she opened them, Kurt saw desire and something else, something that made his heart quicken and his soul sing.

"Yes, darling Kurt. Please fuck me."

He needed no further encouragement. Without another word he found her entrance with his cock. She was so hot and wet Kurt shivered with anticipation. He slid inside her slowly, but with one smooth thrust to the hilt, and Leah moaned deeply in delight. Kurt had to take several deep breaths to gain control of himself.

"Tell me," Valentine whispered, staring at Kurt.

"She's so wet and hot, my love, so tight. I cannot last long, I think. She feels so wonderful." His accent grew thicker with his passion.

"Yes, I do," Leah whispered back, a trill of laughter in her voice. "I want to feel even better. *Le petite mort*, please."

Kurt couldn't stop his snort of laughter, and he saw Valentine grinning like a fool beside them. "We have created a monster, I think," Kurt told him. Leah laughed again.

Her laughter had a strange effect on Kurt. He felt his eyes fill with tears. This laughter, this wonderful closeness, would this be their future? Suddenly that future was bright and filled with promise, and Kurt felt lighter than he had since the war. Was this what Leah would bring them? God, he hoped so. He leaned down and buried his face in her neck, clutching her to him and thrusting deeper into her.

Leah gasped. "Kurt?" she asked breathlessly, concern in her voice.

He couldn't look at her. "Love me, Leah," he whispered. He felt Valentine's hand on his back, Valentine's lips on his shoulder as Leah ran a gentle hand through his hair.

"Yes," she whispered, "I think I shall."

She began to move beneath him, her movements untutored, and Kurt moved with her. He reached one hand down and firmly moved her hips in a smoother motion, showing her how to match him. When she caught the rhythm he pulled his head back from her neck with a gasp. Leah moaned at the exquisite feeling.

"There, yes," Kurt panted, his thrusts gaining in intensity and speed.

"Kurt," she said, over and over, like a prayer. He felt the same. It was perfect, everything about it. He'd never felt a fuck so right except for Valentine. Being in Leah was as good as being in Valentine—tight, hot, intense. Suddenly Leah's movements became more frantic, and Kurt knew she was close.

"Oh God," she cried, "it's going to happen again! Fuck me, Kurt, harder," she demanded, and he complied. He felt her muscles clamp down on him and begin to pulse almost before she began crying out as she climaxed. He held himself deeply inside her, pressing hard against her, trying to make her pleasure last, and then to his surprise without any further thrusts his climax came. His back arched with the force of it and he felt his seed shooting out endlessly, his body racked by shudders of ecstasy. Leah clutched him to her with arms and legs wrapped tightly around him, and then he felt her come again, not as hard but deeper, and she moaned.

"My God," he heard Valentine whisper. "That was beautiful."

75

Chapter Nine

&

Kurt collapsed atop Leah after his climax. His face was buried in the crook of her neck, his arms still wrapped possessively around her. Valentine felt tears on his cheeks and quickly wiped them away. He'd seen Kurt come many times before in many ways, most often with or inside Valentine himself, but this time was different. Before Kurt had always seemed almost melancholy afterward, his mood slightly dark. Valentine didn't doubt Kurt's love for him, but he'd known something was missing. This time Kurt had looked euphoric, sated, happy.

Thank God his plan had worked. When Kurt first mentioned the notion of taking a wife, Valentine had been surprised to say the least. But the idea had taken root in his mind and his heart. A wife who would bring children and softness and the kind of nurturing only a woman possessed. He needed that. He didn't have nightmares from the war, having Kurt had saved him from the war grief and madness that afflicted so many of his brothers in arms. But he lived with the memories every day and so did Kurt. They needed someone to help them start anew, a beginning that didn't come with death and violence.

Valentine knew from the start that Kurt believed he was doing it for Valentine, that he, Kurt, didn't need or want a wife. But Valentine knew Kurt better than he knew himself, and Kurt did need the laughter and light of a wife and children. Just a few hours with Leah, and Valentine could see the difference in him. Valentine had pretended to reluctantly go along with Kurt's plan, all the while hoping they could find a woman Kurt could love.

Then, in London, Valentine had confided in Stephen Matthews. Stephen had agreed with Valentine that Kurt's dark moods were getting worse. He also agreed a wife was a wonderful idea. And it just so happened, Stephen had offered with a wink, that he knew the perfect woman. Valentine thought Stephen had been joking or at least exaggerating, but after meeting Leah he realized Stephen had been completely serious. She was the perfect woman for them.

He owed Stephen a great deal, he thought with a smile, as he gazed with wonder at Leah's perfect profile, her strong chin and aristocratic nose. Her sensual mouth and those eyes, those pale blue eyes, bright with wonder and self-knowledge; she turned her head and those eyes were looking at him.

"Kiss me, Leah," he whispered. She leaned toward him and he raised himself on his knees to better reach her mouth. She was all willing submission and softness beneath his lips. He realized this was their first kiss. She opened for him at a slow swipe of his tongue on the plump curve of her lower lip, and he delved inside her mouth. He felt rather than heard her sharp intake of breath as his tongue met hers. Her hesitation and innocent response revealed her inexperience with this kind of soul kiss, a kiss Kurt had taught him.

Valentine went deeper into the kiss, applying more pressure with his lips, moving his tongue farther into her mouth, sucking as he played with her tongue. Leah moaned and moved one arm from Kurt to wrap it around Valentine's neck, hugging him close. Her hand dove into his hair and fisted it tightly, and Valentine felt his cock twitch in arousal again. Just as he began to entertain thoughts of another bout of lovemaking, perhaps fucking Leah himself, Kurt let out a gentle snore. Leah snorted into the kiss and pulled back with a quiet laugh, and Valentine let her, smiling.

"Our first kiss," Leah whispered, reading his mind.

"The first of many," Valentine assured her, leaning forward to kiss her forehead softly. "Rest for a bit, then we will see you home, my love."

* * * * *

Valentine roused Leah and Kurt after a short rest, as the hour was getting late and he wanted to take her home before her mother started to worry. Kurt was endearingly embarrassed that he had fallen asleep while still atop Leah, and inside her. Leah hadn't cared at all. It was wonderful—the weight of a hot, sated, naked man covering her, his cock still warm in her.

She felt like a different woman. She was a different woman thanks to these two men. She would never again settle for the kind of half-life she'd been living, now that she knew what she'd been missing. The smile was permanently attached to her face as she thought of all the wonderful years of fucking and coming ahead of her with Valentine and Kurt.

They were in the carriage with the lamps lit, and all three were squeezed onto one side, Leah in the middle. She was half draped over both of them, and Kurt was rubbing her feet while Valentine placed little kisses on her neck and nibbled on her ear.

"What are you grinning about, little cat?" Kurt asked quietly, and she opened her eyes to see him regarding her with a lazy smile, his own head resting on the back of the seat cushion.

"I've got the canary rubbing my feet," she answered just as lazily, and Valentine chuckled in her ear, sending sweet chills down her back.

"Mrs. Westridge," Valentine murmured, "you have a quick wit."

"The better to eat you with," she growled teasingly, and then laughed with the other two. She couldn't remember a time she had ever engaged in such silly banter with a man. Thomas had had no sense of humor at all.

She settled more deeply into the seat, snuggling back against Valentine and rubbing one foot on Kurt's thigh. "When will we marry, Valentine?"

"As soon as possible," he sighed, licking her neck right below her ear. She giggled. "I've got a special license already. I obtained it in London, hoping you would say yes."

"Sight unseen?" she asked lightly.

Valentine winced. "That seems so cold now that we know you," he admitted, "but Stephen said you would make a good wife to us, and marriages have been based on less."

"Oh I'm not upset," Leah hastened to assure them. "I'm planning on thanking Stephen profusely when he gets back." Both men smiled.

"Stephen returns from London on the fifth," Kurt said. "We can be married soon after." He grinned mischievously before adding, "Or we could have a longer engagement and get married on your birthday, Valentine. Very romantic."

Leah felt Valentine tense behind her, and she turned slightly to regard him with incredulous eyes. "Don't tell me?" she asked, laughter in her voice.

"Where on earth did you think I got the name?" he asked roughly. "Yes, February fourteenth, Valentine's Day." He jostled her so she was facing front again. "And I've bloody well had to endure enough teasing about it to last me a lifetime. And no, I'm not waiting months to marry Leah."

"Well, at least you wouldn't forget our wedding date," Leah teased, and Kurt laughed aloud as Valentine teasingly bit her earlobe.

"Where will we live?" Leah changed the subject.

"Well, we thought here, at Cantley." Valentine got a horrified look on his face. "Surely you don't want to live in London, do you?"

Leah had to laugh at his expression. "No, not really, although I've never been and would like to visit one day. What's so horrible about London?"

Kurt had a very serious look on his face when he answered. "We're afraid London would be very bad for your health, my love."

"Is it so very dirty then?" Leah asked curiously.

"Yes, the refuse and air are bad particularly when combined with madmen running around assaulting our friends' wives."

"What?!" Leah was aghast at Kurt's comment. "What do you mean?"

"We have several friends in London who have married as we will, a marriage of three. One group made a very unfortunate enemy several years ago, and despite his rather outlaw status after attempting to kill one of them he managed to get back into the country. He has since attacked the wife of two other mutual friends."

"Oh my God!" Leah exclaimed. "Is she all right?"

"Now, yes, but she was rather badly beaten and frightened. I won't have you put at risk that way." Valentine's arms snaked around her more snugly, and his voice was hard.

Leah felt a frisson of fear. "Should I be worried?"

Kurt reached over and took her hand. "No, at least we don't think so. We believe we'll be well out of his sights here in the country, and would like to keep it that way."

Leah relaxed at Kurt's assurance. Then she focused on the most interesting part of his story. "There are others like us?"

"Yes, indeed there are, my dear," Kurt told her with a smile. "When we go to London you shall meet them, but not for a while."

Leah silently agreed. She had no desire to travel into danger if she could help it. The conversation made her think of their other friends. "What is the duke like?"

"Freddy?" Valentine sounded a little startled at the change of topic. "He's, well...he's Freddy."

Kurt laughed. "That says it all, and says nothing." He shrugged in his usual manner, the movement speaking volumes. "He is young and inexperienced, but a good man I think. He likes to laugh and that is always good in a peer."

"He must be very aware of his position if he is at all like his mother." Leah couldn't stop her moue of distaste.

Both Kurt and Valentine burst out laughing. "Freddy?" Valentine said with good humor. "No, he is nothing like that. Brett spends half his time reminding Freddy who and what he is."

"Brett?" Leah inquired.

"Brett Haversham. He's Freddy's constant companion. He was good friends with Freddy's older brother Bertram during the war, was injured in the same incident where Bertie died. Since he came back Freddy's hardly left his side."

Kurt's tone was neutral, so Leah had to ask. "Are they lovers, like you two?"

Kurt looked thoughtful for a moment. "No, I am sure they are not, although Freddy I think would like to be. But Brett, he puts Freddy off." Kurt shrugged again in bewilderment.

"Will he like me?" Leah didn't want Kurt and Valentine's friends to look down on them for their marriage to a simple country widow with children. Their friends sounded so sophisticated. No matter what they said, a duke was a lofty friend indeed.

"They will love you," Valentine assured her, kissing her neck, "if only because we do."

* * * * *

"What the hell?" Valentine muttered behind her, and Leah opened her eyes. She'd dozed off to the rhythm of the carriage, in the security of both men's arms.

"What is it?" she asked groggily, sitting up and stretching. She followed his gaze out the window and saw the cottage ablaze with lights.

"Oh my God!" Leah was frantic. Something must be wrong. The cottage should be dark this time of night, the children in bed.

81

The carriage came to a halt, and Valentine threw open the door, jumping down and turning to lift Leah out. She ran for the door, Valentine and Kurt close behind her. Before she could reach it, the door flew open and Sir Horatio stepped out in her path. She barely had time to stop before his arm drew back and delivered a ringing blow to her cheek, knocking her down. She saw stars and lay there dazed for a moment.

"You filthy slut, I had to lie to the Duchess to cover up your whoring," he hissed. "I'm taking these children tonight. I will be back in the morning to discuss your punishment."

"You pathetic bastard," Valentine ground out, and Leah's vision cleared in time to see him haul Sir Horatio off his feet by his cravat. "Do you gain your pleasure by abusing those weaker than you? Do you dare take on a man instead of women and children?" Valentine held him suspended on his toes with one hand and backhanded him across the face with the other.

"You foul whoreson," Sir Horatio gasped. "You'll pay for that, and for what you and your foreign lover took from me tonight." Valentine threw him on the ground as if he were trash. The older man's face was livid with fury. "Leah was mine, mine. I was willing to marry her, but now I won't. She's not good enough now. I'll get everything I want without having to wed the whore. And you will be driven from the neighborhood, from England if I have my way."

Kurt and Mrs. Northcott had rushed to Leah's side as soon as she went down, and she now sat on the ground, her mother's arms around her. Kurt walked over to stand in front of Sir Horatio for a moment then he bent his knees to squat in front of the fallen man. His voice was all the more menacing for its quietness.

"It is you who will be leaving, Marleston, if you value your life. By next week, Leah will be Mrs. Westridge. As of tonight both she and her mother, and the children too, will be at Cantley with us. You will never touch them or see them again. I will make sure the Duke knows of this incident, and you will no longer be welcome at Ashton Park. And yes, Valentine and I do have that power. You are through being the bully. There is nothing left for you here."

Kurt stood and turned his back on the older man, completely disregarding him as a threat. Sir Horatio was left gasping like a fish on the ground. Kurt turned to the door and saw Bastian and Esme there. "Come, *meine kinder*, let us go and pack your things," he said gently, and Esme let him pick her up and carry her inside.

Valentine picked Leah up in his arms and her mother hurried inside ahead of them. As he walked past Sir Horatio, Leah's head on his shoulder, he paused and looked down. "By the end of the week, or I will kill you," he said in a flat voice, and Leah didn't doubt his words. She buried her face in his neck and wrapped her arms tightly around him. She didn't want to see Sir Horatio ever again, not even lying on the ground in defeat.

"I think I will love you too," she whispered, looking up at Valentine after he kicked the door closed behind them.

He smiled down at her. "Of course you will, my dear. It's all part of the plan."

Sir Horatio was livid. He waited until the door closed and then started to rise. It was only then that his footman hurried over to help him. The man had been standing off to the side near Sir Horatio's carriage, hidden in the shadows. He'd wanted to surprise Leah when he confronted her with her treachery and perfidy. He hadn't counted on the two unnatural bastards being with her.

"Get away!" he snarled at the servant. He hoisted himself to his feet with difficulty, his tight corset making it hard to do. "I see you didn't rush to my assistance when I was being assaulted by that ruffian."

"Well, I..." the footman stuttered, clearly afraid to continue.

"Never mind, you fool," Sir Horatio ground out. "I don't need your assistance. I have my own ways of making them pay."

Chapter Ten

෨

Two days later Leah and the children were settling in at Cantley nicely. Bastian and Esme were enthralled with the nursery, which contained some old toys left by the previous owners. Their pleasure at such tawdry cast-offs nearly broke Kurt's heart. He'd sent off two of the footmen to buy every toy available in the village. He was firmly determined to make them the two most spoiled children in Christendom.

Valentine had taken over Bastian's lessons until a tutor could be found. He'd sent off a notice to the *Times* and was hopeful he'd have some decent inquiries soon considering the salary he was offering.

And Leah was finally letting herself relax. Being free of worry was such a new concept to her she was having trouble adjusting. She'd actually pinched herself so hard that morning trying to make sure it was all real she'd left a bruise on her arm. She was also trying to learn how to take care of a household the size of Valentine's. Yesterday at breakfast she'd asked Valentine what would be required of her as his wife.

"You will take care of the house I should imagine," he'd told her vaguely.

Leah had sighed with impatience. "Yes, but what exactly does that entail, Valentine? How many servants do you have? Have you a housekeeper? Will I be responsible for the household accounts as well?"

He'd looked at Kurt, lost. "I, I don't really know Leah. Kurt handles all that."

Leah had seen then how it would be. "I see. And now I will too."

Valentine had smiled ingeniously. "Exactly, my love."

Kurt laughed. "Valentine wishes to have a pack of dogs and a stable of hunters, my dear, and perhaps a racehorse or two. And in his free time he shall also raise children. The other details of his life he leaves to you and me."

Rather than be annoyed Leah was euphoric. To be able to oversee a house like Cantley was a dream come true. She needn't worry about money, they'd made that clear. Between the two of them they were quite solid financially, their money invested well and growing daily.

She'd spent the morning with the housekeeper, as it turned out Valentine did indeed have one. She was a no-nonsense woman with a bit of a cockney accent and she made no secret of her origins with Leah.

"Mr. Westridge and Mr. Schillig hired me out of the stew," she told her baldly. "I ran my own house there with a few girls, but was needing to go on the up and up you see. They give me a chance, and a couple of my girls as well."

To say Leah was startled was putting it mildly. "I see." She decided to speak as plainly as Mrs. Cadwalter. "Will they be a problem, do you think?" She'd heard tales of street girls lying their way into a position in a good house only to pick up their old ways with the other servants and their masters.

"Not at all, mum," she'd firmly declared. "Hired us because they served with our misters they did. All died in the war you know. Looked us up to see how we were doing, and being the gentlemen they are offered us a better way. We'd never do nothing to embarrass them."

Leah was moved almost to tears. How like Valentine and Kurt to do something like that. She felt petty for thinking ill of these women for even a moment. She knew how hard it was for a widow with no means in this world.

"I'm quite glad to hear it, Mrs. Cadwalter," was all she said. "Shall we begin with a tour of the house?" Her head was spinning by teatime with all the information she'd received. Linens, menus, accounts, servants—she could hardly keep it all straight. She finally realized what it meant to be the wife of a wealthy man, and the responsibilities it entailed.

Leah took tea with her mother in the back garden. "I wonder if I should send someone for the boys," she muttered as she poured her mother a cup.

"Is that what we're calling them?" Marjorie said archly. "I wondered."

Leah slowly put the teapot down and looked at her mother. "I'm sorry. I guess I haven't really discussed anything with you. I failed to see that this affects you too."

Marjorie instantly put her cup down and took Leah's hand. "No, darling, I'm sorry. I didn't mean anything by that remark. It's just, this is rather..." She flapped her hands in the air and then gave up. "I'm not sure what this is quite frankly."

Leah bit her lip and contemplated a lie, but in the end opted for the truth. Her mother would be here quite a lot, even after she moved back to her cottage. She would figure it out eventually. Leah was uncomfortable with the idea of lying to her anyway. She'd stood staunchly by her side through her disaster of a marriage and the calamity of Thomas' debts.

"I'm going to marry Mr. Westridge," she started, "as soon as possible."

"I gathered that from Mr. Schillig's comments last night," Marjorie replied. "But what of Mr. Schillig? What is his role here?" Her look was shrewd.

"He is Valentine's lover and will be mine as well." Leah's voice was steady, her tone perhaps a touch defensive, but she felt her face flame as she spoke.

"I see." It was Marjorie's turn to be startled. She looked away for a moment. When she looked back she too was blushing, but she forged ahead. "And is this what you want?" She reached for Leah's hand again and gripped it tightly. "No one's forcing you? We can find another way to thwart Sir Horatio, if this is against your will."

Leah grabbed her hand with both of hers. "Oh no, Mama. This is what I want. They are both good men, and they need me. I care for them both already. True, I entertained their proposal at first because of our circumstances, and because almost anything was better than Sir Horatio. But now, now I can see a happy future here for me and the children. They are honorable men, and they respect me and care for me in return. We can make it work, we can."

Marjorie closed her eyes briefly, and when she opened them Leah saw the love and determination that had always supported her. "All right then," Marjorie said briskly. "If this is what you want, then we shall all make it work."

Leah leaned over and hugged her. "Oh thank you, Mama, thank you."

Marjorie cleared her throat and asked Leah about her morning. She was telling her all about Mrs. Cadwalter when they were interrupted by Esme's shrill, frightened scream from somewhere in front of the house. Leah dropped her cup to the ground and was running before she even thought about it, Marjorie close behind. They rounded the side of the house to see Sir Horatio dragging a screaming Esme toward his carriage. There were several soldiers standing near him and the maid who'd been assigned to watch Esme was nowhere to be seen.

"Esme!" Leah shouted, running to her.

"Mama!" Esme screamed and tried to pull away from Horatio toward Leah. Before Leah could reach her she was grabbed roughly by one of the soldiers and shoved back. Her mother caught her before she fell.

"She's my daughter!" Leah cried. "What are you doing?"

"Esme?" Leah heard Kurt cry out and turned to see him charging through the front door, the maid who'd been watching Esme close behind. Kurt bellowed with rage as he saw Sir Horatio dragging the little girl and he didn't break stride as he tackled the older man to the ground. Horatio let go of her and she tried to run to Leah but was snatched up by the same soldier who'd grabbed Leah. She was screaming hysterically by now, and Leah was crying, trying to get to her, but another soldier blocked her path.

"Let go of me, damn it!" Leah heard Kurt shout, anger and desperation in his voice. She looked over and saw two soldiers hauling him off Horatio.

"What the hell is going on here?" Valentine's voice rang with authority.

Leah turned to him with relief. "Valentine! They won't give me Esme!"

"Release her at once," Valentine demanded, his face suffused with cold rage.

Horatio ignored him. "Find the boy," he ordered the soldier in front of Leah.

"What did you say?" The tone of Valentine's voice caused the soldiers holding Kurt to look at one another nervously.

"You have no rights here, Westridge," Sir Horatio informed him snidely. "I've a writ from Sir Appleton, the presiding Justice of the Peace in the duke's absence. It gives me custody of the children, and was approved by the Duchess. They are mine now."

"This is my property," Valentine ground out. "It is you who have no authority here. Give me the writ, and after it has been validated, I will consider the situation."

"Do you think me a fool?" Sir Horatio spat out. "If I allow you to keep the children until the writ has been verified you will spirit them away. As for your authority here, that is why I brought the soldiers. They are here expressly to see that justice is served."

"Justice, to steal children from their mother?" Kurt's tone was as virulent as Sir Horatio's. "This is not justice, this is cruelty."

"Sir?" Bastian's voice came unsteadily from the doorway.

"You, boy," Sir Horatio ordered him. "Come here. You are to go with me."

"No, Bastian," Valentine told him quickly as he hesitatingly started down the steps.

The soldier holding Esme passed her off to another and turned to Valentine with a look of contempt. "If you interfere, Westridge, you or your lover," he spat the word out as if it were an insult, "I have the authority to arrest you, and I will do so with pleasure. Your kind has no business around children."

"You cannot take them!" Leah cried out. "Valentine! Valentine, tell them! Tell them they can't take the children!"

Valentine stepped forward menacingly and the soldier reached for his sword. "Give me a reason, Westridge," he snarled. "You disgust me, and I'd like nothing better than to end your sorry life right now."

"Captain," Sir Horatio said with great satisfaction as he watched Valentine go still, "fetch the boy and let us leave this place. We are here to protect the children. I do not believe, unless he attacks us, we have the authority to kill Mr. Westridge, or Mr. Schillig for that matter."

Leah stood helpless as Kurt cursed and raged and struggled, and Valentine stood still as stone as the children were led away to Horatio's carriage.

Before he climbed in Sir Horatio turned to Leah. "You know what you must do, Leah. I'll expect to hear from you shortly."

Chapter Eleven

ᵴᴑ

"We must wait for Freddy," Valentine said again in a weary voice. For two days he had held Kurt back and listened to Leah's sobs. His heart was breaking at what was happening to them, to the children. The future had looked so bright, everything so perfect. He should have known it would all fall apart.

"We cannot wait anymore, Valentine!" Kurt argued. "Marleston is wrong, yes, in the head? If we do not get the children now, there is no telling what he will do to them. What he may already have done!" Kurt paced restlessly on the carpet, running his hand impatiently through his hair. He hadn't slept for two days, none of them had, and it was showing. His accent was heavy, his eyes wild.

Valentine sat forward and resting his elbows on his knees, he rubbed his face roughly. "If we attempt to take the children it may be seen as an illegal act that could outlaw us, Kurt. Considering the behavior of the soldiers it could even kill us. Where would Leah and the children be then? For now Marleston is forced to play the rescuer. He can do nothing to the children or it will weaken his claim. So we wait."

"How do you know the duke will come?" Leah's voice was raspy and weak from her tears and exhaustion. "What if he doesn't come?" She leaned against the door frame of the study, broken. She hugged herself as if she were cold. "I must give in. I must go to Sir Horatio and give him what he wants."

"No, Leah! You can't," Kurt told her in an anguished voice. "You can't, or you will never be free of him. Can you so easily turn your back on what we could have?"

"How can you ask me that?" Leah tone was just as anguished. "You show me a glimpse of heaven, and now I must return to hell. You ask me to choose between you and my children, Kurt, and I must choose Bastian and Esme." She covered her face with her hands and her shoulders shook with her sobs. Valentine rose to go to her, but Kurt beat him there.

"I'm sorry, my love, I'm sorry," Kurt whispered as he took her in his arms. Leah grabbed the back of his coat in tight fists as she burrowed into his chest, still crying. Valentine went to them both, he couldn't stay away. They were his life, his loves, his tomorrows. He gathered them both close in his embrace and they separated, Leah's head on his right shoulder, Kurt on his left.

"I will fix this," he whispered. "I will take care of it."

"Then do it." Marjorie Northcott's voice cracked through the quiet room. "He has stolen our children, and you sit here crying, waiting for some flighty duke. If he's that powerful, he will help us after we have the children back."

All three turned to look at her in astonishment. "Mama!" Leah cried. "Surely you don't blame Valentine!"

Marjorie shook her head sadly and closed her eyes in grief. "No, I blame the one responsible — Horatio." She opened her eyes. "He is evil, Leah. You know it. You know what he's done in the past. Even now he could be beating those children. Do you want them to suffer as you did? I did nothing to help you when you needed me most. I won't make that same mistake with Bastian and Esme. I won't let you make that mistake."

Kurt turned to Leah with a growl. "He hit you before the other night? Why did you not tell us this?"

Leah sat down wearily on the settee. "To what avail? What good would it have done to tell you my marriage was a nightmare? That while my husband was busy gambling away every cent we had, his brother stepped in and made my life a living hell? That he beat me? Can you change the past? I think not. It was enough that you offered me a future free of him."

"Leah—" Valentine began, his face distorted with rage, but Leah cut him off.

"Mother is right. I'm going to Sir Horatio. I will make him give me the children. I can't let him control my life anymore. I won't let him." She looked at Valentine and Kurt. "Take your rage and come with me. If you want to confront him, I won't stop you. But I won't wait with you anymore either." She stood and moved to the door.

Before she could reach it, both Valentine and Kurt intercepted her. Valentine took her in a fierce hug as Kurt stood beside them, vibrating with intent. "Yes, Leah, we will go. We will go now."

Valentine turned his head so that he spoke into her hair. "Yes, I have been a fool to wait for Freddy. If we must we will leave with the children. The world is quite large, and surely we will find our place in it. But my place right now is at your side, protecting our children."

He pulled away and Leah reached for both his and Kurt's hands. "Let us go and bring our children home then."

"Thank God," Marjorie whispered as she sank down on a chair, "thank God."

* * * * *

Valentine and Kurt reined to a stop in front of Sir Horatio's house. They were alarmed to see servants carrying boxes and luggage out to waiting carriages.

"Here, is Sir Horatio at home?" Valentine called to one of the coachmen.

"Eh? Sure he's home, but he's leaving within the hour. Taking the poor mites to school he is, far away from their mama." The coachman shook his head as he spoke. "And who are you?"

"I am the children's father," Valentine told him as he dismounted. His voice was low and ragged, shaking with his rage.

"Thought 'e was dead," the coachman said suspiciously. "Their ma's getting ready to marry again."

"She is marrying me." Valentine's steps didn't slow as he answered the astonished coachman. The servants who moments before had been busy scurrying about were now quiet and watchful. More appeared as Kurt followed Valentine to the steps.

Suddenly the front door flew open and Sir Horatio appeared with the same Captain who had been at Cantley the day they took the children.

"What do you want, Westridge?" Sir Horatio demanded. "You are not welcome here."

"I want my children." Valentine had come to a stop at the bottom of the steps, Kurt on his right. His voice rang with malice and authority, and the stance of both men clearly showed they were familiar with violence and not afraid to use it.

Valentine saw that the Captain was armed with gun and sword, and he looked ready to take them down on the spot. Valentine was glad he'd insisted Leah stay home and let him and Kurt handle this. She didn't need to be involved in a bloody confrontation. If he and Kurt were killed, they would at least take Sir Horatio with them, and Leah would have the children back.

"Mr. Westridge! Mr. Schillig!" Bastian's voice rang from inside the house. They heard running and then a scuffle, and Bastian cried out. "Bugger it, let me go!"

Valentine could feel his rage radiating out from his body, turning the air thick with tension. Next to him, he felt rather than saw Kurt prepare to move on Sir Horatio and the Captain. After so many years fighting by each other's side he knew instinctively what Kurt would do. The Captain's battle experience showed as he too anticipated Kurt's move.

"Don't even think about it," the Captain snarled. "If you put one foot on these steps I have the authority to kill you, and I will do it."

"You are welcome to try," Kurt snapped back. "But it will not be I dining with the devil this eve."

Both men took a step forward, and Valentine's pulse sped up as he prepared to do whatever was necessary to rescue his children and protect Kurt. But further action was suspended by the rattle of carriage wheels and the pounding of horse's hooves nearing the house.

All four men looked to see a large ornate carriage pulling through the gates. Valentine felt the tension leave his body and breathed easier as Kurt stepped back to his side. From the corner of his eye he saw Sir Horatio put a hand on the Captain's arm and pull him back. Good, he knew who it was too.

Kurt stepped forward and opened the door of Freddy's carriage before the footman could do so.

"Kurt!" The duke's jovial voice came from within and a second later his red head poked out the door. He shared a delighted smile with all those assembled and descended from the carriage without a care in the world. His clothes as usual were the height of fashion and impeccably tailored to accentuate his tall, leanly muscled frame. *His shoulders are bigger*, Valentine thought, *and his eyes wiser. Freddy is growing up.*

A handsome man with curly auburn hair and a serious face looked out of the carriage, his stern gaze lighting briefly on each participant in the tableau before him. He went to step out of the carriage and Freddy turned back to him instantly.

"Do be careful, Brett. Watch your leg." Freddy reached a hand back to help him down the steps.

Brett Haversham frowned at Freddy and shook his head. "You make me feel like an old woman, Freddy. Have I ever fallen out of the carriage before?" In spite of his words he took Freddy's hand and leaned on it as he jumped to the ground.

"No, but that's because I always lend you a hand." Freddy's reply was unrepentant and accompanied by his charming smile, yet there was a hint of tension in his voice. Valentine knew Brett could not stay mad for long when Freddy looked at him that way. He thought back to their conversation with Leah and for the first time wondered why Brett denied Freddy. Clearly he cared for him. Sir Horatio's voice brought him back to the present.

"Your Grace, how delightful to see you." The man's unctuous tones made Valentine's hackles rise.

"Yes, yes, of course it is," Freddy trilled. "Valentine! There you are. We come from London with Stephen at your urgent request, and arrive to find you gone! When we stopped at Cantley we were told we'd find you here." He walked over to Valentine and the two men shook hands like old friends.

"Freddy, it is good to see you. We missed you in London." He turned to the carriage. "Hello, Brett." He extended his hand and Brett limped over to shake it. He knew the other man hated when people made concessions to his injury. Freddy and Brett greeted Kurt while Valentine watched Sir Horatio seethe on the steps.

"Sir Horatio," Freddy addressed him, "what is this I hear about kidnapped children? Surely I have misunderstood." Valentine started at the thread of steel in Freddy's voice. When had he acquired that?

Sir Horatio was made of stern stuff, however, and stood his ground. "My niece and nephew are hardly kidnapped, Your Grace. They are here safe and sound with me, as I'm sure my brother would have wanted."

Ah so that's going to be his argument here, Valentine thought with satisfaction. It was weak and easily surmounted.

"Children should be with their mother, Freddy," Valentine smoothly countered. "My fiancée Leah, the children's mother, is most distressed."

"I quite agree, Valentine, at least in this instance." Freddy turned once again to Sir Horatio. "Bring the children to me, Marleston. I shall question them."

For the first time Sir Horatio seemed uneasy. "Your Grace, it would unduly distress them, to be sure. Their mother has chosen a, shall we say, unfortunate future with these two gentlemen, and the children were only too glad to be taken away from such unnatural goings-on. Your mother — "

Freddy interrupted him with a frown. "My mother is no longer in the neighborhood. Upon hearing of my imminent arrival she very wisely took herself off to parts unknown. Produce the children."

For the first time the Captain spoke. "Sir Horatio speaks the truth, Your Grace. You are clearly unaware of the disgusting nature of the relationship between these two or you would not call them friends."

When Freddy turned to the Captain, Valentine took a step back at the regal fury in his gaze. "Do not presume to inform me of the private lives of my friends, Captain. If I desire your opinion I will address you. Until then you are to keep your mouth shut."

"Freddy," Brett said quietly. Freddy's head whipped around to him. "Do not start with me now, Brett." He turned away, dismissing the other man in a way Valentine had never seen before. He was dismayed. What was going on between them?

A mask of congeniality fell over Freddy's features, and he addressed someone over Valentine's shoulder. "Hullo. And who are you, poppet?"

Valentine and Kurt both spun around. "Esme!" Kurt cried, and fell to his knees, his arms outstretched. The little girl flew down the stairs toward him. The Captain moved to intervene, and Esme slammed to a stop, huddled against the stone railing.

"If you touch her, Captain, you will find yourself escorting the refuse of Newgate to Australia." Freddy's tone was colder than Valentine had ever heard, and he knew without a doubt that if he were ever addressed in that tone, he would not hesitate to do whatever Freddy asked. The change in the heretofore easygoing young duke was nothing short of amazing, and a little alarming. Kurt had risen to rush the Captain but was stayed by Brett's hand on his arm.

"Your Grace!" Sir Horatio blustered. "I have a writ of custody for the children, approved by your mother. Surely you do not rescind that?"

"I do indeed, Sir Horatio. You seem to have forgotten the same thing my mother frequently overlooks. I am duke here, not her." He looked down as Esme quickly scurried down the stairs past Valentine and Kurt to tug on his coat jacket. As he looked down Esme held up her arms in the age-old childish way that indicated she wished to be picked up. Freddy obliged, and she leaned in and kissed him on the cheek. "Hmm, you've a smart girl here, Valentine. She knows where the man of true worth is."

Valentine was so relieved he could hear his heart pounding, and suddenly he felt the perspiration running down his temple from nerves that had been taut with tension. He laughed shakily. "Yes, indeed, Freddy. A very smart girl, like her mama."

The light moment was interrupted by Sir Horatio's furious hiss. "Fine, take the girl, she is useless to me. But the boy stays. He is my heir, after all, and British law favors my custody."

"No!" Kurt burst out in anger. Valentine knew it had taken great self-control to keep quiet until now. "You have no claim to these children. They are ours. Leah does not want you, accept this. We will not allow you to abuse the children as you did her. For that alone I should kill you." Brett had stepped in front of him and was holding him back with both hands on his shoulders.

Valentine heard an indrawn breath from within the carriage and turned to see Leah leaning out. He was as surprised as he was angry. What was she doing here? He'd told her to stay home.

"Mama!" Esme cried, and dove out of Freddy's arms. Leah caught her as Freddy let go. "Esme, baby," Leah said, kissing her face and hugging her tightly.

"Ah, and so you see, gentlemen, they always return home to mother," Freddy said dryly. "A chap has no chance against dear mama."

Leah laughed weakly. "Many a maid has no chance against a mister's mama, Your Grace. She is always to be found wanting, and he is the one who runs home to her skirts."

Freddy made a face. "You have met my mother, haven't you?" he asked teasingly.

"Your Grace!" Sir Horatio's tone was clearly admonishing. "Your mother is a great woman, and you should not malign her in front of these people." "These people" was said in the same tone as one might say "these vermin", and Freddy tensed again.

"Do you dare to take me to task, sir?" Freddy thundered, and Valentine winced. He looked at Kurt and the other man's eyes were wide in astonishment. "You who have so much to answer for?"

"Mother?" Bastian rushed out the door, his appearance disheveled. An angry footman followed, his eye beginning to black, his wig askew. Bastian eluded him and bounded down the steps, only to be brought up short by Sir Horatio's hand on his arm. He dragged the boy back, holding his arm tightly so only his toes touched the step.

"Ow, you're hurting me!" he cried, and Valentine rushed up two steps before Sir Horatio's words stopped him cold.

"One more step and I shall throw the boy down the stairs. He will be maimed for life."

"No!" Leah cried, and Kurt growled behind him. "You are a madman!"

"It has all been decided," Sir Horatio told them, his voice low and angry. "The Duchess promised me Leah. She said it was my duty to protect her from her base nature, to punish the children until they learned right from wrong. She promised me." He turned eyes glowing with hatred to Leah. "She was right about you. I should have known. You were always a whore. I couldn't beat it out of you when you were married to Thomas. I tried so hard to train you, to make you worthy of me. Look how you have repaid me."

Leah sobbed, and Bastian kicked out at Sir Horatio. "You bastard!" the boy screamed, struggling. Sir Horatio looked at him with distaste and Valentine's heart stopped. He started running up the stairs just as Sir Horatio flung Bastian away. He wasn't close enough, damn it! As if in a slow-moving dream Valentine saw the Captain reach out and snag Bastian, hauling him back from danger. With a roaring in his ears everything went back to normal, and Valentine didn't break his stride as he rushed Sir Horatio on the steps.

"You're a bloody dead man," he growled, grabbing Sir Horatio by the lapels and throwing him against the stone wall on the side of the steps. He drew back his fist and punched the smaller man with all the rage he felt and he could hear bones crunch at the contact. Sir Horatio fell to the ground, but before Valentine could hit him again he was grabbed from behind. It took a moment for the voice to register.

"Valentine, stop," Freddy kept saying over and over. When he was calm, Freddy released him and gently turned him away from the fallen, broken man. "Bastian is fine, and Marleston will not touch him again. I shall see to it, all right? Go get your boy."

Valentine walked over to the frightened boy, still huddled against the Captain. Valentine looked at the Captain, who was as pale as a ghost, his eyes wide. "I'm sorry, sir, I didn't understand. I didn't see." Valentine could only nodded in acceptance, overwrought. "Thank you," he whispered to the Captain, and knelt in front of Bastian. The boy threw himself in Valentine's arms sobbing and Valentine held him close.

"Valentine," Leah sobbed, and he looked down to see her and Esme in Kurt's arms. He picked up Bastian and went to them, went to his family.

When Valentine and Kurt had loaded the children into the carriage, Freddy bent down and hauled Sir Horatio up. He roughly dragged him down the stairs and threw him to the ground.

"You will leave here, Marleston. You will leave Derbyshire altogether. I do not want to see or hear from you again. Do you understand?"

Sir Horatio spit the blood out of his mouth, the left side of his face beginning to swell. "You have no right to throw me off my land." His voice wavered, with fear or hatred Freddy wasn't sure, and didn't care.

Freddy's vision dimmed with rage. "I am the bloody Duke of Ashland, Marleston. I not only have the right, I have the power. I have more money than God, land and influence, and when I choose to use it I can do damn near anything I want." He crouched in front of the now frightened older man. "I could wipe you from the face of the earth right now if I so choose, and not a hand would be raised against me. Instead, I will have my agent call on you within the next day and make arrangements for you to sell your estate. I have quite a few friends who are looking for country homes. It will not be hard to find you a buyer. By the end of the month I want all trace of you gone from my domain. Do you understand?"

When Sir Horatio made no reply Freddy stood and then suddenly kicked him in the chest, knocking him all the way to the ground. Freddy placed his foot against his throat and applied just enough pressure to make it hard for Sir Horatio to breathe. "I asked if you understood. Answer me."

Hatred burning in his eyes, Sir Horatio nodded awkwardly, struggling to breathe. Freddy stepped away and the older man coughed.

"Good. Pack your things and leave a forwarding address with the footmen I am leaving here to assist you in your departure. I will have my agent call on you."

"Leave now?" Sir Horatio croaked. "I must take care of my affairs here first, oversee the packing of my belongings."

"Someone else will take care of those things," Freddy said airily, waving his hand carelessly and already moving toward the carriage. "I simply cannot allow you to stay and ruin the wedding. Brett, do take care of it." Freddy climbed into the carriage then leaned out to say to Brett, "We shall wait a few minutes, my dear, for you to clear this up. Then we're off to Ashton Park."

Epilogue

∞

Valentine's head fell back against the carriage seat as Leah moved exquisitely above him, fucking his cock slowly, trying to find a rhythm. She moaned, and Valentine hissed as she bore down deeply, hilting his cock. Kurt was busy kissing her, and his hands were touching both her and Valentine anywhere he could reach.

They'd only just left their wedding luncheon at Ashton Park and she was still wearing her wedding dress. Freddy had insisted they be married at his ducal estate. Leah had been overwhelmed at first, but she had quickly formed a friendship with Freddy, and Brett had given her away at their wedding.

"Oh," Leah cried softly, pulling away from Kurt's mouth and grinding down on Valentine. "God, I've been going mad this past week with you two refusing to touch me. This feels so good."

"Freddy locked you up at Ashton Park. And I wanted to wait," Valentine gasped, "for our wedding night."

"Well, you made it to the wedding afternoon anyway," Kurt said wryly, his own voice rough with lust.

Valentine tried to laugh, but it came out a groan as Leah slid back up his cock. "Oh, sweet Christ, yes, Leah," he panted. "Fuck me just like that."

Leah licked her lips and then grabbed both her breasts in her hands, squeezing them roughly. It was Kurt's turn to groan, and he kissed her again before running his lips down her neck to the tops of her breasts.

"You've gotten rather good at that," Kurt noted, kissing her hands on her breasts.

"Oh I've been practicing." Leah's voice was slow, wicked honey dripping from her lips. "I decided the day after we first made love that for the rest of my life I would climax at least once a day." She looked slyly at him out of the corner of her eye. "With or without you." She closed her eyes as she pressed down hard on Valentine's cock. "Vive *le petite mort.*"

Both men laughed, their voices strained with desire. "Absolutely. I quite agree," Kurt assured her. "But even if it's without our help, please let me know so I can at least watch."

Leah's laugh turned into a groan as Valentine's hips suddenly surged up hard and fast into her. She bit her lip and matched his rhythm, throwing her head back.

"That mouth," Kurt whispered, falling back on the seat beside Leah and Valentine. "I'm going to put it to good use sucking my cock as soon as we get home."

"Which," Valentine paused to catch his breath, "one?"

"Both," Kurt growled, and Leah came. Her cry filled the carriage, and Valentine slammed hard into her, pulling her hips tight against his. It was his turn to bite his lip, trying desperately to hang on to his control and not come as her tight, slick walls pulsed around him.

"That's one," he ground out as Leah began to collapse against him. He immediately pulled almost all the way out and then fucked hard and deep again, making Leah cry out and clutch his shoulders. "I'm not done fucking you yet."

"Thank God," Leah groaned and Kurt laughed.

Valentine grinned wickedly. "Consider it a wedding gift," he said. Then he turned to Kurt. "I've got one waiting at home for you too." Kurt leaned over and sank his mouth down on Valentine's. Valentine opened his lips and devoured Kurt's mouth, his passion making the kiss rough and wet.

Leah shivered in ecstasy. "Oh God."

Valentine pulled slowly away from Kurt, giving him one last nip on his bottom lip, and Kurt groaned. Then Valentine moved Leah up and down on his cock, his hands at her hips.

"Remember what we originally told you, Leah? We want this with you, while we remain lovers."

"Do I get to watch?" Leah whispered, her voice trembling.

"That's the plan," Valentine told her, and this time when she came, he followed right behind her.

The End

LOVE'S SURRENDER

ଛଠ

Dedication

ॐ

This one is for my readers. Merry Christmas! And for my editor, Raelene Gorlinsky, who said, "Why don't you write a Christmas story?" And, as always, for my ever-lovin' husband.

Acknowledgments

ॐ

I'd like to thank reader Annette Pascual, who won the chance to name a character in one of my books in a charity auction. She went above and beyond to help out a romance book blogger in need, and I was thrilled with her enthusiasm for the project. Annette named one of the heroes in this book, Oliver Gabriel, using her two favorite male names. Thanks again, Annette!

Chapter One

℘

No one had asked to partner her in a dance.

It had been happening more frequently. And it was glaringly obvious here in this small drawing room, where the furniture had been pushed back for dancing. There were no potted palms or columns to hide behind.

She never would have come if she'd known there would be dancing. It was supposed to be a small Christmas Eve dinner, nothing more. Ordinarily she wouldn't have accepted an invitation from the Shelbys, but it had been last minute and she hadn't wanted to stay at home on Christmas Eve. She should have known there were ulterior motives behind her invitation. There always were. Tonight's agenda seemed to be to humiliate her while showcasing young Melinda Dorsett's popularity and vivacious beauty.

Lady Vanessa Carlton-Smythe felt all the weight of her ponderous name and her equally weighty ancestors. Not to mention The Incident.

Lady Dalrymple chose that moment to take pity on Vanessa and sidled over to where she stood alone.

"No partner again, my dear? What a pity." Lady Dalrymple languidly applied her fan as she surveyed the ballroom. Curls the color of a cold, gray dawn barely moved in the tepid breeze she made. "Perhaps you can convince your father to...*lower* his standards a bit, hmm?" Lady Dalrymple continued mercilessly. "You are getting on, my dear. If he isn't careful you'll be on the shelf, like poor Miss Peasbody over there." The old woman tsked as Vanessa choked on a horrified gasp.

Miss Peasbody was *old*. And unwed. And unwanted.

"Certainly one would think with your bloodlines that some gentleman would come up to scratch," Lady Dalrymple mused unkindly. "The Carlton-Smythe connection alone is enough to forgive any deficiencies in character or looks."

Vanessa pasted on a brittle smile. She'd forgotten Lady Dalrymple was Miss Dorsett's great aunt. Which reminded her, where was her Aunt Grace? Her job as chaperone was to help Vanessa avoid situations just like this. "It does seem to make a difference," she agreed coolly. "Dancing and coy artlessness are not required of a woman in my circumstances. My name alone recommends me, as good breeding, impeccable manners and intelligence are understood in any Carlton-Smythe."

Lady Dalrymple was not so stupid that she didn't recognize the censure in Vanessa's words. Other than a thinning of her already thin lips, however, she did not acknowledge the set down. "Surely a man requires more than a name, my dear. It might be enough to attract, but to secure him you must display the warmth and sensibility that a man wishes for in a wife. Wit, dancing, intelligent conversation are all required to keep a man's attentions."

Vanessa gave Lady Dalrymple the coldly blank look she had achieved at a young age, after rigorous training with her mother. The look reserved especially for those who did not know their place when addressing a Carlton-Smythe. "A Carlton-Smythe has no need to snare a man through posturing, Lady Dalrymple. While some young ladies," she glanced over at Miss Dorsett, laughing a little too loudly while she was spun around the dance floor, "feel a less refined manner will attract and secure, it is not required of me."

"Perhaps the handsome Duke of Ashland would argue that point." Lady Dalrymple drove that nail home with undisguised malicious pleasure. "Her Grace is well-known as a lively young woman who enjoys dancing and laughing and the pleasures to be found in such endeavors."

Vanessa took a quiet, dignified, deep breath. Of course Lady Dalrymple would bring up The Incident. "Then His Grace was quite right when he felt we would not suit. As I have said to Ashland," she used the familiar address to show she was intimate with the Duke and Duchess while Lady Dalrymple was not, "if he had not behaved so badly when he broke our engagement, neither of us would enjoy the happiness we do today." She inwardly cringed. Happiness, indeed. She hardly knew what the word meant these days.

"If you will excuse me, Lady Dalrymple, I believe I see my aunt. Good evening." Vanessa hurried in the direction of her Aunt Grace, whom she'd spotted gossiping near the far end of the room. She passed the dance floor on her way to her aunt's side, and noticed Miss Dorsett was no longer displaying her dancing and wit there. She caught her aunt's eye and the small older woman excused herself from her companion and stepped forward to greet her niece.

"Is something the matter, my dear?" she asked quietly, taking Vanessa's hand and tucking it in her elbow as she slowed Vanessa's steps to a stately walk around the room's perimeter. To most observers it most likely seemed as if the two had met deliberately to stroll around the room and chat.

"I was ambushed," Vanessa said softly as she smiled politely at Mrs. Crusher and her two daughters. The girls were rather plain but very sweet and well dressed, ensuring at least one offer for each of them this season, Vanessa was sure. She always made it a point to show her approval of them when they met. The opinion of a Carlton-Smythe was enough to sway many families in favor of a match they might not have sought otherwise.

Her smile grew brittle as they passed the Crushers and strolled into enemy territory. Lady Dalrymple now stood with her sister and niece, Miss Dorsett's grandmother and mother, all three glaring at Vanessa and her aunt.

"I saw. Keep smiling," Aunt Grace said. She nodded at the ladies, forcing them to acknowledge her and Vanessa. She knew they couldn't afford to risk a falling out with the Carlton-Smythes. They all nodded back politely.

Vanessa felt a spurt of disgust. She knew they disliked her and resented her family, and yet they all put on masks and pretended an affinity none of them felt. Including Vanessa. But she was reluctant to ruin their family and Miss Dorsett's chances for an advantageous match, simply because she disliked them. As a Carlton-Smythe she may wield a great deal of power, but Vanessa had been taught from a young age to use it wisely and judiciously. It simply wasn't in her nature to be so spiteful.

"Do you need a moment, Vanessa?" Aunt Grace asked, continuing their stroll, smiling and nodding as she went. She had been raised a Carlton-Smythe as well and knew how to maintain appearances. She also knew how this life sometimes suffocated Vanessa, and she was sympathetic. Aunt Grace had never married, not by choice but because her father and brother had never found a suitor worthy of her. She had once confided in Vanessa that were the grocer to offer for her at this point, she would say yes without a moment's hesitation or consideration.

"Yes." She did need a moment alone. She needed to regroup and settle her nerves. It wouldn't do for anyone here to see her flustered or in a temper. She lived her life in a glass bowl. Her thoughts and feelings were her own, however, and not for public scrutiny.

Suddenly her aunt stumbled and caught her heel on Vanessa's hem, tearing it. "Oh, dear!" Aunt Grace exclaimed. Several ladies and gentlemen standing nearby rushed over to help her unsteady aunt. "Oh, I've torn your hem, Vanessa," Aunt Grace said sadly. "I'm so sorry."

Vanessa wanted to applaud her masterful performance. Instead she smiled warmly. "I'm fine, Aunt Grace. As long as you are all right?"

Her aunt was glancing around the floor. "I'm fine, dear. I just can't fathom what I must have tripped on," she mused. By now there were at least ten people searching the floor in vain for the offending article. "Run along and get your hem fixed, Vanessa," Aunt Grace begged. "I shall be well cared for, I'm sure." A chorus of assurances came from her aunt's rescuers as Mrs. Crusher pressed a glass of lemonade into her aunt's hand and she was led to a chair.

Vanessa didn't answer. Instead she slipped out without anyone noticing.

She had almost reached the relative seclusion of the retiring room when a small noise to her right made Vanessa stop. It had sounded a little like distress, but not quite. Was it a man or woman? Again, Vanessa wasn't sure. It might have been a cat, even.

The noise came again and Vanessa turned her head slowly until she gazed into the dark shadows of a small hallway, partially hidden by a chest of some sort. She couldn't immediately discern what was happening. There appeared to be a couple, or perhaps more? They were hiding in the shadows, and a gentleman was holding a woman up. The dark material of his coat sleeve stood out in stark relief against the lady's pale dress. Vanessa took a step toward them, still silent. The man raised his head from the woman's shoulder and his eyes met Vanessa's.

Her heart stuttered and then beat erratically. His eyes were black, one speck of light burning in each, mesmerizing her. She was frozen in place by the heat and intensity of his stare.

The moment was broken when the woman in his arms squirmed and sighed. The sound was the one that had caught Vanessa's attention. Breaking eye contact with Vanessa, the man bent over the woman's shoulder, one hand cupping the back of her head to hold her steady. Then he licked her neck.

Vanessa's breath caught in her throat. It was an assignation. She'd stumbled upon lovers, it seemed.

Embarrassment burned in her cheeks. Only the man was aware of her. Vanessa was uncharacteristically flustered. Should she turn and hurry on to the retiring room, probably alerting the woman to her presence? Or should she quietly back out the way she'd come? That seemed somehow like a retreat, a surrender to the challenge she'd seen gleaming in the gentleman's dark eyes.

When a second man stepped out of the shadows and took the woman's hand from the first man's shoulder, Vanessa gaped like a green girl. He, too, was watching Vanessa as he kissed the woman's hand. His hair gleamed in the faint light from the hallway sconce; it was obviously golden, though light or dark she couldn't tell. He was taller than his companion. The woman giggled and it was then Vanessa recognized who it was. Miss Dorsett. Not a woman then, but a girl too young to understand the trouble that had found her. With a sigh, Vanessa realized it was up to her to rescue the foolish chit.

Before she could make her presence known the blond gentleman spoke quietly. "We must return you to the drawing room before you are missed, Melinda." His voice was a deep whisper, a mere rumble that carried across the hall to Vanessa, and she shivered. The dark-haired man smiled at her as if he'd seen the telltale sign of her discomfort and it amused him.

"Oh pooh," Melinda said, sounding like a spoiled child. "I was told you two were dangerous, a threat to my virtue. A few kisses and a pinch or two and you're sending me off? That hardly signifies. I shall have to tell everyone your reputations are much exaggerated." Vanessa could picture her pouting, though she faced away from Vanessa.

The dark-haired man laughed quietly. "So now you know our secret. We are truly saints in disguise." He untangled her arms from around his neck. "Go now. We shall follow after so no one suspects your virtue was threatened."

"Well, it wasn't," Miss Dorsett declared testily. "I was hoping for some fun with you two this season before I must settle into a staid marriage with someone appropriate. God knows I can't encourage you as suitors, but I thought at least you could satisfy me in private. I begin to think I shall have to find a different lover to do so." She patted her hair. "Don't ask me to dance again. Mama had a fit when I agreed earlier. You are not marriage material, after all."

Miss Dorsett turned toward the drawing room and Vanessa swallowed a gasp and stepped back quickly, pressing against the wall behind her as if she could blend into the garish oriental print on the paper there. Even though Miss Dorsett faced the opposite end of the hallway from where Vanessa stood, she feared the girl would detect her presence. She needn't have worried. It was apparent the young lady was quite put out and too self-interested to notice her surroundings.

"I shall send for you if I want you," Miss Dorsett said dismissively. "Until then, stay away. I won't have you two ruining my chances at a brilliant match. Mama says I am the catch of the season."

The dark-haired gentleman bowed over her hand as if in agreement, keeping her attention focused on him while the taller one moved to stand between Vanessa and Miss Dorsett as if to help her hide from the girl. "Of course," he said in reply. Vanessa recognized the amused disdain in his voice. It was quite confusing as to who had been using whom in their little assignation, for there was clearly no love lost between the three.

Without a word or look in Vanessa's direction the two men ushered Miss Dorsett between them down the hallway, leaving Vanessa feeling like an eavesdropping fool as she hurried to the retiring room.

Once they were out of sight of the blonde beauty, Nick watched as Oliver grabbed Miss Dorsett's hand, slowing her retreat to the drawing room. "Melinda, my dear, a question, if you will."

Miss Dorsett turned to Oliver, her look smug and self-satisfied. Nick almost laughed at her misconception. Oliver had never been interested in her at all. Nick had been randy, and Miss Dorsett obviously willing. Though she had preferred Oliver's blond good looks, it had been Nick playing at seduction while a bored Oliver looked on. But someone else had clearly caught Oliver's attention.

"There was a blonde woman, tall and rather cool, talking with your aunt earlier. Who is she?" Oliver asked. He placed a tender kiss upon Miss Dorsett's palm, as if the question was merely meant to delay her and not the only reason Oliver hadn't walked in the opposite direction when they parted ways.

"A cool blonde?" she asked with a frown. Then she laughed, and there was a wicked gleam in her eye. "You must mean Lady Vanessa Carlton-Smythe." The way she said the name clearly indicated she did not care for the quiet, blonde beauty.

When Nick heard the name his heart sank. Even he had heard of the Carlton-Smythes. Lady Vanessa, the daughter of an Earl, was as out of reach as the moon to fellows like him, no matter what Nick had seen in her eyes as she'd watched him. His sinking heart turned to an acute pain in his stomach as he recognized the look on Oliver's face. Oliver wanted a new toy, and he wasn't going to take no for an answer.

"Don't bother," Miss Dorsett said dismissively. "She won't grant you an audience. The high and mighty Lady Vanessa is too good for the likes of you. She thinks she's too good for the likes of just about everyone." Her look turned spiteful. "But I'd like to see you try. Wouldn't that set everyone's tongues wagging?" She laughed. "Lady Vanessa, unwed at twenty-two, reduced to accepting you two as suitors. How rich!"

Nick didn't care for her tone. Actually, he didn't care for her at all. When she kept her mouth shut she was only tolerable. When she spoke she became completely intolerable.

With a sigh he realized he wouldn't have wanted to go any further with her than he had, even if they hadn't been interrupted. He'd lost interest in her almost immediately. That had been happening more and more lately to both him and Oliver. It was the reason they'd come back from the continent after almost three years abroad. Nick was beginning to think there wasn't a woman alive who could hold their interest for more than an hour.

"Yes, how rich," Oliver agreed in a pleasant tone. "Now, off to the drawing room with you." He dismissed her lightly with a little tap on the bottom, as if she were a naughty child. With a huff, Miss Dorsett turned and stalked out of view.

"I hope you don't come to regret that rather cavalier dismissal," Nick observed, leaning his shoulder against the wall.

"What could you have been thinking to choose that one out of all the women here tonight?" Oliver asked, exasperated. "A ready quim is one thing, of course, but I know for a fact you are not that desperate. I distinctly remember sharing a rather nice fuck just the other night."

Nick shrugged with one shoulder. "I wanted to fuck tonight. I wasn't aware there were limitations on that particular pastime."

"There aren't." Oliver leaned his back flat against the opposite wall and crossed his arms while he regarded Nick. "But you aren't one to indiscriminately fuck when the urge strikes. Care to tell me why tonight was different?"

"It wasn't." Nick looked away, toward the drawing room. "I was very discriminating. I determined that this party was a crashing bore and the only thing that could save the evening was a nice, clandestine fuck. With my best friend, of course," he added, bowing slightly in Oliver's direction. "And I chose the most willing, and likely, candidate in the vicinity."

Oliver bowed back. "I thank you for the thought. But next time, let me choose the candidate."

"Oh no," Nick said, standing up straight. He pointed at Oliver and glared. "I choose young ladies with loose morals and absent chaperones. You choose wide-eyed, innocent, well-bred young ladies who get us shot."

"I got shot. Not you. And you have never been disappointed in any of my choices."

"I was greatly disappointed in Mathilde, since she got you shot."

Oliver sighed. He sounded so long-suffering that Nick had to grit his teeth against his annoyance. "Before I was shot, you were not disappointed," he pointed out, irritatingly patient. "And I readily admit she was an ill-conceived choice, but how was I to know her ancient husband was such a good shot? Spaniards aren't known for their accuracy, after all."

"But they are well-known for their passionate tempers," Nick ground out. He shook his head. "I knew that too, and should have said no."

Oliver grinned conspiratorially. "She was worth it, no?"

"No." Nick's reply was flat but adamant. "And neither is this one." He pleaded, his hands outstretched. "Please, Oliver, not again. There are plenty of merry widows who would gladly share our bed. Please leave this Lady Vanessa alone."

"She looked so...isolated," Oliver mused. "As if she lived separate from the world." He looked at Nick then, and Nick was frozen by the desolation in Oliver's face. "I know that feeling. She's very lonely."

And that was that, wasn't it? If Oliver wanted Lady Vanessa, then Nick would help him get her. For both of them.

Chapter Two

ഇ

"May I have this dance?"

Vanessa turned to the unfamiliar voice, relief warring with trepidation. Trepidation won out when she saw it was the tall, blond gentleman whose illicit interlude she'd interrupted not long ago.

"We have not been introduced, sir," she stalled politely. She was frantically trying to find her wayward aunt without appearing the least perturbed. From the knowing look on the gentleman's face she'd failed miserably.

"Mr. Oliver Gabriel, at your service," he replied with a small bow.

There was nothing untoward in his speech or manner, and yet Vanessa felt as if her defenses were being assailed. How she hated being unsure in these situations, her hands tied by polite manners and societal mores.

She sketched a slight curtsey. "How do you do?" she murmured.

"And you are?" he asked, amusement written in his devastatingly attractive half smile. His good looks alone made her wary of a mere dance. He'd had the delightfully witty and vivacious Miss Dorsett very nearly throwing herself at his feet but a half hour past. His interest in Vanessa must surely be motivated by a desire to ensure her silence.

"Lady Vanessa," an irritating voice trilled to her left. Lady Dalrymple was hurrying up to them, resembling a startled, plump dove in her gray watered silk. "Let me introduce you to Mr. Oliver Gabriel. A friend of Mrs. Shelby's nephew, isn't that right, Mr. Gabriel?" He nodded, but didn't take his eyes off Vanessa. "And this is Lady Vanessa Carlton-Smythe," she continued, breathless from her rush to reach them, and from the thrill of introducing Vanessa to someone unsuitable, in all likelihood. "You should dance, my dear," the older woman crooned sympathetically. "You haven't had a partner all evening."

At that comment Mr. Gabriel's eyes flicked to Lady Dalrymple and then back to Vanessa. Vanessa wasn't sure what his look meant. Agreement with Lady Dalrymple? Horror that he might have asked a social pariah to dance? Distaste for Lady Dalrymple's obvious efforts to demean Vanessa in front of him? Vanessa dearly hoped it was the latter.

With an effort Vanessa tore her gaze away from Mr. Gabriel and saw with growing discomfort that they had attracted an audience. Her gaze clashed with that of the dark-eyed, dark-haired, frowning gentleman who'd been holding Miss Dorsett. The one who had licked the girl's neck. Vanessa could see the wicked caress in her mind as clearly as if she were watching it again, and her cheeks heated as perspiration broke out on her brow and between her breasts. He frowned harder at her and then his gaze cut to Mr. Gabriel.

Mr. Gabriel just stood there. It took Vanessa a moment to figure out that he was waiting on her answer. The entire room was waiting. Suddenly her mouth felt as if it was stuffed with cotton wool. She couldn't utter a sound. She just stood there, biting her lip, staring back at Mr. Gabriel.

From the corner of her eye she saw the dark-haired man turn away in anger. There was something about his rejection of the whole scene, of her in particular, that spurred her to answer.

"Yes," she blurted out. The smile that slowly spread over Mr. Gabriel's face had butterflies dancing in her stomach.

Lady Dalrymple's reaction was worth the nerves now besetting Vanessa. The older woman stood there gaping, her mouth hanging open. Vanessa belatedly realized she hadn't been trying to demean her by pointing out her lack of partners, but by showing her incapable of accepting an innocent offer of a dance from someone socially beneath her. Now that she had, Vanessa was sure Lady Dalrymple would find a way to twist it into something unpleasant.

Without acknowledging Lady Dalrymple or any of the other observers of their introduction, Mr. Gabriel took Vanessa's hand and led her out to the dance floor. They passed the dark-haired man, who stopped to watch them walk by. His look was enigmatic now and Vanessa found herself inordinately curious as to what he made of her acceptance.

It wasn't until they were facing each other on the dance floor that Vanessa realized she didn't know what dance they were supposed to be doing. She peeked up at Mr. Gabriel, who was still watching her, that ever-present amusement on his face. His eyes were brown, so light they were almost gold. With his wavy blond hair, it was a potent combination. Vanessa sternly reminded herself to keep her head about her. She had a feeling there was a great deal more to Mr. Gabriel than attractive features.

"It's a waltz," he told her. Her eyes widened in surprise at his apparent ability to read her mind. "You haven't danced all night," he told her as he took his position next to her and held his hand out for hers. "I assumed you hadn't been paying attention to the dances."

"I have not," she agreed truthfully. "Thank you." With a deep breath Vanessa found the composure that had abandoned her earlier. She placed one hand in Mr. Gabriel's and her other arm on his shoulder, which was no mean feat as he was so tall. She should have found out the dance before agreeing. A waltz was far too provocative to dance with a complete stranger. Especially this dangerously compelling stranger.

The music began, a slow French waltz. That meant a *Sauteuse* waltz and a *Jetté* would follow, all with Mr. Gabriel. As they performed the march steps, the introduction to the dance, she could tell that in spite of his size he was an excellent dancer, light on his feet with a gentle hand to guide his partner. For the first time since he'd asked her to dance, Vanessa relaxed and began to enjoy herself.

She loved to dance. The music, the feel of her partner's hand in hers, moving her body vigorously — the entire act pleased her. It was a freedom she rarely enjoyed in any other endeavor. And conversation was most often kept to a minimum. She needn't utter an endless stream of platitudes, merely one or two when the dancing brought her face-to-face with her partner.

She had to reach high in order to grasp Mr. Gabriel's hand over their heads as they spun in a *pas de bourée*, and with a genuine smile he lowered his arm to accommodate her without missing a step.

"You are quite dainty," he observed admiringly. "I feel like a great elephant next to you."

Vanessa laughed. "I am not so dainty as you believe, but you are indeed greater in size. Your dancing, however, makes you appear as a gazelle rather than an elephant."

He frowned. "I'm not sure I wish to be a slight gazelle. But I think you meant that as a compliment. Did you not?"

"Indeed I did," she said on the next pass around, and they switched hands over their heads. He had very masculine hands.

He inclined his head. "Thank you. And may I return the compliment. Your dancing is as graceful as I imagined it would be."

Vanessa just smiled. She'd heard many such empty compliments. She concentrated on the dance and the music, and the feel of Mr. Gabriel's big, strong hands.

When the *Sauteuse* began Mr. Gabriel placed his hands on her waist and she nearly flew through the air in the first up-tempo *pas de bourée*. If she hadn't been holding onto his shoulders she would have. It felt so wonderful she laughed out loud.

"Ah, there it is," he said with light laugh. "Now I know you are enjoying our dance."

"Oh, yes," she said breathlessly, "very much." When she realized what she'd said she looked at him in alarm. He just smiled and spun her again. So Vanessa ignored her better judgment and lost herself in the dance.

She was a dream to dance with. So light and dainty, and yet full of energy and delight as he spun her about the floor. Oliver hadn't enjoyed a dance this much in years. She hadn't wanted to dance with him. He'd seen her hesitation. Thank God for busybodies like Lady Dalrymple, interfering where they were not wanted and ignorantly playing right into his hands.

Lady Vanessa's hold on his hands was firm and assured. Each time they grasped hands she practically caressed his palm, and then wrapped her elegant fingers around his like a kiss. She liked the way he felt. He knew it. He took a deep breath, not allowing his desire for her to get out of control. They were on display here, after all. He wanted her. He didn't want to drive her away by embarrassing her with his lack of discretion.

He wished the French waltz was danced in reverse, fast to slow rather than slow to fast. He wanted to tease her some more, to pull her close to his side and feel the rise and fall of her rapid breathing. When the dance called for her to place her hands behind her back as he slid his hands around her waist and grasped them, he had to fight the urge to yank her against him and kiss her.

Her eyes widened and she looked like a startled doe. Something must have shown in his expression. Her manner cooled considerably for the remainder of the dance and Oliver inwardly cursed. Rather than retreating when the dance came to a close, however, he went on the attack.

"You didn't run when you saw us," he said as they began to leave the dance floor. "Why?"

Only a brief hesitation in her step gave away her surprise at his question. Without looking at him she said, "I was too shocked. I wasn't sure what to do. I didn't at first realize what was happening."

He had to admire her forthrightness. She hadn't tried to pretend ignorance. "And when you did?"

"I didn't wish to embarrass the lady involved."

Now that did surprise Oliver. From Melinda Dorsett's words he'd assumed the animosity between them was mutual. Apparently not. Lady Vanessa's sensitivity to how the situation might have affected the other woman was admirable. It also showed an unexpected depth of understanding concerning the consequences that could occur were one to be caught in such a compromising position. For many reasons, Oliver thanked God it was Lady Vanessa who had discovered them, and not someone else. It would have been Nick who paid the price and Oliver could not have tolerated that.

Lady Vanessa began to move in the direction of an attractive older woman who had been watching them closely. Oliver refused to let her go. Instead he steered her in the opposite direction.

"Mr. Gabriel," she said firmly. "Our dance is at an end. To walk and talk privately with you now could be construed as a declaration."

"Perhaps it is," he said cheerfully. He practically dragged her over toward Nick. Not that the rest of the room could tell. Her composure never faltered, and he was sure onlookers saw nothing amiss in their pleasant conversation. Nick watched them approach, his expression wary. Nick was oblivious, as usual, to the longing glances cast his way by the young ladies idling nearby. His dark good looks drew them like bees to nectar. His complete disregard for them also attracted them, perverse creatures that they were. The more he ignored them, the more they wanted him. It was amusing, really.

He gauged Lady Vanessa's reaction. She had looked mesmerized by Nick earlier in the dark of the hallway. Was it him or what he had been doing with Miss Dorsett?

As they drew up in front of Nick, Lady Vanessa grew agitated. Although, again, it was hard to tell unless you were watching her closely. Her cheeks turned a becoming shade of pink and she refused to look at Nick. Interesting.

"May I present Mr. Nicholas Wilkes?" Oliver said. "Nick, this is Lady Vanessa Carlton-Smythe."

Lady Vanessa reluctantly held out her hand and Nick shook it, bending over in a slight bow. "How do you do, Lady Vanessa?" Nick murmured. His face was set but his eyes were stormy. Nick didn't understand. He thought her reluctance was just that, and not the result of an unwanted attraction. Oliver wanted to laugh in delight. Oh, seducing Lady Vanessa was going to be so much fun.

"And now we are three," Oliver said with satisfaction. "Surely no one can criticize us now if we promenade around the room together? Hmm?"

Nick cast a startled glance his way.

"I dare say they should not," Lady Vanessa agreed stiffly. "Although they surely will."

Oliver laughed. "Let them talk. Come." He began walking again and Nick fell into step on the other side of Lady Vanessa. He said nothing, clearly letting Oliver lead the way.

"Are you enjoying the holiday season?" Oliver asked, keeping the conversation impersonal. For now.

"Yes," she replied politely. "Although it has only just begun." She cast an amused look his way. "Truthfully, I would prefer the old ways, I think. Games, Yule logs, Christmas candles, mummers and greenery." She blushed on the last.

"Mistletoe?" Oliver teased.

"And others," she said sharply. "Rosemary and holly, ivy and bay."

"Of course," he murmured. After a minute or two of silence he tried again. "I enjoyed our dance immensely," Oliver commented, watching Lady Vanessa nod politely to just about everyone they passed. "Do you dance often?"

"I like to dance," she answered simply. "I do not get the opportunity as often as I would like."

"Why not?" Nick asked, startling both Oliver and Vanessa. His voice was low and harsh. "Why did no one ask you tonight?"

Lady Vanessa's hand tightened on Oliver's arm. "I'm sure I don't know," she replied, her demeanor composed. "Why don't you inquire of the men in attendance?"

"I think they're frightened of you," Oliver said sincerely. "You are too self-possessed for a woman. It unmans them."

She turned shocked eyes on Oliver. "What?"

"He's right," Nick agreed. "You gaze at them all as if daring them to approach you. Not many men are up to a challenge of that sort."

"Just Mr. Gabriel?" she asked lightly, not looking at them again.

"I cannot resist a challenge like that," Oliver murmured, not wanting to be overheard. "You dare a seduction of the most dangerous and rewarding kind."

She stumbled and then quickly righted herself. "I do no such thing," she argued just as quietly. "Pray put it right out of your head. I desire nothing of the sort."

Nick laughed, a quiet huff that drew Lady Vanessa's eyes. "Don't bother to deny it or try to circumvent it," he advised her. "Simply accept that the attempt will be made, and try to resist it."

"Resist it I most certainly will," she said in steely tones. "Believe it or not, other men have tried and failed miserably, as you will."

Oliver and Nick both laughed this time.

"What is so amusing?" she demanded, stopping to glare at them both, once she determined no one was near to overhear them.

Oliver exchanged an amused glance with Nick. "I never fail where I am determined to succeed," he told her, not caring how arrogant he sounded.

Nick nodded. "Never."

Her eyes narrowed and a small smile curved her delicious, pale-rose-colored lips. "Neither do I," she said firmly.

The gauntlet was thrown.

Chapter Three

ஐ

Vanessa scanned the room as soon as she entered. It had been seven days since the Shelbys' Christmas Eve dinner party. In spite of her original plan to stay at home this holiday season, Vanessa had gone out every night. And at each party she'd attended the determined faces of Mr. Gabriel and Mr. Wilkes greeted her. It was both irksome and flattering.

With a disgusted huff she forced herself to stop looking for them. Let them dance attendance on her in an embarrassing display of interest and possession. She needn't play along. Seduction required two parties. Or, in this particular case, three. Which was quite disconcerting.

Vanessa was not ignorant of those sorts of relationships. Through their mutual charity work, she had grown quite close to Veronica Tarrant, who, with her husband, had taken a second lover. Vanessa saw the three of them across the room, laughing together as they conversed with two other gentlemen. Vanessa was not privy to the details of their relationship, but it was obvious the three were...intimate. All of them. With one another. The possibilities had kept Vanessa awake many, many nights.

Not that Vanessa wished to have a relationship of that sort herself. It seemed to her that one man was more than enough to deal with. Her mother lived in a constant state of vexation with her father. There were examples of frustrated couples wherever Vanessa went. She imagined the frustration was twofold when two men were involved. It seemed like an awful lot of work for one woman. Truly.

And yet, several times over the last few days Vanessa had put herself in Miss Dorsett's place in that dark hallway seven nights ago. Held in Mr. Wilkes' arms, his carnal kiss on her neck and Mr. Gabriel's hands on her. She shivered.

"Come over by the fire, Lady Vanessa," a voice drawled in her ear from behind. "It's much warmer there." A hand appeared in front of her holding a bouquet of rosemary. She knew instantly who it was, of course. Each time she'd seen them since their first meeting, Mr. Gabriel and Mr. Wilkes had presented her with gifts of traditional greenery and other Christmastide delights. She'd received holly, ivy and bay in addition to candies and Christmas candles, and now this. She both dreaded and anticipated the appearance of mistletoe.

She met Mr. Wilkes' gaze at her side. He was watching her as Mr. Gabriel stood too close behind her, whispering to her. He was always watching with his too-knowing, intense, dark eyes.

"I'm fine, thank you," she replied politely. "A momentary chill, nothing more." She took the bouquet and held it to her nose.

A footman passed with a tray of champagne and Mr. Wilkes took two glasses. He silently handed her one with his customary slight bow. She took the glass with a nod and sipped it. "You do not talk much, Mr. Wilkes."

"I prefer to do other things with my mouth," he answered slyly. "If you'd care to engage in that type of conversation, I am more than willing."

Behind her Mr. Gabriel gave a surprised snort of quiet laughter. "Hear, hear. Let's. I like that idea."

Vanessa glanced around the company and saw that no one was paying them any attention. She should have been worried about her lack of alarm at their outrageous suggestion, but she found herself amused instead.

"And if I said yes?" she asked conversationally. She watched them share an eager look as she sipped her champagne.

"Are you?" Mr. Gabriel asked as he walked around to face her.

"No," she said, even more amused at their obvious disappointment. She shrugged. "I was just wondering how you would go about finding the privacy for such a...conversation." She gestured with her rosemary to the room full of holiday revelers.

Mr. Wilkes drank his champagne as if it was whiskey. He tipped the glass too far and took a large swallow, his big hand wrapped around the flute, his thumb pointing toward his mouth. She enjoyed watching him. She sometimes got the impression he was like a caged lion in these drawing rooms, pacing around his prison, waiting to take a swipe at anyone who dared get too close to the bars.

It was Mr. Gabriel who answered her question. "We would all leave the room separately, of course, and meet in a designated spot far from prying eyes. It would not be difficult."

Vanessa pretended to consider it. "Something like a dark hallway, perhaps? Close enough to reach quickly from the drawing room, but far enough not to attract undue attention?"

Mr. Wilkes actually smiled. "Something like."

Vanessa shook her head sadly. "You are very unimaginative. Did I not catch you in just such a place during another ill-fated assignation?"

Mr. Wilkes' eyes narrowed. "That was but a dalliance. You're right. A true seduction such as yours would be would require much greater privacy."

Vanessa felt her cheeks grow warm. "I see. And what is the difference between seduction and dalliance?"

Mr. Gabriel lifted her rosemary-laden hand and placed a soft kiss against her wrist through her glove. "To dally is merely to enjoy a brief encounter, nothing more. A seduction is a prolonged act of temptation and surrender. A prelude to possession. There is nothing brief about a seduction, neither its implementation nor its rewarding conclusion."

She frowned. "You have made a study of the two, I take it?"

"Are you jealous, Lady Vanessa?" Mr. Wilkes said softly, his glass hovering in front of his lips, half-tipped as if to take a drink. "You needn't be." She was almost holding her breath as she waited for him to take a mouthful of that lucky libation. He smiled before he drank, as if he knew what she was thinking.

"I am not," she said indignantly, taking a sip of her own drink as she turned away to survey the room again.

"Good." Mr. Gabriel let go of her hand. She blushed because she'd forgotten they were standing there holding hands. Is that how seduction proceeded, then? Inure the lady to your touch until she doesn't realize you're making love to her? She laughed quietly in amusement at her thoughts. The idea that she could ever get so used to the touch of either of these men that she wouldn't notice if they were making love to her was preposterous.

"Surely you know you are the only woman who holds our interest, Vanessa," Mr. Gabriel continued. "Since we first saw you we have not looked at another."

"Why?" She really was puzzled. She had never inspired devotion of any kind in any man, nor feelings of a baser nature as far as she knew, mild or otherwise, unless motivated by greed or social advancement.

"Your eyes spoke to me." Mr. Gabriel was quite somber as he made such an extraordinary pronouncement. As if realizing he'd revealed too much, he laughed lightly and looked away for a moment before turning back to her. But his smile seemed forced. "You looked lonely, my dear. I wished to remedy it. That's all."

She looked lonely. Vanessa took that blow rather calmly. Yes, she supposed she did. She *was* terribly lonely, after all.

That Mr. Gabriel had sensed something no one else had, neither family nor friends, did indeed reveal a great deal about him. Was it possible he felt the same? Did it matter? Should it be enough that he had seen that about her and wished, if only for a short while, to make it better? She turned expectantly to Mr. Wilkes.

"I wanted you immediately. I saw you watching me with that silly girl, and it wasn't her in my arms, but you. At least, I wished it were. There was such longing in your gaze, Vanessa." He said the last so softly she had to strain to hear. He closed his eyes as if remembering. "I have not seen someone want me so much in a very long time." His eyes opened and burned her with their intensity. "Passion would not be a game with you. I can feel you straining at the leash every time we are together. You crave our touch. You cherish it, relish it even. And those are simple, polite touches—a glide of palms in a dance, a hand at your elbow as we promenade, a brush of fingers on your nape as I help you with your wrap. I have not slept well the past several nights thinking of how you would react to a surer hand and far more intimate touches."

Vanessa was breathless. It was by far the longest speech she had yet to hear Mr. Wilkes make. And what a speech it was. He bared her soul with it. He was right, damn him. Their touches were water upon her parched skin. She wanted more. There was a passion blooming in her under their attentions she had not truly understood she possessed. And she wanted to give in to it.

"Take it, Vanessa," Mr. Gabriel said fervently. "Take what we are offering you. There is no ulterior motive, no strings or complications involved. There is only passion and need between us. We want nothing more. You needn't fear that."

Of course they wanted nothing more. Because they knew Vanessa could not give it to them. They might argue otherwise, but it was a dalliance, plain and simple.

Vanessa did not have to answer. Veronica Tarrant interrupted them. "You are all so serious! This is a holiday party, isn't it? Where is your Christmas spirit? Twelfth Night is days away! It is time to make merry." She grabbed Vanessa's hand. "Come and play cards, my dear. We need a fourth." She dragged Vanessa away, and Vanessa only had time to pass her half-empty glass into Mr. Wilkes' outstretched hand and give them both a brief smile. They smiled back and she knew they wouldn't be far from her for the rest of the evening.

"Are you all right, Vanessa?" Veronica asked when they were out of the gentlemen's hearing.

Vanessa replied warily. "Yes. Why?" Had she unknowingly revealed something when she was talking to Mr. Gabriel and Mr. Wilkes?

Veronica sighed. "I'm probably not supposed to tell you, but I've actually known you longer than those two, so I shall." She stopped and faced Vanessa. "They asked for my help to court you. I agreed. But then I thought about it and I just want to make sure it's what you want before I assist them."

"You did what?" Vanessa asked incredulously.

Very bit her lip. "I agreed to help them seduce you. Oh, not actually seduce, although I'm sure that's what they have planned, but help them see you more often and cover for you should you all, ahem, disappear for a while."

"Is that why your aunt and uncle invited me this evening?" Vanessa asked stonily. She'd thought Very was a friend, but it looked as if her friendship had ulterior motives, like so many of Vanessa's so-called friends.

"Yes, and don't look so sour." Very rolled her eyes. "You told me months ago that you wanted a man who wanted you for yourself, didn't you? Well, here they are. I want you to have an illicit passion, Vanessa. You are too unhappy by far."

Vanessa actually sputtered, at a loss for words.

"See?" Very said nonsensically. "Just the thought of such a daring adventure has you speechless." She leaned closer after casting a furtive glance around the room. "I can tell you that there is nothing better than illicit passion. Truly. And I want you to have that." She took Vanessa's arm and continued across the room. "It's settled then. When you give me the signal I shall divert everyone's attention while you three slip out." She leaned toward her again, while still walking, and spoke quietly out of the corner of her mouth, as if imparting a great secret. "There's a small, unused linen closet on the third floor, second door to the left, that makes an ideal trysting spot. Here we are!" she trilled gaily as they came to a stop at the card table. Mr. Tarrant and Lord Kensington, Very's husband and lover, stood at their arrival. They'd clearly been waiting for them, cards at the ready. "I've found her." Very plopped herself down in one of the empty chairs. "I shall partner Wolf and Kensington will partner you, Vanessa."

Lord Kensington held her chair as Vanessa obediently sat down.

"It is a pleasure to see you again, Lady Vanessa," Lord Kensington said, his smile genuine. Vanessa wondered if he knew of Mr. Gabriel's and Mr. Wilkes' plan and blushed. Lord Kensington looked puzzled by her reaction and sat down with a slight hesitation. "I do hope you wish to play cards, Lady Vanessa," he said politely. "I know Mrs. Tarrant can be rather domineering."

"I'm right here, you know," Very said from across the table. "I can hear what you're saying."

"That's why I'm saying it," Lord Kensington responded, picking up his cards as Mr. Tarrant dealt. "What good would it do if you couldn't hear it?"

"Be careful, or I'll domineer you," Very said with a mock fierce look.

Mr. Tarrant made a clicking noise, as if settling down a hissing cat. "He would roll over and submit, as usual, my dear. Play cards."

Very laughed loudly. Lord Kensington did not dispute Mr. Tarrant, however, and Vanessa thought she might have actually seen him wink at the other man.

They drew a crowd as they played, mainly because Very was laughing contagiously the whole time as she bantered with Lord Kensington while Mr. Tarrant tried to mediate their conversation. Vanessa felt her loneliness grow as she listened, a fierce longing for an intimacy of affection such as the three obviously shared.

"I was sorry that your parents couldn't join us this evening, Lady Vanessa," Very's aunt, Lady Randall, said at one point from where she watched their game.

"They're not in town," Vanessa said, distracted by her cards. "They are attending a house party in Kent. I feared I was coming down with a fever last week and didn't accompany them."

"Oh," Very said, full of concern. "Are you all right now?"

Vanessa was startled by her concern. "Yes, thank you. It passed within a day." She gestured across the room to where Aunt Grace sat, deep in conversation with the dowager countess, Lord Randall's mother. "My aunt came to take care of me, and has graciously agreed to celebrate the holiday season with me."

"I'm glad you are not alone this holiday," Very said, grasping her hand. "You and your aunt must come to our house tomorrow night for dinner." She looked around the table. "You all must come! We shall have a wonderful evening." She looked back at Vanessa. "You can see the baby. Say you'll come."

Vanessa laughed at her earnestness. "I'll come." Very clapped in delight, quite pleased with herself.

Mr. Tarrant barely glanced up from his cards as he commented, "It's a good thing the household is used to your impromptu dinners, my dear."

"You all love them, you know you do," Very said looking at both Mr. Tarrant and Lord Kensington. Lord Kensington murmured his agreement while he glowered at his cards, seemingly unaware he'd just admitted to being part of the

Tarrant household. Vanessa took her cue from the rest of the company and ignored his comment.

Vanessa had to amend her acceptance. "I'll come if I can. I'm pledged to the orphanage tomorrow, to hand out charitable gifts."

"Oh, do you need help?" Very asked, biting her lip worriedly. She often helped at the orphanage with Vanessa. It was how they'd become acquainted.

"We shall help, won't we Nick?" Mr. Gabriel said with a smile at Vanessa. "If you would like?"

"Oh, good," Very said in a tone that implied the discussion was over. "I had planned to do some holiday preparations tomorrow. Wolf's parents are coming for Twelfth Night."

"It's settled then," Mr. Gabriel agreed with satisfaction. Vanessa raised her brows at his high-handedness but said nothing. She saw Mr. Wilkes smile.

It wasn't long before Vanessa grew agitated with Lord Kensington's play. "My lord," she said calmly after they'd lost another hand due to his poor play, "I must insist that you stop cheating. For the other side."

Her comment drew guffaws from around the room as Lord Kensington stammered out a denial. Very threw down her cards. "Oh drat. She's figured us out." Her comment caused even more laughter.

"Well, you don't have to live with her when she loses," Lord Kensington defended himself. "She's impossible."

Mr. Gabriel plucked a protesting Lord Kensington out of his chair and sat down. "I'll take over." He waved at Very. "Go on."

Very raised an eyebrow. "Think you can beat us, do you? Well, we shall see, Mr. Gabriel."

He wasn't looking at Very. He was looking at Vanessa with a question written on his face. "We don't have to cheat," she told Very. Mr. Gabriel's answering smile was victorious.

"Oh, that is a challenge if I ever heard one," Very said, smartly dealing the cards. "Did you hear that, Tarrant? She thinks to humiliate us."

The play was even for a bit while Vanessa and Mr. Gabriel learned each other's style of play. Mr. Wilkes had been idly wandering around the table while they played, perusing everyone's hands. On the sixth hand he stopped opposite Vanessa just as she was about to play a card. He shook his head very slightly. Vanessa wasn't even sure at first she'd seen it. She tapped the card again, and again he barely moved his head from side to side. Hmm, Very must have another heart, then, and a high one at that. Which meant Vanessa would have to play her ace to win the trick. She touched the ace and Mr. Wilkes smiled. Before playing it she glanced across the table to Mr. Gabriel. His eyes met hers for a moment and a half smile crooked his lip before he looked back down at his own cards.

Vanessa played her ace and won the trick before she realized they were cheating for her. And it had seemed so natural to follow their lead. She ought to feel remorse for resorting to the same sort of trickery she'd called Kensington out for, but instead she was elated. It was the first time she'd ever felt this sort of communion with a member of the opposite sex. They shared a secret, the three of them. It was a heady thought and she was drunk on her own audaciousness. She had to take a drink of champagne to keep the smile off her face.

And so it went for the next half hour, until Very threw her cards down in disgust and frowned ferociously at Vanessa. "We shall defeat you tomorrow night. You are fairly warned."

Vanessa laughed and held her hand out across the table. "Peace, friend. I look forward to another game tomorrow."

Very shook her hand. "We meet at dusk."

The crowd laughed and clapped good-naturedly as Mr. Tarrant and Mr. Gabriel also shook hands. As Vanessa stood up, Mr. Wilkes appeared behind her to pull out her chair. "An excellent game, Lady Vanessa. Well played."

She smirked at him conspiratorially. "Thank you."

The crowd was breaking up around them and Vanessa waited a few moments before she smoothed a hand down her skirt and looked pointedly at Mr. Wilkes and then back at Very. "I think I shall go and refresh myself." It took a moment for Very to catch on. Then she insisted quite loudly that she must, this very minute, have some music or her Christmastide was ruined. Half the party moved off into the adjoining music room.

Vanessa waited until they had a small space of privacy. Then she said softly, "Very told me there's a small…retiring room on the third floor." Her voice was so quiet both men had to lean over to hear her. Mr. Wilkes' wide eyes flew up to meet hers, and Mr. Gabriel winked. He was outrageous. But then, so was she, wasn't she?

Vanessa slowly made her way out of the room, sharing a word here and there with acquaintances and smiling at her aunt, who immediately went back to her conversation. Just before she went out the door she nonchalantly turned back to survey the room, sniffing her bouquet of rosemary. Mr. Gabriel stood at Mr. Wilkes' side, and both men were watching her retreat. At her look Mr. Gabriel smiled and looked up at the ceiling.

Her heart pounding, Vanessa went in search of illicit passion.

Chapter Four

ᘒ

Nick tapped lightly on the door. It had been left ajar, so both he and Oliver assumed this was it. If not, they would have to do some quick explaining.

The door was yanked open and a disembodied hand came out of the interior darkness and grabbed Oliver's arm, yanking him inside. Oliver laughed and in turn grabbed Nick and dragged him right behind. Once they were in there he only got a quick impression of Vanessa before she slammed the door and they were all lost in the dark.

"Are you mad?" she hissed. "Knocking on the door? What if someone heard?"

"Well, just in case they didn't, it's a good thing you slammed the door behind us so they'd be sure to hear that," Oliver drawled with a thread of laughter beneath his words.

Vanessa moaned as if in pain. "I'm not very good at this sneaking about business," she confessed in a miserable tone. "Perhaps this was a bad idea."

"It was a brilliant idea," Oliver said soothingly. "Now where are you?"

Nick felt a hand on his hip and he caught his breath at the thrill that shot through him. Here in the dark he could enjoy Oliver's touch without anyone noticing or caring. He stepped closer, but Oliver patted his buttock and pulled away.

"That's the wrong person," Oliver quipped lightly. "Ah, there you are, my dear," he purred, obviously having found Vanessa. There was some rustling in the dark and then a soft, fragrant shape was pressed against Nick.

"Oh," Vanessa said softly. She squirmed, and Nick forgot his disappointment over Oliver moving away. He bent his knees and pressed his hips into Vanessa's soft bottom. He gave a little rub and a slight moan escaped him.

"Oh," she said again, and the wonder and uncertainty combined in her voice hit Nick hard. His heart was suddenly pounding in excitement, his cock hard. The transition had been so quick he ached from it. He hadn't been this aroused from a simple touch in a very long time. Was it the thought of Vanessa's innocence? Her trust in them? More likely simple anticipation. He'd seen the fire in her. Now he wanted to taste it—to possess it and be consumed by it.

Vanessa made a little distressed sound and started to move away. Her steps were clumsy and Nick could tell Oliver was blocking her retreat.

"Don't," Nick rasped. He reached out and put his hands on her hips, holding her against him. "Please don't."

"Open the door," Oliver demanded. "It's too dark. I want to see you two."

"No," Vanessa gasped. "They'll see."

"Who? There's no one up here but we three."

Oliver's argument was sound, but Nick wanted it dark for reasons of his own. "No," he said. He wrapped one arm around Vanessa's waist and with the other found Oliver's arm. "No. Leave it be. I like the dark."

For a moment they all stood still, their harsh breathing cutting the air. There was heat arcing between them, and Nick felt like the conduit. He was burning up inside. Giving in to temptation, he leaned down and breathed in Vanessa's scent. His nose found her hair and he followed the curve of her cheek down to her neck. When he put his mouth on her sweet-smelling skin, she whimpered.

"Kiss me, Vanessa," Oliver whispered. "Please."

Her neck arched under Nick's lips as she tilted her head up, and he nibbled on the taut tendon along the side. He felt her tremble under his hands. And then he heard it. Heard the sound of their lips meeting, the gentle sounds of a sweet kiss. His fingers tightened on Oliver's arm and he pulled Vanessa closer against him.

"Have you never been kissed before, pretty Vanessa?" Oliver murmured.

"I...yes, yes, I've been kissed," she stammered breathlessly.

"Not *really* kissed," Oliver said. His hand brushed Nick's cheek as Nick nibbled on Vanessa's ear. Oliver pulled his hand back, and it hovered near Nick's face for a second before he brought it back again and finished the caress, just a fleeting touch. Then he must have used his other hand to caress Vanessa's cheek. She sighed and tilted her head as if leaning into his hand.

"What does that mean?" Vanessa asked softly.

Nick pressed his finger against the corner of her mouth. "Open up," he whispered. "Let Oliver taste you. And you can see what love tastes like."

"Love has a taste?" she whispered skeptically. He liked the feel of her mouth moving against his finger and he slid it along her lower lip, outlining it. His breath caught when her tongue dashed out to lick her lip and found the pad of his finger. She gasped lightly and he slid the tip of his finger into her mouth, just a little, and then dragged it over her lip as he took it out, pulling her lip down slightly.

"It has many flavors," he told her kissing her cheek down to her jaw. "But I don't think we'll get to all of them tonight."

"Why not?" Nick was amused by the haughty tone in her voice, as if she were affronted that they had the temerity to withhold something from her.

Oliver laughed. "We don't have the time or space to do things properly here," he told her. "But what we share tonight will make you crave another taste, I promise."

"I think it is you two who crave, not I," she said coolly. She tried to slide out from between them, but neither he nor Oliver budged an inch. There was no way she could move.

"Why are you angry, little dove?" Oliver murmured. "Don't fly away."

"I am not angry." Her words said one thing, her voice another.

Nick was confused. What had they done? "Don't play games," he told her roughly. "Speak plainly. If you don't tell us what we did wrong, we won't know not to do it again."

She stilled between them. "Is it that easy?" she asked incredulously. "Just tell you, and you won't do it again? You are very unusual men if that is all it takes to mend your ways."

"Mend what ways?" Oliver asked patiently.

Vanessa sighed, clearly defeated. "You seek to make me crave you. Why? What do you want from me?"

Her question was like a blow to Nick. He hadn't realized what it must be like for her. Did she have no friends, no lovers, who wanted her just for herself? Was she so accustomed to being used and deceived she could no longer see the obvious? "You. We want you. Like this."

He turned her face to his with two fingers on her jaw and pressed his lips to hers. In the dark he missed, his lips only half covering hers, but she drew in a sharp breath and it gave Nick the opportunity to slide over her open mouth and lick inside. He didn't kiss her like she was an untried virgin, but as if they were already lovers. Some instinct told him that was the way to have her. Not with kid gloves, but with assurance and vigor. Vanessa wanted to be craved, not wooed. She wanted to be possessed, not have a man ask permission with delicate kisses. If they wanted this to work, and right now Nick desperately wanted this to work, then they couldn't afford to give her time to have second thoughts.

Vanessa responded as he'd known she would. She opened her mouth and let him in, and once she'd learned how to kiss him back she battled to dominate the kiss. He didn't let her, and he could feel how his mastery aroused her. Her breath was quick on his cheek, her heart pounding beneath the arm he had wrapped around her as she moved restlessly between them, seeking more but not sure how to get it.

She tasted like champagne and sweets. Her mouth was small, her teeth straight and smooth against his tongue. He wanted to lift her up and throw her down on the nearest soft bed, mount her and fuck her until she admitted he owned her. He wrapped his hand around the back of her head and held her mouth to his, breathing her air and drinking her desire until she whimpered.

It wasn't until Oliver put his arm around him, buried his hand in Nick's hair and forcibly pulled him away from her that Nick realized how rough he was being. "I'm sorry," he gasped. "Damn, you just...you feel so good."

Oliver kept his hand in Nick's hair, although his hold was gentle now.

"How do I taste?" Vanessa asked, as breathless as he was.

"Taste?" Nick asked stupidly. He was having a hard time thinking with Vanessa in his arms and Oliver's hand petting him like that.

"Do I taste like love?" she asked. "Did I do it right?"

Nick found her hand pressed up against Oliver's chest and he dragged it down between his own legs. He pressed her palm against his erection. "Yes, you did it right. Feel how right." He thrust into her hand and held his breath, waiting to see how she'd react to his crudity.

She cupped her hand around him and her fingers explored the length and width of him. He groaned and grabbed her skirt, trying to yank it up.

"Nick," Oliver said roughly. He grabbed Nick's wrist, stopping him. "Don't."

"Do," Vanessa said, her voice unsteady. "I want you to touch me."

"Damn me," Nick murmured. "Yes."

"May I kiss you again, Vanessa?" Oliver asked. He sounded hesitant, which was so unusual for Oliver in these situations it momentarily took Nick's mind off getting under Vanessa's skirts.

"I wish you would," she responded with an ingrained politeness that made Nick smile. Then she added, "Just like Nick, please," and Nick began pulling up her skirt again.

Oliver let go of Nick's head and Vanessa moved against Nick as if adjusting to something Oliver was doing. Nick had a moment of pity for her, trying to accommodate two men who were desperate to touch and taste her. His pity died quickly, replaced by pure unadulterated lust when she moaned and it was muffled by Oliver's mouth on hers.

"Tell me what you're doing," Nick growled. He wrapped his hand around Vanessa's bare thigh, above her stocking. He'd taken his gloves off before they'd reached the little room they were in. Previous experience with these sorts of clandestine encounters had taught him well.

"She has the most delightful breasts," Oliver said. Nick's hand tightened around Vanessa's thigh at Oliver's tone. He loved to hear it like that, so heavy with need it sounded almost painful for him to talk. It had been so long since Nick had heard him sound like that. What was it about her? Why were simple kisses and touches driving both him and Oliver mad with lust tonight? "Soft and plump." Vanessa gave a little whimper. "Her nipples feel like small raspberries. I have to taste them." The last was said with a near desperation that ignited something in Nick. He let go of Vanessa's thigh and reached for her shoulders, tugging the sleeves of her silk gown down her arms, until he could reach around and pull it under her breasts. Like all women, she wore a multitude of undergarments to protect them. But with a tug on a string or two, Nick and Oliver managed to pull it all down under her breasts, until those soft mounds were propped up on her clothing, an offering for both men.

Nick slid around to her side and Oliver made room for him. Then Nick pressed Vanessa until she rested against his hand on her lower back. He put his mouth on her, didn't really care where he landed as long as it was bare skin. And it was. She tasted so fine, like nothing he'd ever tasted before. Her skin was soft and fragrant and he thought he could spend days just licking her. His mouth encountered the curve of her breast and he was as excited as a young boy at his first taste of love. With an eagerness that had been lacking in recent encounters he sought her nipple. When he sucked it into his mouth and wrapped his tongue around it, Vanessa cried out. Then he moved and his head bumped into Oliver, who was clearly suckling her other breast. Nick wondered if they were moving too fast, but then Vanessa slid her hand into his hair and held him on her breast with a fierceness that drove his desire higher. No, it wasn't too much.

She moved restlessly between them, and both men knew what she wanted. Nick parted his legs and let her hip rub against his engorged cock while she squirmed. It felt so good he had to take his mouth from her just so he could breathe. He rested his cheek on her breast, panting and humping her still-covered leg and he felt like a fool, but he was too gone to care. Suddenly Oliver's breath was on his cheek.

"Are you close, Nicky?" Oliver whispered. Nick thought he might have felt Oliver's lips on his cheek, he was that close to him. He shuddered with desire at the thought, and could only nod his head as he gripped Vanessa's hip and rubbed his cock against her, hard.

"Oh God," Vanessa said weakly. "I'm sorry."

Oliver laughed. "Don't be sorry. It's marvelous. You're marvelous." He kissed her then. Nick heard the sound of their mouths sliding against each other, their tongues tangling just over his head. It was almost too much. He had a sudden, harsh desire to see them fucking. He wanted to watch Oliver fuck Vanessa, slowly, the way he liked, to watch Vanessa writhe beneath the bigger man. And Nick would slide up next to them and they would both service him with their mouths while they fucked, and fucked, and fucked.

He whimpered with the need to come, like a green schoolboy.

Suddenly the door was opened and Nick jerked his head up, but it was Oliver's hand on the latch. Dim light penetrated the closet and Vanessa's cry of fright was cut off sharply.

"I have to see you both," Oliver said roughly. He had his hand over Vanessa's mouth as she stared at him with wide eyes. "I want to watch you both come. I swear, Vanessa, no one will see. Trust me." He looked at Nick. "And next time, remember to bring a light."

"Have you ever seen a man come, Vanessa?" Oliver asked her. He slowly took his hand from her mouth and kissed her apologetically. "Have you?" She shook her head while biting her lip. She looked overwhelmed. Desire warred with fright in her eyes as she glanced between the door and the two men. "Would you like to?" Oliver asked in a devilishly seductive tone. "Would you like to watch Nick come? Would you like to see his bare cock as he does it?"

"Yes," she whispered. She'd covered her breasts with her hands, and the sight of her holding her own breasts was terribly erotic even though Nick knew she didn't mean it to be. He covered one of her hands with his own, tightening her grip until the small mound pressed out along the sides of her hand and then he licked the sweet, exposed flesh.

"Oh God," Vanessa moaned as she let her head drop back in surrender. "Yes, I want to see him. I want to see you both."

"I want to see you first," Nick said. He'd still been rubbing his cock against her, she felt so good, but he forced himself to take a step away. "Lift your skirts for us."

"W—what?" she stammered.

"Show us," Oliver said, his voice hard, demanding, yet at the same time teasing and seductive. Nick didn't know how he did it. He made you do things with that voice, things you wouldn't ordinarily do. Things that felt so damn good. "Show us how much you want it."

Vanessa hesitated, but then she slowly retreated from them. Nick could tell she wasn't trying to get away. Some instinct told him she was going to give them what they wanted, what they all wanted. She leaned against the wall and after another small hesitation, let go of her breasts. There was a thin line of light from the hallway cutting across her right breast that caught Nick's eye. He couldn't look away, watching it rise and fall as her breathing accelerated. He heard the rustle of her skirt and his heart kicked in his chest as he recognized the sound. His eyes dropped down.

She was clutching the skirt in both hands, slowly pulling it up in front. By the time the hem reached her thighs Nick realized she was bare under her petticoat. For a long moment she held the skirt there, and then with a final yank pulled it to her waist.

It wasn't bright enough. Nick wanted to see her in the harsh light of day, see every sweet valley and luscious pink curve of her cunt. Even in the dim light he could see she had a light covering of hair. Was she wet? He wanted to drop to his knees and put his mouth on her to see.

"Gorgeous," Oliver purred. He stepped up next to her, leaning one shoulder against the wall, and put his hand over her mound. Vanessa moaned and Oliver moved his hand against her. "Wet," he said quietly. "Very wet." Oliver turned and pierced Nick with his glance. "Your turn."

Nick backed up until he leaned against the wall opposite Vanessa. He began unbuttoning his pants, his cock throbbing with the need to come for them.

"While Nick pleasures himself for us," Oliver whispered in Vanessa's ear, loud enough for Nick to hear, "I'm going to pleasure you with my fingers. Have you ever come, sweet Vanessa?"

She nodded jerkily. "I ride horses, don't I?"

Oliver and Nick both laughed and Vanessa smiled at them.

"Has a man ever touched your cunt?" Nick asked bluntly. "Has a man ever made you come? Ever fucked you with his fingers?"

Vanessa licked her lips and squirmed against Oliver's hand. She shook her head. "No," she whispered.

"You like it when Nick talks like that, don't you?" Oliver asked, kissing the side of her head and then nuzzling behind her ear. "You are very naughty, aren't you, Vanessa?"

She nodded, caught in his spell, in the heat and seclusion of their little closet. "Yes," she whispered.

Nick had his pants open now. "Look at me," he growled. He shoved his pants down to mid-thigh, exposing his cock, spreading his legs as wide as he could with his pants binding them. "Look at my cock."

She was looking. Oliver was watching, too, as enthralled as Vanessa. Nick wrapped his fist around his cock and Vanessa whimpered.

"Next time you'll do this for me," Nick told her. "Tonight you'll watch and learn how I like it." He knew it wasn't going to take long, not with both of them watching him, wanting him. He knew what Oliver wanted. Why couldn't he give it to him? What held him back? He shook off those thoughts and concentrated on the here and now. On making it good for all of them. On the feel of his hand on his cock, the heat in his sac, the eyes watching him, the sharp, panting breaths of all three of them in the small space.

"I'm going to slide my finger inside you now, Vanessa," Oliver told her. "Tell me if it hurts."

"Tell me," Nick said to both of them. "Tell me how it feels." He moved his fist up and down, from the sensitive crown of his rod to the base, where his fingers brushed his balls. The pleasure made him shiver. He moved his hand faster as he watched Oliver's hand on Vanessa's cunt. It slid deeper between her legs and she spread them wider, giving him the freedom to do as he willed to her. And her eyes never left Nick's cock.

Oliver's wrist moved and Nick could see his hand was moving in a rocking motion. "God damn it," Nick said between clenched teeth. "Tell me."

"She's so damn tight, Nicky," Oliver whispered. "And deliciously wet. We have to get her alone again so we can taste this."

"Talk to me," Vanessa said breathlessly. "Don't talk about me, talk *to* me."

"Fine," Oliver said. "I want to lick your cunt. There. Better?"

"Oh my God," Vanessa whispered. "Do you?"

Nick couldn't contain a burst of laughter. "Oh yes. We'd love it. So please, next time let us lick you."

"Together?" she asked in a trembling voice.

"Together," Oliver promised.

"Yes," she said with a moan.

"Mmm," Nick rumbled, loving the heat and ache rushing over him, his climax hovering just out of sight. "More. Tell me more."

"It feels so odd," Vanessa whispered. "I can't decide if I want him out or I want him deeper." Her voice trembled on the last word. "Yes, deeper," she cried out softly.

"Let me show you," Oliver murmured and Nick looked over to see Oliver slip behind Vanessa, his arm wrapped around her, his finger moving in and out of her more deeply now. He put his other hand on her hip and pushed her down, then up.

He was showing her how to fuck.

"Yes, that's right," Oliver continued encouragingly. "Tell me what you're doing, Vanessa."

"What," she paused to lick her lips, "what I'm doing?"

149

"To his finger," Nick ground out, deliberately holding his climax back, his hand wrapped around the base of his cock, strangling it.

"You're fucking it," Oliver whispered in her ear. "Say it."

"I'm...fucking it," Vanessa whispered.

That was it. That was all it took. Nick released the pressure on his cock and gave it two quick strokes. "Vanessa," he moaned, "now." He covered the end with one hand, trying in vain to catch all his come, but it was useless. He'd been hard for days thinking about this and his climax shook him and stole his breath and overflowed his paltry attempts to contain it.

"Show her," Oliver demanded.

Nick opened his hand and watched as the last few spurts of come pumped out of his rigid cock and ran down onto the hand wrapped around it.

"Oh," Vanessa said, then she moaned and Nick looked up to see her head thrown back on Oliver's shoulder as she ground her cunt into his hand.

"Damn," Oliver whispered in awe. "You're so tight and hot darling, so incredibly gorgeous when you come."

Nick's hips jerked, moving his cock one more time in his fist, at Oliver's words. He could imagine it, imagine Vanessa's sweet little cunt gripping him as she came.

She rolled her head against Oliver's shoulder, biting her lip as her hips continued to undulate in Oliver's hold. "Still coming," Oliver whispered in delight. "What a treasure you are." He was so clearly enchanted by her, mesmerized by her passion. "Just look at you two," he said with satisfaction, surprising Nick. He rubbed his cheek in Vanessa's hair as he glanced up at Nick with a little smile and then kissed Vanessa's cheek.

As Nick watched them, he knew. Knew that tonight he'd finally give in to his desire for Oliver, and that tomorrow they would have Vanessa. They would make her theirs and that was all there was to it.

Chapter Five

ဏ

"She's perfect," Oliver said with a moan as he fell back against the very wall Vanessa had been leaning against as he'd pleasured her. She was so sweet, the way she let him touch her, her trust and passion. And that incredible climax. He cupped his still-hard cock. "We've got to have her again."

Vanessa had left first. She was going to a real retiring room to repair her appearance and then she'd go downstairs. They were to wait about twenty minutes and then go down.

"We will." Nick sounded so sure of it. Oliver looked over at him finally. He'd had a hard time meeting Nick's eyes while they'd help redress Vanessa. Did Nick know how much Oliver enjoyed watching him touch himself? That he'd wanted to see Nick come as much as he had Vanessa?

Of course he did. He'd always known. But they'd never spoken of it. It was the one thing they were silent about, the one thing they didn't share. Nick's gaze was enigmatic. Oliver didn't know what he was thinking. He looked away and ran both hands through his hair. He'd put enough on Nick as it was. He didn't need to add unwanted desire to Nick's burden.

"Are you hurting?"

It took Oliver a moment to figure out what Nick was talking about. Oliver laughed ruefully. "A little. I was so focused on you two, I didn't take care of myself." He closed his eyes and thinned his lips at his slip. He shouldn't have told Nick he'd been watching him. What was wrong with him tonight?

"I know." Nick didn't say anything else, and Oliver couldn't read his tone. He didn't sound evasive, as he usually did when Oliver let something slip. Nick took a step toward him and Oliver turned to face him directly. "Come here," Nick said roughly.

"What?" Oliver was confused. Where did he want to go?

Nick sighed and took another step, until he was a breath away from Oliver. Then he leaned down and kissed Oliver's neck, right above his collar. Oliver was frozen in place. When Nick put his hand on Oliver's stomach and ran it down to his crotch, where he cupped his cock, Oliver tried to push Nick away. "What are you doing?" he croaked unevenly.

"Taking care of you," Nick told him. He nuzzled Oliver's neck and then licked him.

Oliver had seen Nick perform the same seductive routine on countless women. And taking care of him? Did Nick feel that responsibility, too? It wasn't enough that he couldn't be out of Oliver's sight or Oliver couldn't function, hell, couldn't even breathe? Now he had to "take care" of his unfulfilled passion? Oliver shoved harder.

"No," he ground out.

This time Nick moved away. "Why not?" Nick asked in a hard voice. "We've been dancing around it for years. Dammit, I want you. There, I've said it."

"What?" Oliver was beginning to feel as foolish as he sounded. He rubbed his hands over his face in frustration. "I'm not your responsibility, Nick. I know...I know I have a...problem. But I'll get over it. I know I will. It doesn't mean you have to take care of me. Not like this."

"Is that what you think?" Nick asked. His voice was a harsh whisper. "You damn idiot. I've wanted you forever." He grabbed Oliver by the back of the neck and pulled his head down to touch his forehead to Oliver's. "Tonight? When I came, that was for you *and* Vanessa. It's always been for you, idiot."

"What are you saying?" Oliver whispered, afraid to believe Nick's words.

"I'm finally saying what I should have years ago. Something held me back until tonight. Being with Vanessa together this way pushed me beyond it. Suddenly it seemed so stupid that we'd never been with each other, as if we were afraid what would happen if we touched. But I've always known what would happen. It would be *good*. So fucking good we'd never go back. And I'm ready. I'm ready to never go back."

"Now I know why you don't talk very much," Oliver joked weakly. "You don't make any sense when you do."

"I'm in love with you." Nick's declaration was said with such conviction, yet Oliver was still afraid to believe it. Nick understood his silence. "Believe me, Oliver. And this isn't a sudden realization. I've known it for years. But like you, I thought it was the same problem that would eventually go away. I thought you'd taken your need to be near me and misinterpreted it as desire. But it isn't that, is it? It's amazing and glorious and I want you. I want to touch you, be with you."

"Right now?" Oliver attempted to defuse the situation with humor as he always did. He was off-balance. Nick's confession was essentially the stuff of Oliver's dreams—although Nick had been slightly more eloquent in his dreams—but it was so unexpected he didn't know how to respond.

Nick kissed him. That was unfair. How was Oliver to step back and give Nick the room to think it through when he was kissing him? And he was such a good kisser. Oliver had watched him for years. Had even, on a few rare occasions, snuck in and shared his kisses with whatever woman they were with. But this was the first time he'd been the sole recipient of Nick's expertise, and it was devastating. He grabbed Nick by the lapels of his coat and held on while he dove in to the pure pleasure of Nick's mouth.

Nick moaned and fell against Oliver, pinning him to the wall. Instinct had Oliver thrusting into the hard planes of

Nick's stomach. When his cock made contact with Nick he had to break the kiss and suck in great gulps of air as he fought the urge to come in his pants like a schoolboy.

Nick reached down and began to open Oliver's pants clumsily.

"What are you doing?" Oliver asked in between panting breaths.

"I've got to taste you," Nick muttered. "You're going to come, aren't you? Just from my kiss?"

Oliver would have liked to say no, to claim more control than that, but Nick knew him too well to believe him. "Yes," he said desperately, hoping with all his might that Nick meant what he'd said when he'd used the word "taste".

Nick fell to his knees and yanked Oliver's pants down to mid-thigh. All right then, apparently he'd meant it. Before he could do anything, however, Oliver cupped his jaw and forced his face up. The raw desire he saw there nearly knocked him to his knees with Nick. "Are you sure?" he rasped, hating to ask but feeling it necessary.

"Yes, dammit," Nick snarled. "Let go of me so I can suck you."

"God, Nick," Oliver said, dropping his head back against the wall with an audible thump. "Do you have any idea how long I've waited for you to say that?"

Nick laughed. "Not words of love, but 'let me suck you'?" he teased. "That's my Oliver."

"Yes, I am," Oliver agreed. "Now suck, before it's too late."

Nick didn't waste any more words. He'd already said more in the space of a few minutes than he had in years. It was enough. It was almost too much when Nick grasped the base of Oliver's cock in his fist, but then he put his mouth on him, sucking on the full head of his engorged rod, and Oliver cried out before he bit his lip. He slammed his palms against the wall to keep from grabbing Nick's head and fucking his gorgeous mouth hard, which is what he'd always wanted to do.

Nick sucked cock like he kissed. He licked around the head and nibbled and sucked lightly on it, savoring it, in between hard pulls on it, nearly sucking Oliver's soul out.

"Dammit, Nick," he growled. "I can't last. It feels so damn good."

Nick hummed around the cock in his mouth, and Oliver trembled. Then Nick slid his mouth down to meet his fist, engulfing nearly all of Oliver's cock in the warm, wet cavern of his mouth, and sucked deeply. He moved his fist and his mouth in tandem, and Oliver was lost. The only warning he could manage was a strangled moan.

Instead of pulling off, Nick stayed and Oliver came in his mouth. After an initial gag as Oliver shot into his throat, Nick drank him down smoothly. Oliver wasn't proud of the whimper that escaped, but he was too intoxicated from his orgasm to care much. Nick continued to suck his head gently, his tongue sliding over the sensitive ridge beneath it, as Oliver softened in his hold. Even when he'd gone soft, Nick licked and sucked him as if he couldn't get enough. Oliver was shaking from the intensity of the feelings, both physical and emotional, coursing through him at Nick's attentions. He put his hand on Nick's head and ran his fingers through his hair while he caught his breath.

"How did I taste?" he asked finally.

Nick chuckled and let Oliver slide out of his mouth. He stood up and rubbed his lips on Oliver's. "You tell me," he whispered right before he kissed him.

Oliver pushed his tongue into Nick's mouth and tasted the sharpness of his come. It was bitter, perhaps a little salty. So different from a woman's. Nick took over the kiss, holding the back of Oliver's head, sucking his tongue before shoving his own past Oliver's, into Oliver's mouth, filling him and devouring him. Oliver suddenly couldn't breathe, but instead of wanting to break the kiss it made him want to hold on tighter and let Nick be his air, his lifeline, his anchor.

Nick's hold gentled as if he understood what Oliver needed. He slid his hands down and around Oliver's chest, hugging him, nipping at his lips now with a soothing swipe of his tongue along the sting after. Oliver wrapped his arms around Nick's broad shoulders and let him do whatever he wanted.

"I liked it," Nick said against his lips. "I liked the way you felt and the way you tasted. I liked being in control of you like that, and making you come for me."

"Oh God, Nicky," Oliver said with a weak laugh. "Now you've done it, you're going to go all out, aren't you? You're going to drive me mad with your love talk."

He could feel Nick smile against his mouth. "I hope so. Are you hard again? I want you hard all night, you know."

"I know," Oliver whispered. But there was a worry in the back of his mind, and he wasn't going to pretend. Things had gotten too serious for that, now. "What about Vanessa?"

Nick let him go then and retreated to the far wall. He gestured at Oliver's pants. "Better get dressed. You're right. We're supposed to be down there in a few minutes."

"No," Oliver said, though he started straightening his clothes. "I mean what about her? I love you, Nick, and I loved what we just did. I've been dreaming about it for years. But I still want her. There's something about her...I don't know."

"Her eyes speak to you?" Nick asked. He didn't sound disappointed. "I feel the same way. I think that if we hadn't found her and been with her tonight, I might not have found the courage to finally tell you how I feel."

"Why?" Oliver tugged his coat into place as he waited for Nick's answer.

"I'm not sure," Nick said, clearly frustrated. "But I know that I can't imagine this with you without her involved in some way."

"Does it make it easier for you to want me knowing there's a woman you want, too?" Oliver tried not to let his hurt show.

"No," Nick said dismissively. "Don't be an idiot again. It's just that she wants us. She wants us both. Not you, not me. Both of us. I like that. I like being part of something with you, part of a whole. Does that make sense?"

Oliver laughed in disbelief. "Actually, yes. I think that's what drew me to her so strongly. When she caught us with that girl, what was her name?" He shook his head. "Never mind, it doesn't matter. But when she saw us there was no censure, no shocked dismay. If anything her eyes showed even more longing. Did you see, that first night?"

"Yes, yes I saw." Nick straightened from the wall and dusted Oliver's shoulders off, tightening his cravat before patting him on the chest. "And it's more fun. I'm not going to pretend that wanting you has ruined my attraction to women. I still want to fuck a quim, too."

"Thank God," Oliver said with relief. "I feel the same. I like women. I like the way they smell and taste and feel. But I think we both know we like them better together. There's nothing better than being with a woman with you, Nick. It's everything I want."

"And I have a feeling that once we're with Vanessa like that, we'll never want another woman," Nick said matter-of-factly. "We've never reacted to a woman like this. Whatever it is that makes Vanessa perfect for us…well, there it is. She is. Perfect, I mean." He opened the door and peered up and down the hall, then gestured for Oliver to follow.

As Oliver closed the door behind them and followed Nick to the stairs, he hoped that Nick was right. He wanted that for them. He wanted someone who wanted them both and could accept them as they were. He'd never thought to find that. It might be too much to ask of an overworked deity, but Oliver asked anyway.

Vanessa was shaking by the time she found some privacy and a mirror to repair her appearance. She had to sit down.

That hadn't gone at all the way she had planned.

She covered her face with her shaking hands and took several very deep breaths. It succeeded in settling down her racing heart a little.

That had been the most exhilarating, terrifying, magnificent experience of her life. They had been with her. Well, of course they were with her. But they had noticed her, enjoyed her, in a way no one ever had before. There was nothing perfunctory about their attentions upstairs. Oh no. On the contrary, every move, every breath, every touch was inspired by passion. Passion for her. They'd desired her responses, had demanded them and indeed had climaxed from them. Touching her body and kissing her had excited them beyond their control.

Vanessa bit her lip and shoved her hands between her knees to stop herself from laughing out loud and dancing around the small room like a lunatic. She'd never felt this alive. Her body was still sensitive from their lovemaking. Her breasts were tender as they rubbed against the muslin of her undergarments. The place between her legs — God, she'd nearly swooned to hear Nick call it her cunt — tingled and throbbed, wanting one of their hands there again. Or their mouths. They'd promised mouths, and licking.

Vanessa spun around on the small stool to face the mirror. Her cheeks were flushed. Her usually plain brown eyes sparkled. Her hair was a mess. When she saw the tangled disaster of her coiffure Vanessa gasped and sent a prayer of thanks that no one had seen her on her way downstairs. How Very had managed to keep everyone away was a mystery, but Vanessa would have to find some way to repay her. She took the pins from her hair and used the brush beside the mirror to tame her hair. What dull hair she'd always had, long, straight, blonde. Incredibly boring. Until Nick had buried his hand in it and kissed her breath away. Until Oliver had pressed his nose to it and inhaled her scent and rubbed his cheek on it. Now it was the hair of a siren.

Vanessa laughed at her fanciful thoughts. Siren, indeed. She was very aware of her inexperience after being with them. How they must hate having to hold back, waiting for her to catch up. They didn't have much time for that, did they?

She slowly lowered the hairbrush to her lap as her smile disappeared at that sobering thought. Just Christmastide, really, and that was half over. As soon as her parents returned the rounds of parties would end. There would be dinners and teas, of course, with the right sort of people. Not at all the gay crowd of holiday revelers she'd enjoyed the past week. And no Oliver and Nick. Her father would never allow them to call upon her.

Perhaps one of them? Perhaps her father would find one of them acceptable. But which one? Vanessa didn't possibly see how she could choose. They'd become rather entangled. Oliver was so playful and flirtatious, and Nick was so serious and quiet. But when he did talk, he was outrageous and took her breath away. Oliver seduced her and Nick claimed her. She wanted both. What did that mean? Perhaps they weren't right for her, then, if neither was enough alone.

She shook her head and frowned at her reflection. No, that wasn't right. If she'd only met one or the other she'd have been just as attracted to them. She was drawn to Nick when he first stared at her over Melinda Dorsett's shoulder in that dark hallway, when she didn't know Oliver was there in the shadows with him. And when she and Oliver had danced that night she'd loved the feel of his hands, the way he danced, the way he made her feel. But there was something about them together…the way they complemented each other and satisfied all her desires. She was able to have the light and the dark, the sweet and the demanding all at the same time, in two men who were as close as brothers.

Closer even, perhaps. Though they'd given no indication of it tonight, Vanessa wondered if they were lovers, as Very's two men were. She wasn't sure how she felt about that. She tried to imagine Nick kissing Oliver the way he'd kissed her. She nearly fell off the stool as she lost her balance at the decadent thought. Maybe they'd do that for her if she asked? After all, this brief affair with them was certainly the only chance she would have for decadent pleasures like these. She couldn't imagine any of the staid gentlemen she knew engaging in such pleasures of the flesh.

Determinedly she twisted her hair up and pinned it in place. If this was the only time she would have, then she would use it wisely. She would enjoy as much of their company as possible over the next six days. Surely they seemed to want her company, as well? Starting with their help tomorrow at the orphanage. This was Vanessa's holiday gift to herself. She would surrender to passion and desire and all those things she'd been taught to repress since birth. For six days. And then she would go back to her life as if it hadn't happened. She would seek a respectable husband that her father would approve, however. She did not wish to be on the shelf, alone and never again having the intimacies she'd shared with Nick and Oliver. She couldn't imagine doing those things with anyone else, had no desire to do so at this point, but a future without any love at all seemed quite, quite bleak now that she'd tasted it.

She wanted them. For whatever reason, for as long as she had them, she would give in to her deepest secret desires and have them. And then, when Christmastide was over, she'd give them up. She had to. Nothing in her life, neither her family nor her social position, would allow her to have the two men forever. But six days? That just might work.

161

Chapter Six

ဆ

"Miss, there are two gentlemen here to see you. Mr. Wilkes and Mr. Gabriel."

Greely's voice was perfectly modulated, as always. The butler had been here longer than Vanessa. Longer than her father, actually, although he'd been a lowly footman in his youth. He never gave anything away. Vanessa knew almost nothing about him. It seemed a sad state of affairs that she'd known someone her whole life and didn't really know him at all. How tragically typical of her life.

She sighed. Then she straightened her shoulders and serenely folded her hands in her lap. "Thank you, Greely. Show them in."

"Oh, are these your two suitors?" Aunt Grace asked. "Chasing you to ground at home, hmm?"

Vanessa made a face at her aunt, who seemed pleasantly surprised at her playful attitude. "They are here to escort me to the orphanage and help hand out gifts."

"Oh, good," her aunt said with relief. "With my hands and knees aching so today, I was feeling terribly guilty for not accompanying you. I'm so relieved you'll have help."

"We shall have to marry you off to your grocer while you can still walk," Vanessa teased. Her aunt's mouth opened in shock at the suggestive comment. Vanessa just laughed.

"Good morning," a pleasantly deep male voice said. Vanessa knew that voice and it slid like silk over her skin, leaving goosebumps behind.

"Good morning," Aunt Grace said as she held her hand out to Oliver. "Mr. Gabriel, is it not?"

Oliver bowed slightly and took Aunt Grace's hand. "Yes, Lady Grace. We met at the Shelbys'." He turned to Nick. "And Mr. Wilkes."

"How do you do?" Nick said with a small smile. He too shook Aunt Grace's hand.

"Very well, thank you," Aunt Grace replied with a twinkle in her eye. She smiled mischievously at Vanessa. "Here to take Nessa to the orphanage, are you? You are the best of men to do so. My old bones are tired today, and it is rather cold, so I'm afraid I had to cry off. I'm quite relieved she won't be trying to do it all herself."

Oliver was bending over Vanessa's hand as Aunt Grace talked. His back was to the older woman so she didn't see him turn Vanessa's hand and lick the pulse at her wrist. Vanessa had to repress her gasp of awareness. Oliver stood with a satisfied smile and turned to her aunt while Nick took his place.

"We were glad to offer our services," Oliver told her aunt.

Nick took her hand and rubbed his thumb over the spot Oliver had licked, as if smoothing the damp remains of his kiss into her skin. Then he looked up at her. "Are you well today, Lady Vanessa?" he asked quietly. "Nessa?" he whispered with a roguish grin.

She blushed at the childhood nickname. "I'm fine," she mouthed, not wanting her aunt to wonder at their conversation. "Quite well," she said aloud. "Would you care for some tea before we leave?"

"I insist," her aunt said in a tone that brooked no refusal. She indicated the sofa and empty chairs about them. "Sit. Please."

Both men glanced at Vanessa, but she had no idea what her aunt was up to.

"Do you have any family in London over the holidays?" Aunt Grace asked after they'd taken seats. She poured tea for both men and handed them their cups while she waited for an answer.

After thanking her, Oliver replied, "No, ma'am. I have no family here. An aunt and uncle reside near Thornby, in Northamptonshire. But that is the only family I have left."

"I see," Aunt Grace said sympathetically. "I'm so sorry." She turned to Nick. "And you, Mr. Wilkes?"

"My family is from Gloucester, ma'am, although my parents now reside in Cheltenham. For the restorative waters."

"Are they ill?" Aunt Grace asked, wide-eyed.

Nick shook his head with a smile. "No, ma'am. A fact they attribute to the waters." He chuckled and her aunt followed suit.

"I see," Aunt Grace said. "Have you no brothers or sisters?"

"Several through the years, but alas, I am the only one still living."

"Why are you not with your parents this Christmastide?"

"They do not care to celebrate the holidays, ma'am. They find the excess to be bad for their health."

Her aunt laughed outright. "Yes, well, ill health or not, it is good for the soul. I am glad you've chosen to stay in the city with us, then."

Nick's eyes met Vanessa's. "As am I, Lady Grace."

"I understand you both served against Napoleon," her aunt said after taking a sip of tea.

"Yes, at Waterloo," Oliver said. Nick's look had turned hard and inscrutable.

"And since the war?"

Ah, thought Vanessa, that's what this is about. She's trying to determine their situations. She almost laughed aloud. Surely Aunt Grace knew her father would never condone either man as a suitor? Her inquiries were a waste of time.

"We've been traveling on the continent," Oliver said. "Neither of us had a tour as young men and so we took the opportunity after selling out to travel."

"And now that you are back in England?"

Nick's expression softened with amusement. The look he gave Vanessa from the corner of his eye was sly. "We haven't decided, Lady Grace," he answered. "Perhaps I shall take up trade."

Her aunt's eyes widened. "Surely not?" she said, scandalized. "Have you no property?"

Oliver laughed. "Oh, he was just teasing, my lady. Nick is a man of property, indeed. He has a small estate in Oxford. And is, of course, his father's and his uncle's heir."

"Oh, really?" Aunt Grace said, leaning closer to Nick. "That sounds promising." She turned to Oliver. "And you, Mr. Gabriel?"

Oliver held his empty hands out to his sides. "You see the extent of my wealth here before you, ma'am. I own my soul and little else."

"Well, in these times a man is lucky to still lay claim to that," Aunt Grace said soothingly. "Perhaps Mr. Wilkes can give you some advice about your finances. You two seem bosom beaus."

Vanessa had had enough. She stood abruptly, and Oliver and Nick set down their cups and followed suit. "Now that we have established that neither Mr. Gabriel nor Mr. Wilkes will be holding me for ransom, we really must go, Aunt Grace."

Aunt Grace's look was reproving. "We have not established anything of the sort. Mr. Gabriel may very well profit from such a scheme."

Nick bowed low. "I shall endeavor to keep her safe from Mr. Gabriel's nefarious plans, Lady Grace."

Oliver put his hand over his heart, sighing dramatically. "My name is impugned. I must protest my innocence."

"You may protest," Aunt Grace said with a stern look, "but we shall judge your name on your actions."

At that Oliver looked horrified. "Well, I daresay that's a sight worse, wouldn't you?" he asked Nick.

Nick shook his head sadly. "You're done in, Oliver. You may as well give up now."

Vanessa put her hands on her hips. "I shall be doing the kidnapping if we don't leave immediately. I'll not have the orphanage staff waiting on us."

Vanessa seemed rather melancholy today. Nick didn't care for that at all. It was hard to woo a sad woman. Or so he imagined. It was also hard to woo a woman — one you planned to know carnally as soon as possible — when her wide-eyed maid was in attendance. Nick glowered at the girl sitting next to Vanessa in the carriage, across from him and Oliver, and she shrank back against the seat as if she wished to disappear.

"What are we handing out at the orphanage?" Oliver asked Vanessa. "Should we stop and pick something up?"

"Food and clothes," Vanessa answered. "I had them sent ahead. The wagons should be waiting for us there."

Nick frowned. "Shouldn't they already have those?"

"They do," Vanessa said with a nod, "but traditionally they receive a new set of clothes at Christmastide, and some special treats, such as sweetmeats and chestnuts."

"Why today?" Oliver asked. "I would have expected that on Twelfth Night instead."

"Yes, well, many of the orphanage workers are with their families on Twelfth Night. The children attend church and are put to bed. It's thought that giving them the gifts now is better for everyone."

Vanessa's argument was a solid one, but Nick couldn't help but feel sorry for the children and their sad Twelfth Night. On the other hand, he'd never gotten a gift of any kind at Christmastide from his parents. Not out of spite or dislike, but because they simply didn't think about it. Nick had been six before he realized he was missing out.

"We have chestnuts?" Oliver asked hopefully. Nick grinned.

"Yes," Vanessa said, dragging the word out a bit. "Why?"

"I like chestnuts." Nick laughed outright at the anticipation in Oliver's voice.

"There may be one or two extra for you," Vanessa promised. "But only if you behave."

Oliver solemnly crossed his heart. "I swear, Lady Vanessa, I shall be on my best behavior."

Vanessa laughed then, and Nick relaxed. Whatever had been bothering her had been washed away with Oliver's teasing. Thank God for Oliver.

When they arrived Vanessa sent her little maid back with the carriage. "Return in about two hours," she told the carriage driver. Nick was elated. Two hours of unchaperoned time with Vanessa.

An hour later his elation began to wane. They had not had a moment's peace. Vanessa was very well liked by the children and staff at the orphanage, and she clearly doted on them all. Nick couldn't begrudge them her time. She was so happy here, and free with her smiles and laughter. He hadn't seen her like this before. Her work here was obviously important to her.

The children accepted Nick and Oliver because they came with Vanessa. The staff was not quite so welcoming. Nick found judgmental eyes watching him at every turn. He could almost hear them talking amongst themselves later, trying to decide which of them was more worthy of Vanessa's attentions. If they only knew they were both having an affair with her, how shocked they would be. Nick would have laughed at the thought except for the grave implications were they to actually find out. Vanessa would be branded a whore or worse, and the chances were quite good that she wouldn't be allowed back into the orphanage. Nick knew how devastating that loss would be to her.

And yet he still wanted her. Even though he knew the situation was unusual and society would brand them unnatural for their desires, he still wanted her.

"I missed you last night," he whispered to her at one point when they had a modicum of privacy as the children frolicked in the yard. "I thought of you while I lay in my bed." Which was true, though he'd been with Oliver at the time. Actually, they'd talked about her while they were together and how much they wished she were there. He'd tell her that tonight. Not here, not now.

"I missed you too," she whispered back with a sultry look. "I wish I'd been in your bed with you."

Nick caught his breath at her confession, mirroring his and Oliver's wishes from the night before. "Do you?" She nodded. "Tonight," he promised fervently. "I shall find a way for us to be together."

"With Oliver?" she asked. "I want to be with you both."

He nodded. Yes, he wanted the same thing. He wanted them both.

Oliver smoothed his palms on his thighs yet again. He caught himself and forced his hands down to his sides while he smiled at a young girl saying something to him. He couldn't hear her in the din of the orphanage, but the smile seemed to be the right response, and she ran off happily.

It wasn't that he didn't like children. He did. He just had no idea what to do with them. He glanced over at Vanessa where she stood with a little toddler on her hip. It was easy to imagine that was his or Nick's child she held. He liked that idea. He liked thinking of her big with their child, creating something inside her that came from the three of them together. The image, and the desire, shook his composure.

He'd never wanted that before. Never imagined getting any woman with child and being happy about it.

He turned away from her, trying to appear nonchalant. His nerves were frayed this morning. Last night with Nick had been shattering. He'd never felt like that. When Nick had taken him in his mouth he'd felt complete for the first time in his life. Nick had been with him all night and Oliver had relished it. Nick was his lover. Not just his best friend, but also the man he loved. A delicious shiver raced down his spine. It was almost perfect.

Except the whole time both he and Nick had talked about how much better it would be if Vanessa had been there to see it. And they'd both meant it. They'd gone so far as to put off fucking each other until Vanessa could be with them.

Oliver hadn't expected to feel that way. He'd loved Nick for years. He'd fantasized about fucking him. He'd always believed that Nick would be enough when they finally consummated their relationship. Oliver shouldn't want anyone else. But he did. Whether he deserved them or not.

And there was the rub.

The inquisition by Vanessa's aunt this morning had brought home his inadequacies with startlingly clarity. He was a man with nothing to recommend him except his charm and his prowess in bed. He doubted that was what either Vanessa or Nick truly wanted in a mate. Could men even mate with other men? And if there were three of them, were they mates? Or was there another word for a union of that nature? Triumvirate? No, the Latin clearly referred to "three men", and was far too political. Tripod? Again no, as one of them was clearly lacking the extra "foot". The linguistic semantics of the situation were mind-boggling.

Oliver took a deep breath. He was babbling in his head, as he was wont to do when he was nervous. He looked up at Nick...

Nick wasn't there.

He spun in a circle and didn't see him. Where was he? Had he left? Was something wrong? Why couldn't he see him? This was a small room. Perhaps he was in the hall. Yes, he'd go look there. He began walking toward the door, but there were so many children. He tried not to step on them or push them aside. The walls seemed to be closing in on him and he couldn't catch his breath.

Stop it, stop it, stop it, he screamed in his head. He knew he was being irrational. Nick had told him time and again that he'd never leave him alone again. He promised, damn it. *He promised.*

"Oliver."

He froze, his eyes closed. It was Nick. He turned around, breathing as if he'd run a mile. Nick stood there, his eyes apologetic. He touched Oliver's arm lightly and then let his hand drop. "I was right over there," he said, pointing to the far wall. "I just bent over to help some children. I'm sorry."

"Mr. Gabriel, are you all right?" Vanessa was at his side, a worried frown on her face. She linked arms with him, hugging him to her side.

He should have been embarrassed. Instead he was vastly relieved at her physical reassurance. He held her arm tightly so she wouldn't slip away, as Nick had had to do. "Yes, yes, I'm fine," he lied. "A bit of a headache, but nothing to worry about." He rubbed his temple for effect.

"Shall I send for the carriage?" she asked. "I think it should be arriving soon as it is."

"Of course not," Oliver protested, loath to make her leave too soon. She was clearly enjoying herself. As a matter of fact, he hadn't seen her enjoy herself this much before.

She smiled and Oliver relaxed a little more. "Come then. The children have exhausted me. I simply must sit down."

Nick immediately cleared a path through the children and led Oliver and Vanessa to some benches along the wall. Vanessa sat down with a relieved sigh, pulling Oliver down next to her. "Shoo," she said affectionately to some children who tried to climb into her lap and they ran off laughing as one of the matrons came and herded them off by waving her big white apron at them. "I love them, I do," Vanessa said as she leaned back against the wall, "but they wear me out rather quickly. One or two children at a time are preferable, I think."

"Do you want your own children one day, Nessa?" Nick asked from where he stood beside them, his arms crossed and his feet spread wide in a stance that spoke more of guard than patron as he surveyed the children settling down at the tables for their chestnut treats.

"Of course I do, though I shall have to find a husband first," she said pragmatically.

"Of course," Oliver murmured his agreement, though her comment, spoken so casually, indicated that he and Nick were not being considered for the position. He didn't care for the sharp sting of jealousy and resentment that gripped him. Hadn't he just been lamenting his unsuitability as a mate? Her agreement was hardly unexpected.

Nick was frowning now. Apparently he didn't like the implications either.

"Nick says he shall find a way for us to be together tonight," Vanessa said under her breath, watching the room as she studiously avoided his gaze. "Do you still want that?"

"Of course," Oliver responded, worried he'd frightened her away from further involvement with them. God knew that was the last thing he wanted. "More than anything."

"Together," Nick said, his voice rough and low. He, too, was looking out at the room as if commenting on what he saw. "All three of us. I have an idea how it can be done."

Chapter Seven

ფა

"This way," Nick whispered, pulling Vanessa through the door behind him. She was wearing a voluminous cape that covered her from head to toe, although there was no one in the vicinity who might see her. They were sneaking in a back door of Steven's Hotel, where Nick and Oliver were staying. Vanessa's heartbeat sounded so loud in her own ears it was difficult to hear Nick.

Steven's was well known as the hotel of choice for officers and former military men. Vanessa hoped and prayed they didn't see any. She may not be a notorious beauty, but because of who she was, she was relatively well known by a large number of people. What had she been thinking to agree to something so foolish? She had gone mad, obviously. What if Aunt Grace came looking for her in the middle of the night? True, she did not make a habit of checking on Vanessa in the wee hours, but there was always a first time, wasn't there? Vanessa had pleaded exhaustion after they returned from the Tarrants' dinner party, however, so that should keep her away.

Getting out of the townhouse had been torture. Never before had Vanessa realized how many floorboards creaked and doors squeaked. She'd planned to try to sneak out the kitchen door into the yard, but Nick said it would actually be easier to leave by the French doors in her father's study. He and Oliver waited in the garden for her and then spirited her out the gate to a waiting hackney.

The whole thing was ludicrous. So many things could go wrong. And all for the thrill of a forbidden carnal experience? Now that she was living the scenario, Vanessa better understood the tales about ladies and gentlemen who had fallen from grace out of an ill-conceived lust. She sympathized.

Because the truth was she wouldn't miss this opportunity for the world. The chance for someone like her — someone forced by station to lead an exemplary if extraordinarily dull life, no beauty or wit or vivacity to recommend them — to be with two such handsome, sought-after gentlemen? Vanessa was no lackwit. She knew this was her one and only chance to experience this kind of passion.

"Why is there no one here?" she whispered, the deserted hallways rather ominous.

"It's early yet," Oliver said from beside her. "Everyone is still out, and the hotel is half-empty as it is."

"And when I leave?" Vanessa asked as she and Oliver waited in the shadows at the end of the corridor while Nick unlocked the door to his room.

"We'll be careful, Vanessa," he promised as he kissed her gloved hand. "We wouldn't have you hurt in any way."

She believed him. She trusted them both more than she could remember trusting anyone, except perhaps Aunt Grace. "All right," she said, not really sure what her response meant, just knowing she wasn't going to worry about it. She'd let them take care of it all.

Nick beckoned them from the doorway and they hurried forward. She rushed into the room and spun around as Nick closed the door behind Oliver.

"I can't believe we made it," she said breathlessly, throwing back the hood on her cape.

"Believe it," Nick said with seductive grin. "Now the real excitement starts."

Oliver laughed. "First, let me take the cape. You are completely lost in there."

Vanessa laughed with him as she looked down at the cape pooled on the floor. "Yes, I am. Whose is it?"

"Mine," Nick answered. "A gift from my mother. I'm not exactly sure what she was thinking when she bought it. I have never worn a cape in my life."

Vanessa admired his broad shoulders in his greatcoat. "No, I think I prefer you in a coat. It shows off your shoulders quite well."

"Like my shoulders, do you?" he said with a waggle to his eyebrows as he shrugged his coat off that made her laugh again.

"His are indeed broad. But he is a lumbering beast on the dance floor," Oliver commented. "Unlike my svelte and graceful self."

"Nonsense," Vanessa scoffed. "Your shoulders are just as broad as his, and he is just as graceful."

Oliver cupped her jaw and angled her head up as Nick pulled the cape from her shoulders. "My dear," Oliver said sweetly, "you look through eyes blinded by lust."

He kissed her then. Vanessa had been breathless with wanting, and she was ever so grateful he'd seen that. She slid her arms around his shoulders, still covered in the thick wool of his greatcoat. It was slightly damp, but the smell and feel of it only added to the atmosphere of intrigue and excitement.

The kiss turned passionate as Oliver stroked his tongue into her mouth and she buried her hands in the hair on his nape. She rose on tiptoe and fit her body to his and his hands slid from her upper back to her bottom, squeezing. No man had ever handled her like that until Nick and Oliver. She liked it, liked being the object of their desire.

Nick came up beside them and pulled one of Vanessa's arms down. She was startled and began to pull away from Oliver, but Nick murmured, "No," and with a gentle hand on the back of her head pushed her toward Oliver again. So she kissed Oliver, not caring that Nick was right there, that she could feel his breath on her cheek as she kissed another man. It was all so exciting and forbidden. She knew it was, even more so than her being here at all. And then Nick leaned in and licked at the corner of her mouth as it was pressed to Oliver's.

Oliver moaned and his lips moved to the side of Vanessa's mouth with a little nip on her lower lip. And then Nick was kissing her too. Both of them licking and sucking her lips, dipping their tongues into her mouth as she licked back. She wasn't sure whose tongue and lips she was kissing at any given moment, just that it was Nick and Oliver. It was wildly arousing. She had to break away to catch her breath, only to forget to breathe as she watched Nick and Oliver kiss each other. As they'd been kissing her. Open mouths slid across each other and she saw their tongues tangle. Oliver pulled her closer to him, settling her between his legs, and Nick's hand rubbed her back and then slid down to cover Oliver's on her bottom. Nick bit Oliver's lip as he had Vanessa's and then he turned to her with a smile. He leaned over and kissed her again, and she let him. She wanted to taste Oliver on him. Oliver let her go and stepped away and she moaned in distress against Nick's mouth.

"I've got to get this damn coat off," Oliver said.

Nick stepped in to take his place and he roughly pulled her close so they were touching from chest to groin. He rubbed his erection against her stomach and she gasped into his mouth. He had one hand on her bottom and maneuvered her so that she straddled his leg, and now that hard, hot part of him was on her hip, thrusting and rubbing lightly. He pulled her in with his hand still on her bottom and her sex rubbed on his muscular thigh.

"Oh," she said softly, the tingle from that contact making the hair on her nape rise. She rubbed against him again.

"That's it," he murmured, kissing her neck. She tipped her head back to give him more room. "Feels good, doesn't it?"

She nodded, bumping her chin on his head. "I'm sorry," she gasped as he bent his leg more and dragged her sex along the muscled length of it.

"Didn't even feel it," he said lightly, running his tongue along her collarbone. After another minute of his mouth on her and riding his glorious thigh until she was wet and throbbing between her legs, Nick cleared his throat softly. "Vanessa." He sounded a little pained. "Could we please get these clothes off and move to the bed? Please?"

"What?" she muttered, having a difficult time deciphering what he wanted.

Oliver's hands lightly grasped her shoulders and pulled her from Nick. "Look at Nick, darling," he whispered. She blinked a few times until Nick came into focus. "He's so hard he aches. He wants to bury his cock inside you. Are you going to let him?"

"Oliver," Nick growled. "You go too far, too fast."

"Oh, God," Vanessa said breathlessly. She vividly recalled his long, thick member from their tryst last night. He wanted to put that inside her? Her sex clenched in anticipation. She'd enjoyed Oliver's fingers there last night. She could only imagine she'd enjoy that glorious cock even more. "Yes." She spun in Oliver's arms, shocked to see he was naked already. She had a moment of indecision, whether to ask the question on her mind or simply stare at how classically beautiful his body was, all planes and angles and musculature. And cock. There was quite a bit of that too. "And you?" she asked in an unsteady voice. "Will you put yours inside me too?"

She heard Nick start to remove his clothes, cloth rustling and hitting the floor. Oliver's gaze flicked over her shoulder and then returned to meet hers. "If that is what you want, yes."

"I want," Vanessa moaned. "Dear Lord, how I want."

Oliver chuckled devilishly. "Somehow I don't think that prayer would be condoned by the church." He was rapidly undoing the front ties on the simple gown she'd worn. She hadn't had the benefit of a maid before escaping the house. Neither man seemed concerned with her informal attire, however, merely in getting her out of it. "Up," he said, and he tugged on the dress. She lifted her arms and he pulled it off, catching a couple of pins in her hair in the process.

When she stood in her underclothes she shivered, suddenly cold. Oliver began to take the rest of the pins from her hair. "Nick, build up the fire, would you? Vanessa is chilled. Give me your hand, darling." He picked up Vanessa's hand and flipped it palm up and began to deposit the removed pins there. It was all so...domestic. Vanessa couldn't help laughing quietly. "What?" Oliver asked.

"This," she said, waving her hand to indicate Nick building the fire and the pins in her hand. "It all seems so terribly normal. A fire because it's cold, and taking my hair down like a ladies' maid."

"We're working our way up to excitement," Oliver remarked dryly. "We wouldn't want to overwhelm you."

This time it was Nick who laughed. "I'm afraid we're three quarters domestic and only a fourth excitement. Disappointed?"

"I'll reserve judgment until I've seen the fourth quarter," Vanessa teased. "It may prove too much for me. After all, I can only claim a fourth of a fourth of a fourth of excitement myself."

Oliver took the pins from her hand and set them on top of a washstand in the corner. Then he wrapped her in his strong arms and rubbed his hands up and down her back to warm her. "Nonsense. You are an incredibly exciting woman. The mystery of you nearly had us too timid to pursue you. And then the challenge you presented made you irresistible."

Vanessa snorted in disbelief.

Oliver pulled her head back with a hand in her hair until she was looking at him. "It's true," he said quietly. "So cool and self-possessed in company. If we hadn't seen the fire in you in that dark hallway and taken advantage of the secret we shared by pursuing you that very night, we would never have known how passionate you are. You hide that." He ran his hand gently over her hair, smoothing it back from her face. "Why? Why do you keep the real Vanessa a secret from almost everyone who knows you?"

"No one knows me, really, do they?" she asked. She ran her hands down from his shoulders, toying with the fine blond hairs in the middle of his chest. She hesitated a moment, but when he seemed to enjoy her touch she circled one of his dark nipples with her finger before pressing on it. It was hard, as hers sometimes felt. She could explore his chest for hours and not get bored.

"We will," Nick said from behind her. He stepped in tight against her, his legs tangling in her shift. "We will know every inch of you, everything you desire, before tonight is through."

She was pressed between the two men. It was a delicious confinement. She leaned back against Nick while she played with Oliver's nipple. She wanted to be outrageous with them tonight. She wanted to be bawdy and uninhibited and free to act however she chose. "I desire that you should lick me, as you promised," she said in a voice roughened by trepidation and a healthy dose of bravado.

"I want you naked first." Nick untied her petticoat and lifted it off. She was wearing nothing but her short, thin chemise and her shoes and stockings. She'd left off her stays since she had no maid to lace them. She'd felt positively lewd without them. Now she was glad not to have to bother with another undergarment.

"Yes, naked is a very good idea," Oliver concurred. He knelt at her feet and slipped first one and then the other shoe off.

Nick moved behind her again and cupped his hands around her breasts. It felt so good Vanessa gave a little moan. While Oliver rolled her stockings down Nick played with her breasts, squeezing them, plumping them up, pinching her nipples. It all felt so incredibly decadent, even through her chemise, and so very, very good. Then he slipped the last layer of her clothing over her head and she was naked before them.

She should be nervous, at the least self-conscious of her body. She didn't have much of a figure. Her breasts were no more than a handful, her hips almost nonexistent. But she felt like a veritable goddess the way the two men were touching her and looking at her. She didn't want to change a thing about herself at that moment.

When Oliver stood he trailed his hands up her bare legs, over her hips, and then he held her waist as he dipped his head and licked one of her nipples. Nick held her breast for him, an offering in the palm of his hand, and Vanessa arched her back, thrusting her breast toward him, wanting him to taste it. Would he take it in his mouth?

He did. He wrapped his lips around the sensitive point he'd licked and then he sucked, just a bit. She put her hand on his shoulder for balance and noticed her breathing was labored. And they'd barely begun. Then he sucked harder, and opened his mouth wider so that a little more of her breast went in his mouth and *that* felt so amazing she just had to let out a little moan. His laughter against her breast was shockingly intimate.

Oliver began to sink to his knees, licking her stomach and biting her hip as he went. But her breasts didn't feel abandoned because Nick began to caress them again. Oliver buried his nose in the springy hair covering her mons and Vanessa felt a little trepidation start to invade her pleasure. Was this something he truly wanted to do? What if he didn't like it? Or more precisely, what if he didn't like *her*? She had no idea what that portion of her anatomy must taste like.

"Stop," she said in a panic.

He stopped immediately, settling back on his heels and looking up at her. He was so incredibly unself-conscious. But then, he had no reason to worry, did he? He was physically beautiful in every way. "What is it?" he whispered. He caressed her hip in a soft, soothing stroke. "It won't hurt, you know."

179

She shook her head, because that wasn't what she was worried about. But how to say what she was thinking? She bit her lip as she stared at him.

He sighed. "Do you want me to lick you, Vanessa, or not? I very much want to." He leaned in again, and again he put his nose on her mons and inhaled deeply. "You smell divine. Like aroused woman. My mouth is watering for a taste."

"Really?" she asked in tiny voice, not wanting to make him feel obligated to do it if he didn't want to. But she very much wanted him to.

"Really," he assured her with a wicked smile. Then he tapped the little button at the top of her crease with the tip of his tongue and she gasped at the sensation. Nick reached down and pulled her leg up with a hand on her thigh. He set her foot on Oliver's thigh, exposing her. Her face felt positively crimson with embarrassment, but her new position seemed to push Oliver from playful to intent in the blink of an eye.

He slid his tongue deeper into her crease and Vanessa could feel that she was wet there already, knew he tasted the cream of her arousal. She could feel that tongue gliding and then he licked her lower lips, which felt swollen with want. His hands gripped her thighs, holding her open for his pleasure as his tongue played with her entrance, dipping in and retreating, circling, and she shivered in Nick's arms.

Without a word Nick ran his hand through Oliver's hair and he stopped and looked up. Nick picked her up and sat down on the edge of the bed with her in his lap. He tucked his knees between hers and spread her wide again. Oliver just grinned and crawled over to them on all fours, his eyes never leaving Vanessa's sex. She felt as wanton as Bathsheba. When Oliver put his mouth on her this time she gave in completely to the pleasure, thrusting her hips at him, laying her head on Nick's shoulder and trusting that he'd hold her while Oliver brought her such incredible pleasure.

Nick did more than hold her. He reached under her arm and he toyed with her as Oliver licked and sucked. The sight of his hand rubbing her curls and his finger flicking her small knot of pleasure while Oliver devoured her was the most decadent sight she'd ever seen. Then Nick's cock grew harder between her legs.

Chapter Eight

❧

It was hard to miss the rise of his sex. He adjusted Vanessa in his lap, and suddenly his cock was right there, off to the side, right next to Oliver's face. Oliver brushed it with his cheek and it actually jerked against him, as if trying to catch his attention. Oliver pulled away from Vanessa and looked at it. She held her breath. What would he do? Did men like a mouth on them as well? Did they like to put their mouths on each other? Oliver slid his hand up Vanessa's thigh and stroked Nick's cock, rubbing the end with his thumb, and Nick caught his breath behind her.

"Are you lovers, then?" Vanessa whispered.

"Yes," Nick said, his voice a low rumble in her ear. "We haven't fucked, but we'd like to, if you'll let us."

Vanessa reached down and pushed Oliver's hand away from Nick's cock, and Oliver frowned. Then she wrapped her hand around the surprisingly hard shaft and guided the tip to Oliver's mouth. His gaze flew to hers. "Take it," she whispered. "I want to see." With his eyes still on hers, Oliver opened his mouth and leaned over slightly, letting the tip of Nick's cock slip into his mouth. His lips closed around it and his cheeks drew in as he sucked. Behind Vanessa, Nick moaned his appreciation.

Vanessa had known the power of watching illicit behavior before. She'd been aroused watching Nick pleasure himself last night. But she hadn't truly understood it. Now, watching Oliver suck Nick's cock lovingly, sliding his mouth up and down on Nick's shaft until it was slick and shiny in the firelight, until it was red and hard enough to stand on its own, had her wild with desire. She squirmed in Nick's lap, and he slid his finger down the valley of her cunt until he reached her entrance. She gasped as he circled it, teasing her mercilessly.

"Please, Nick," she begged breathlessly.

"Please what?" he asked. His voice was rough and breathless too, telling Vanessa more than words about how aroused he was by what they were doing.

"Please fuck me," she whispered, remembering how much he'd liked to hear her say that last night.

He shoved his finger inside her a little roughly, as if he couldn't control himself. It went deeper than she'd expected, but the sting of his entry was washed away when he pulled it back and thrust again.

Oliver let Nick slip from his mouth, giving one last, slow lick to the end. A tiny drop of pearly moisture appeared there as Oliver let it go. Just as Vanessa thought he was done he quickly leaned back down and licked the drop away.

"Damn," Nick cursed behind her, but it was pleasure in his voice, not anger.

Oliver returned to Vanessa, licking right along Nick's finger as it fucked her. He spread the lips of her sex with gentle fingers so that Vanessa could see how dark pink she was, how wet, how Nick's finger looked as it went in and out of her. Oliver maneuvered around Nick's hand and took the small red bump at the top of her crease into his mouth and sucked. Vanessa cried out and Nick quickly covered her mouth with his free hand.

"Not too loud, Nessa," he admonished. "We don't want to alert anyone to your presence."

She tore his hand away. "But it feels so good," she said in a strangled voice. "How am I to be quiet?"

Oliver laughed against her sex. "You have to be," he told her, his voice silky but with a thread of command in it. "You must be, or we'll stop. Do you understand?"

She nodded. "Yes, yes," she said panting. "I'll be good."

Her reward was Nick fucking his finger into her deeply while Oliver sucked her again. She writhed and moaned softly, thrusting her hips, craving more and more and more of this shattering pleasure. "Inside me," she begged desperately, hoping they understood what she wanted.

"I'm going to fuck you," Nick growled. "But I want you to come first. It will be easier the first time."

Oliver began licking the same knot he'd been sucking—hard, slow licks, pressing his tongue against her. She trembled violently and Nick put his finger as far inside her as he could reach and she came. She felt the pulsing waves of her climax tighten and release inside her, around Nick's finger, and as Oliver licked her she became so sensitive that the pleasure was almost pain. Her fingers dug into Nick's thighs and she bit her lip to keep her cries inside.

Before the waves receded, Oliver and Nick dragged her up on the bed and Nick crawled on top of her. He looked at Oliver, who lay down beside them. "Is it all right? If I'm the first?"

"Yes," Oliver said with a smile as he brushed Nick's hair off his forehead. "Because I'm going to be a close second. And I like the idea of fucking into her when she's full of your come."

"Oh God," Vanessa moaned, her hips taking on a life of their own as they thrust up against Nick, begging for his cock. He didn't make her wait. He pressed inside her, slowly but forcefully, no hesitation. She didn't feel any pain. She knew there was supposed to be some, but there wasn't. Nick grinned once he was seated fully in her, his pubic hair a foreign feeling against the sensitive flesh of her sex. He rubbed against her and she moaned.

"It didn't hurt?" he asked. She shook her head. "Good," Nick said with satisfaction. He pulled back out and thrust into her again and the pleasure was immediate and electrifying. She started to cry out, but Oliver's mouth crashed down on hers, swallowing her cries as Nick continued to fuck her.

Vanessa's hands needed purchase against the sensory assault and she grabbed Nick's hip and Oliver's shoulder and dug her nails into them. Their only response was a grunt from Oliver and a groan from Nick, both sounding more of pleasure than pain.

Oliver broke their kiss and Vanessa gasped. "Tell me," he urged her. "Tell me how he feels."

"I'm full to bursting with him," she said breathlessly. "It feels so strangely wonderful." She moaned as Nick circled his hips, grinding his cock into her as he sucked her nipple hungrily into his mouth.

"She likes it a little rough, doesn't she?" Oliver said, and Vanessa knew he was talking to Nick. She didn't mind that tonight. Didn't mind them discussing her like some wanton from the street. She felt like one. And she liked it. "I knew she would," Oliver said with satisfaction. "I knew she wanted to be taken, not wooed with delicate lovemaking, but fucked and used by men who knew how to do it."

She came again. Nick laughed through her climax. "You're going to need both of us to keep up with you, aren't you?" he murmured right before he kissed her. She sucked his tongue into her mouth and gave him a wild, untamed kiss, fighting him for control of it. His thrusts lost their rhythm and became hard and fast and he broke the kiss to groan as he ground against her. She felt the jerk of his cock inside her and knew he was coming. She might be inexperienced, but she knew it. And she loved it. She wrapped her legs around his waist and held on, the tremors of a small climax making her throw her head back against the bed. She came knowing he was releasing inside her. She remembered Oliver's words, and greedily held Nick until he was spent so she'd be full of him when Oliver entered her.

Nick's arms gave out on him as he felt the final tremors of his release. He tried to lower himself gently down on Vanessa rather than collapse on her in a stupefied heap, but he wasn't sure he accomplished it.

Vanessa was still moving beneath him, her quim clenching and releasing as she came again. He let out an exhausted laugh. "You come more than any woman I've ever known."

"I'm sorry," she cried out, and from her tone Nick could tell it was true distress.

He raised his head and glared at her. "Don't ever apologize to any man for enjoying yourself in bed, Vanessa," he growled. "You are a treasure. There are many women who are unable to come at all. What you can do is a gift, to yourself and to any man you share it with."

She moaned, partly in distress but mostly in pleasure as her walls continued to tremble around him. "It's not right," she whispered. "I have no shame, and now that I have known this I cannot give it up!" She moved restlessly under him, but he was done for the moment. His cock was too soft to bring her pleasure anymore and he pulled out.

"Nick is right, darling," Oliver purred, nuzzling behind her ear. He bit her earlobe and she let out an undignified squeak. "I love how much you come. I'd like to be able to make you come someday just by whispering wicked suggestions in your ear or licking your beautiful breasts. Do you think you could do that?" Vanessa nodded, the motion jerky and uncontrolled. "Do you want to do that now?" he asked.

Vanessa shook her head violently. "No. No, Oliver. Please. You promised you'd fuck me. Please. I need you."

Nick rolled off her and Oliver wasted no time in taking his place. Vanessa's legs clamped around Oliver's hips, her heels pressing into his gorgeous backside. Nick grabbed her foot and leaned in and kissed the cheek of Oliver's butt before he bit it. Oliver growled and shoved Nick away.

"Damn, that hurt," he complained.

"It was supposed to," Nick said with a laugh, lying back down. "That way you won't come the minute you enter her."

"I'm no green youth," Oliver mumbled. "I can hold back."

Nick just shook his head. "You haven't been inside her yet," he told him with a contented sigh. "She's perfect. And the first time she comes, you'll want to, too. Just remember she can come several more times."

"Oh, Nicky," Oliver said breathlessly, and Nick looked down at his hips to see him easing into Vanessa's damp heat. "She so tight and wet. You were here."

Vanessa was already sliding into orgasm. It was astounding. They barely fucked her and she came. Her body was made for cock. What would it be like when they were both inside her, one front and one back? Would she go off like this time and again? He dearly hoped so. How magnificent it would be to keep her coming all night, until she collapsed from exhaustion. Perhaps not so wonderful for her, but Nick felt his masculine pride swell at the idea of it.

Oliver fucked her slowly, clearly relishing every second of it. Vanessa whimpered and moaned and Nick could see her nails digging into Oliver's shoulders. He'd have half-moon marks. Nick would kiss each one and place his hands over them as he fucked Oliver for Vanessa. He had no doubts now that Vanessa would love to watch them. She was a sensual goddess, desire incarnate. She would love every wicked thing they wanted to do together, every wicked thing they'd ever dreamed of doing but had been too nervous to try. They'd do it all with Vanessa.

"Oh Vanessa, Vanessa," Oliver moaned, burying his face in the curve of her shoulder. She gripped the back of his head with one hand, her fist tangling in his blond hair, pulling it in her passion. She thrust up, giving as good as she was getting. She licked Oliver's ear, kissed his cheek, turned his head and kissed his pouty lips roughly. Nick realized then that Oliver

187

wasn't in charge. Vanessa was. She owned him completely at that moment. He would do anything to keep fucking her.

Vanessa bit Oliver's lower lip and held on, holding him like that as she came. Nick knew she was coming. He recognized it now. Her eyes were closed and her cheeks flushed as she tipped her head back slightly, dragging Oliver with her by the mouth, her hands gripping him tightly.

Oliver whimpered and Nick's cock began to harden again. He loved that sound. He loved the feel and sight of Vanessa coming, and the sound of Oliver's surrender.

"Keep fucking her," Nick ordered him. "Don't come yet. She's not done." Oliver's breathing was hard and erratic but he obeyed. He kept his hips pumping, driving into Vanessa as she moaned. "Yes, hard like that. She likes it hard," Nick murmured. He leaned up on one arm and placed his palm on Oliver's buttock, wanting to feel them fuck. It wasn't enough.

He sat up and straddled Oliver's backside. On each stroke the plump, firm flesh of Oliver's arse tapped Nick's growing cock. Oliver whimpered again and Nick put a hand on his hip, guiding him in and out of Vanessa and back into Nick.

"Oh yes," Vanessa said, her voice rough from her moans and suppressed cries. Nick loved the sound of it. It was the kind of voice that only came from fucking, or from sucking cock. He wanted her to speak like that from now on. "Are you going to do something with him?" Vanessa asked. The last word was high pitched and her eyes closed tightly. He thought she might be trying not to come again. She lost the battle with a moan.

"When you're done with him," Nick said, beginning to rub his cock on Oliver's cheek each time the two met when Oliver pulled out of Vanessa before driving back in.

Oliver made a sound between a moan and a whimper at Nick's words. "I can't last, Nicky," he said desperately. "I have to come. She feels so good. Nessa," he begged, "let me come."

"Yes, yes," she said between panting breaths. "I want you to. Oh God." She threw her head back as Oliver shouted and bowed his back, driving his cock into Vanessa. Nick wanted to be inside Oliver so much at that moment he nearly ignored every consideration and rammed into his beckoning entrance. He was pressed so tightly against Oliver he could feel the contractions of the muscles in his backside as he came with hard, sharp thrusts.

Vanessa was crying. Oliver rolled off her and gathered her in his arms. "Are you all right?" he asked, panic-stricken. "I didn't hurt you, did I?"

She shook her head. "No, no you didn't." She sniffed and looked up at him with eyes as big and beautifully brown as a doe's. "That was the most wonderful thing I've ever done." She reached for Nick and he crawled over behind her, spooning her and kissing her shoulder. "I've never felt this close to anyone. Never." She laid her head on Oliver's shoulder as Nick rubbed her back. "I hate that I can only have you for a short while."

Oliver's heart stuttered in his chest. It was true, wasn't it? They weren't the sorts of men that women like Vanessa married. She'd marry someone with a title, of course. Someone with wealth and power who could give her the life she deserved. He looked up at Nick, and Nick seemed angry and sad and everything Oliver was feeling.

There was one thing they could give her. They could give her passion.

"What do you want, Vanessa?" He tipped her face up to his. "Tell us. Whatever it is, if we can give it to you, we will. Let us do that for you. This night is yours."

Nick rolled away from her onto his back and he lay there in stony silence staring at the ceiling.

"I want it all," was her simple answer. "I don't have enough experience to know what to ask for, really. What haven't we done?"

Nick gave a rather harsh bark of laughter. "A great deal," he answered her. He rolled back over on his side as Vanessa went onto her back. Oliver fought back a smile at the choreography of bed sport. Vanessa looked up at Nick questioningly. "You haven't sucked either of our cocks," he told her in a silky voice as he trailed his fingers up her arm. She shivered against Oliver. "Did you know we could fuck you here, too?" Nick asked, sliding a hand under Vanessa. She squeaked and Nick laughed. "We can both fuck you at the same time if we do that." Vanessa's mouth gaped open and Oliver had never seen her eyes so wide. "And I can fuck Oliver like that."

At his last statement, Oliver's gaze flew to Nick, who was watching him carefully, his eyes heavy-lidded with desire. "I can guarantee no peer of the realm will do that for you," Nick said, his gaze cutting back to Vanessa. "Or whomever you end up marrying. Oh, they'll probably fuck the groom or the footman behind your back, but that's not the same as fucking another man for you, is it, Nessa?" Nick's voice was a growl now, and Vanessa's breathing was harsh, her chest rising and falling in excitement. "Because you'd like to see that, wouldn't you?" Nick asked. He traced her lips with his finger. "I bet you'll come, watching us."

Oliver's heart was tripping over itself in his chest. He'd wanted to fuck Nick, wanted to fuck him while Vanessa watched, even. He'd fantasized about it last night. But it was so soon. He'd hardly had time to accustom himself to being Nick's lover at all, and now this. But there was no denying he was growing hard again thinking about Nick's cock inside him.

"I will," Vanessa whispered. "I'll come for you, if you do that."

Nick and Vanessa turned to him then. He'd never felt so nervous, not even his first time with a woman. "Why me?" he asked, his mouth dry. He licked his lips and Nick's look as he stared at his mouth nearly scorched him. "Why not you?"

Nick gave him a predatory half-smile. "Because I think you want to be fucked by me more than you want to fuck me. Am I correct?"

Damn him. He was right. Oliver didn't even have to answer, Nick knew. He laughed and then he leaned over Vanessa and kissed Oliver to take away the sting of his amusement. "And because I want to fuck you very badly," he whispered.

"Well, who am I to say no?" Oliver replied in a voice too shaky for his liking. He cleared his throat and looked down at Vanessa with a smile. "It's for you, after all."

Vanessa laughed with Nick. "Oh, I don't think it's all for me," she teased, tweaking his chest hair.

Nick reached over and pulled a small box out from under the bed. When he opened it, Oliver saw a bottle inside. He recognized it. Many were the times he and Nick had used similar exotic oils with the women in their bed. "No sense wasting time," Nick said casually as he pulled the bottle out and tossed the box back onto the floor. "Roll over."

Oliver rolled over. That was how he was going to get through this. He'd just do what Nick told him to do. It was simple, really. Then he didn't have to think too much about the fact that Nick was about to fuck him. Then again, he'd just thought about it. He took a deep breath as Nick touched his hole with a slick finger, circling and circling around it, teasing. Oliver tried to relax. He imagined all the times he'd done this to a woman. If a woman could take a cock there, then surely he could. Men and women may be different in other respects, but in that way they were definitely the same.

"Can I touch myself?" Vanessa whispered. Oliver opened his eyes—he hadn't even realized he'd closed them—and saw

191

Vanessa was biting the inside of her lip, looking very hesitant. "I don't want to disturb you two or interrupt what you're doing. But I really need someone to touch me, and it looks as if I'm the only one available."

Oliver laughed and Nick chose that moment to slip the tip of his finger inside him. His laughter turned to a stunned gasp. His initial response was to tighten up and refuse Nick entrance, but he forced himself to relax again.

"Of course you can," Nick answered Vanessa. "I'd love to see you do that. Wouldn't you Oliver?"

"Yes." Oliver wasn't capable of drawn-out conversation at this juncture.

"Knees up," Nick said, and Oliver obeyed. Then Vanessa let out a breathy moan and he looked over to see her rubbing her quim. Damn she was wet, from herself and from both men filling her not too long ago. He lowered his arms and put his cheek on the bed, his head turned toward her to watch. His focus narrowed to Vanessa's hand and Nick's fingers fucking him.

Vanessa came and Oliver nearly cried out with her. How on earth could she do that? She ought to be exhausted. He didn't know how long she could keep this up. Was it just the excitement of her first time? He hoped not. "Again," he whispered. Without hesitation Vanessa spread the lips of her sex with one hand so he could see while she finger-fucked herself with the other.

Oliver's cock was hard. When Nick started he didn't think he could get excited this first time. He was so nervous, and the sensation was almost painful. Now, with Vanessa putting on a show for him and his hole opening for Nick he was getting harder by the second. "Now," he said. He looked over his shoulder at Nick. "Now."

Nick put the stopper on the bottle and rose on his knees behind Oliver. When Oliver felt Nick's cock pressing against him, demanding entry, he closed his eyes and let his other senses take over. He relaxed and pushed back against Nick. He could feel the large head opening him up and it stung, but Oliver welcomed the pain. He wanted it, wanted Nick inside him, and so he pushed back again, harder, and Nick slipped inside with a grunt. Vanessa let out a moan, and Oliver became aware of the smell of her arousal over the soothing scent of the almond oil. He felt Nick pour a few more drops of oil in his crease, so that it ran down to where Nick filled him, and he shivered in anticipation. His erection, which had flagged at Nick's entrance, began to grow again.

"Oh my God," Vanessa whispered. "You two look so incredible. I never imagined that two men doing that would be so beautiful together."

Her voice seemed to come from far away. Oliver was so intent on the feeling of Nick going deeper and deeper inside him with each thrust, the rest of the world was fading. "It feels so good, Nicky," he had to tell him. "You feel so good."

"Yes," Nick whispered back, breathless. He really began to fuck him then, in and out, penetrating Oliver in a steady rhythm. It was divine. After just a few minutes of that, Nick got rougher. He stroked harder and deeper, and Oliver whimpered at the pure, unadulterated pleasure coursing through him. He had to reach down and grab his cock and stroke it.

"Up," Vanessa said fervently. "Lift him up. I want it."

With a hand on his chest Nick pulled Oliver, until his back was to Nick's front. Oliver opened his eyes. Inside him, Nick hit a spot that had him seeing stars. "Just a little more," he begged. Nick obliged him, stroking into him roughly again, and Oliver came.

Then he felt Vanessa. She had her mouth wrapped around the tip of his cock and was sucking him as he came. It felt so right, so perfect to have both of them inside him and around him. He cried out, jerking his hips toward her, and she pulled back, startled. But immediately she returned and licked the end of his cock as the last few contractions of his orgasm rocked through him. She smeared his come around with her tongue and he couldn't stop shivering in Nick's arms. When his orgasm faded, Vanessa sat up and smiled at him. He was beyond words, his entire world shifting under him.

"Good?" Nick asked Vanessa.

She made a face. "Not really," she answered honestly.

"I liked it," Oliver rasped. He clutched Nick's hand on his chest. "When I tasted Nick's. I liked it."

Vanessa walked her fingers up Oliver's chest and pinched his nipple. "Then I shall have to taste Nick's too sometime."

Nick's hips jerked, and Oliver could feel him quivering inside his passage, like a racehorse at the gate, as if the stillness were excruciating for him. "Fuck me," he told Nick. "Finish it."

"Inside?" Nick growled.

Oliver nodded. "Yes. I want to feel it."

Vanessa slipped off to the side and Oliver went down on his hands and knees again. He was barely down before Nick began a punishing series of thrusts that shoved Oliver forward on the bed. Oliver whimpered, and then blurted out, "Good. Don't stop," afraid Nick might misinterpret the sound.

Nick didn't stop, not until he came. Then he thrust as deep into Oliver as he could, until Oliver could feel Nick's balls against his own. The sensation of Nick's cock jerking inside him as he climaxed was exciting and devastatingly intimate. Nick was filling him, fucking him, consummating a love that had gone unrecognized for years. His eyes found Vanessa, her face flushed, her legs spread with her hand buried between them again. Her gaze was hot and possessive as she watched them, as if it truly were all for her. This was it. There was no turning back. Like Vanessa, now that he'd known this he could not live without it.

Chapter Nine

ഇ

Nick helped Vanessa pull her dress down over her head. Women's fashions were a mystery. She seemed to think the lovely little dress was "too informal". What the hell did that mean? She'd snuck out in the middle of the night to fuck two men. Exactly how formal was one supposed to dress for that sort of thing? He wasn't the formal type, anyway. His fingers suddenly seemed too thick to help with the delicate row of ties on the bodice. Oliver gently pushed him out of the way and took over.

"We'll see you tomorrow, won't we?" Oliver asked. "What are we doing?"

"Yes, and I don't know," Vanessa said, laughing up at him.

Nick had wanted her before, when she seemed so cool and confident, hiding a sensuality that had the potential to take on him and Oliver at the same time. But now that he'd seen her laughing and teasing, and so caring at the orphanage, and experienced just how sensual she was, he nearly shook with the need to keep her by their side. Her desires matched theirs in every way. How on earth was he supposed to let her go? Not just tonight, but when Christmastide was over. She'd said as much, that their liaison was temporary. He suspected he and Nick would become something of a half-remembered dream for Vanessa. But Nick would never forget this night. He had taken both Vanessa and Oliver for the first time.

"Why are you smiling at me like a cat with a pitcher of cream?" Vanessa asked suspiciously.

"Just thinking about the hours past," Nick answered with a lascivious grin. "I would like to take you shopping tomorrow," he added. "Will you go with us?" What he really meant was *can* you go with us. So far, they'd limited their association to gatherings of friends, not true public outings. Perhaps he was pushing too hard, but he had to try to keep her.

Vanessa didn't hesitate. "Of course I will! I'd love to. I want to get Aunt Grace something special for staying with me over the holidays. When should we go?" She was so animated as she talked, obviously excited to see them tomorrow. Oliver was helping her into the voluminous cape again. She looked so diminutive in it, as if a good wind could blow her out of their lives.

"As early as propriety will allow," he answered. He stalked over and dragged her to him with the edges of the cape. He swooped down and kissed her roughly. She liked it rough. Oliver had been right. She wanted to be wanted, to be physically desired and conquered. And Nick wanted to do those things to her. He broke the kiss, but grabbed the back of her head and held her face tipped up to his. "I don't want to be apart any more than we have to. The hours without you will be endless."

"Nick," she whispered. "I don't know what to do with you. So silent most of the time, and then you make my heart sing with gruff confessions." In contrast to his rough hold, she slid her arm around his shoulders and kissed his lips sweetly. Her lips clung to his before she pulled away, breaking his hold on her. "Ten o'clock," she whispered. "In six hours' time. I must sleep, at least a little." Her smile was as sweet as her kiss, and Nick just nodded.

"Why shopping?" she asked as she fussed with her hair, pulling pins out and putting them back in. Nick didn't see a difference when she was done, but he was no ladies' maid.

"I want to buy you a gift. Something small and beautiful, like you. So you can keep it with you at all times." He desperately needed her to have something of him, no matter what happened after Twelfth Night.

"And there you go again," she whispered. She blew him a kiss.

"He doesn't waste words, does he?" Oliver asked as he kissed Vanessa's cheek. He winked at Nick. "I think he says those things because he likes to shock us with how sweet he is."

"I am not sweet," Nick responded, offended. "I am honest. There is a great deal of difference between the two." He walked over and opened the door, looking up and down the hallway. "We have to leave now if we are to return our prize before sunrise."

"What happened earlier today?" Vanessa asked Oliver as they sat in the hackney taking them back to her street. "At the orphanage?"

She took his hand and her hand was small and elegant in his. Oliver pulled it to his lips and kissed it, wishing she hadn't donned her gloves. But it was too cold out not to, he supposed. He pretended ignorance of what she was talking about. "When?"

Nick sat across from them, watching. He knew, but he wasn't going to reveal Oliver's secret. It was decent of him, really. Oliver could tell Nick was more than halfway in love with her. It must grate on him not to be able to tell her.

"When you couldn't find Nick," Vanessa said patiently. "Tell me."

Oliver had been avoiding her eyes, but now he looked at her and he couldn't deny the truth. He was more than halfway in love with her too. And it hurt him to keep secrets from her. There was no censure in her gaze, no accusations. She'd accepted so much about them already. This stupid weakness of his was surely the least of it.

"I don't like to be apart from him." He sighed. "That's not true. I *can't* be apart from him. If I can't see him, or at least know he's close, I panic. I can't breathe and I get rather…foolish. The whole thing is foolish." He said the last in disgust and let go of her hand.

She reached determinedly over and took his hand again. "It's not foolish. Why?"

"I don't know," Oliver said in frustration. "That's the damnedest part. I mean, I know he didn't just disappear. He's promised not to do that again. I know he won't."

"Again?" Vanessa asked, picking up on that one word.

"At Waterloo," Nick said. "I was injured and unconscious. They took me on one of the wagons to a private residence turned hospital. Oliver couldn't find me for a week."

Oliver's hand was fisted in his lap. He'd thought Nick was dead. It was a hellish week of trying to get permission to search for Nick and then pawing through dead bodies piled high, expecting to see Nick's ravaged face at any moment. When he'd found Nick, he'd been conscious again but his memory was addled. He'd imagined he was in Gloucester and Oliver was his older brother Tate. Oliver hadn't cared. He would have gladly been called Tate for the rest of his life. His commanding officer had finally found him there with Nick and nearly beaten him black and blue for deserting before dragging him back to his unit.

"That must have been awful for you, Oliver," Vanessa said quietly. She wrapped both hands around his one and cradled it to her cheek before kissing his knuckles. "I wish I had been there to help you."

God, he wished she had too. When he'd had to leave Nick, the nightmares had begun. They had gotten so bad he gave up sleeping. Eventually he gave up eating. Nick recovered enough to be sent home, and Oliver was sent with him. He was less than useless to his company, as his commanding officer had pointed out with disgust.

They hadn't been apart since.

"You helped me today," he told her. He didn't want to remember those days. He didn't want to reopen old wounds.

198

Vanessa had given him hope at the orphanage when her touch had stopped the fear from choking him. Maybe it was that simple. Maybe he just needed that kind of sympathetic touch to make him realize he wasn't alone. And maybe now Nick could do that for him too. He'd been afraid before. They'd both been afraid to show that side of their affection for each other. But Vanessa had taken away the fear.

What would happen to them when Vanessa was gone?

Vanessa watched the flame of her Christmas candle as the sun rose outside her window. Nick and Oliver had given it to her. Tradition said it should burn throughout the holiday, until Epiphany. But she wasn't sure she'd let it. She didn't want it to burn down and disappear. She wanted to keep it, to remember them. She was drying the rosemary and had already pressed some of the other greenery. She would keep them forever, or at least until they turned to dust and she was too old to remember.

They all knew they had only a few more days. Vanessa had alluded to it, but neither of the men had acknowledged her warning. Going shopping with them tomorrow was a mistake, but it was one she had to make. She wanted to spend more time with them. She might rue the day, but first she would enjoy it. She'd wanted to weep when Nick told her he wanted to give her a gift she could keep with her always. Didn't he realize they'd already done that? The memories of their affair would be her constant companions for many years to come.

They'd seen the real Vanessa and they hadn't been disgusted or shocked. Quite the opposite. They wanted to spend more time with her. They wanted her, not a Carlton-Smythe. Just Vanessa. How could she regret that? She didn't know what tomorrow would bring, but she was counting the hours until she saw them again. She felt a twinge of uneasiness over her longing for them. She mustn't need them too much, mustn't rely on seeing them to get through each day. It could only end in disaster if she let herself become too attached.

Wearily she climbed into bed. She had only a couple of hours to sleep before they came for her.

"What a lovely day it's been," Vanessa sighed happily, her arm linked with Oliver's while Nick walked next to her, holding her packages. Except for the very special one nestled in her reticule.

"If you like blustery, cold winter days," Nick said wryly. "Then yes, it's been lovely."

Oliver laughed. "I for one never felt a bit of the chill, warmed as I was by your company, dear lady," he said gallantly, patting her hand. "And memories of last night, of course." Vanessa tugged on his arm in reproach, glancing about to make sure no one was near to hear him. She earned no more than a lascivious look from him for her trouble.

"I was near to melting in the heat of those reminiscences," Nick agreed. "We should get through this winter quite comfortably, I think."

"Shh," Vanessa hissed. "What if someone hears you?"

Nick looked around incredulously at the empty street and sidewalk. "It's freezing out here, Vanessa. No one in his or her right mind is walking about."

"We are," she declared.

"My point exactly." Nick's droll reply had Oliver laughing again.

"Oh, don't be cross," Vanessa begged. "I just wanted a little more time with you. I didn't make you walk me all the way home from Bond Street, did I? I had the hackney stop just around the corner."

Nick stopped and so did she and Oliver. "I'm not complaining," Nick said with such a serious look on his face.

"I'm glad you did. I'd freeze my arse off for one more minute with you, and that's the truth."

"I like it on you," she said seriously, "so let's try to avoid that catastrophe." Nick looked so shocked at her humor that she burst out laughing. "Oh, darling, how I adore you," she blurted without thinking. She quickly turned away, her heart pounding at her slip of the tongue. She mustn't give him false hope. No matter how much she adored him, she would never be allowed to marry him, or Oliver either.

"I adore you too," he said. There was nothing light in his tone, and Vanessa took it for it was — a declaration.

"We are all agreed on it, then," Oliver said lightly. "We are adorable." He paused a moment and then added, "And we do not want Nick to lose his arse."

Nick's smile was reluctant but genuine. "Thank you. Your good wishes are duly noted."

Vanessa's laugh was forced. "Positively adorable," she agreed. "Here we are." They had arrived at her door and were halfway up the steps before Vanessa noticed the knocker in its place. Her feet froze on the steps as denial screamed through her head. She was supposed to have four more days.

"What is it?" Oliver asked with an inquisitive look.

Nick was looking around with a frown, trying to find what was wrong. But Vanessa couldn't answer. If she didn't say the words she could stand here with them all day and pretend.

The door opened and Greely stood off to the side, leaving her room to enter, but not Nick or Oliver. She started to put her hand up, as if to tell him, *no, don't say it,* but he didn't give her the chance. "Good afternoon, Lady Vanessa," he said, reaching for her packages. "Your parents have returned. Your father asked that you see him in his study immediately upon your return."

"Good afternoon, sir," Vanessa said as she entered her father's study. She walked around his desk and kissed his proffered cheek. "I trust you had a pleasant journey?"

"I did not," he replied coolly. He gestured to the chair in front of his desk. How she hated that chair and the hours she had spent there listening to countless lectures about her duty to her family and her station. Deportment, charitable obligations, social obligations, marital obligations, duty to her family, duty to her church, the responsibility she bore them all. And she mustn't forget the servants and the lower classes! God forbid she set a bad example for them. Her head ached with the weight of all those words.

"I'm sorry to hear that," she said politely as she took a seat. "Is Mother well?"

"As well as can be expected," he replied cryptically, and Vanessa's uneasiness grew.

"Oh?" she answered, standing. "Perhaps I should go to her?"

"Sit." Her father's one-word reply brooked no disobedience. She sat. "I have brought a suitor home to meet you. I find him an excellent candidate for marriage. I expect that you shall agree. After you have been introduced tomorrow and the formalities have been exchanged, you will excuse yourself and retire to your room so that I may discuss the details of the marriage arrangement. Do you understand?"

Vanessa's head was spinning. She feared she might actually swoon, which would never do, of course. True ladies did not swoon. "What?" she whispered.

Her father frowned at her. "News of your holiday activities reached us in Kent. Lady Dalrymple is a cousin of Mrs. Bent, another houseguest." He sighed and leaned back in his chair. "After Ashland's rejection, I felt pity for you and did not push for another betrothal as I should have. You have clearly been given too much freedom, and as such have gotten yourself into trouble, which is to be expected I suppose, with only your Aunt Grace to see to you, although it is a great disappointment."

"Where is Aunt Grace?" Vanessa interrupted, fearing what her father may have done in his anger. Vanessa didn't want the dear lady banished to the country because of her poor judgment.

"She is packing," her father said. "She and your mother will be going back to Kent tomorrow." He sighed unhappily. "I took you for a girl with a sense of decorum and a high degree of gratitude for all you have been given. I see this is not the case. A respectable marriage to a man of adequate social standing and impeachable reputation should put any rumors to rest."

"You've found another available duke, then?" Vanessa asked sarcastically. It was common knowledge that she'd been raised to marry a duke, and when the only available one rejected her, her father was too arrogant to accept anything less. Pity for her had nothing to do with it. She knew her anger would not be appreciated, but at that moment she didn't care.

"No." Her father's clipped response indicated he was as angry as she. "Another great disappointment for this family. Because of your failure to secure Ashland, we shall be forced to ally ourselves with a mere baron."

A baron! Vanessa nearly gaped in astonishment. Oh, this was bad indeed. She'd expected some ancient Bavarian duke, at the very least. Marriage or not, she'd be a virtual outcast from the rest of the family as the wife of a mere baron.

"I shall send for you when Lord Wetherald gets here. You are dismissed."

And that was that, Vanessa thought wearily as she got to her feet. Her father was already reading some correspondence, having ended their conversation. It was also the end to all her hopes and dreams, which it seemed she had been harboring despite her own warnings. What a foolish, foolish girl she was.

Chapter Ten

ॐ

"How do you do, Lady Vanessa?" Lord Wetherald said politely as he bowed over her hand.

He was unexceptional. Not offensive in any way, simply one of the hundreds of well-dressed gentlemen out and about London each day, too involved with his own business to smile at the world as he passed. He had unremarkable light-brown hair of which one section had the unfortunate tendency to fall across his forehead—ruining the sartorial perfection of his appearance—and light-blue eyes, which looked rather tired. He was neither tall nor short, fat nor thin. In other words, unexceptional. The only thing that set him apart, Vanessa supposed, was his mustache and beard, which were not all that fashionable. He had the look of a cavalier from an earlier century.

"How do you do," she murmured politely. She glided over and took a seat on the sofa in front of the window, directly in the middle to avoid his trying to sit next to her. A very long night of thinking about marriage to a stranger had made her even more averse to the idea.

"Lady Vanessa is aware of our plans, Wetherald," her father said, surprising her. His comment bordered on rudeness, which was quite uncharacteristic of him.

"Excellent," Lord Wetherald said after a short but noticeable silence. "Then I trust it is permissible to ask to speak with her alone?"

Vanessa turned away quickly so he wouldn't see her dismay, which she was sure showed in her wide eyes and nervous swallow.

"Of course," her father said. "The sooner, the better, I say. No sense prolonging the inevitable, eh?" His joviality was so forced it was painful for Vanessa to hear. He knew she was unhappy with this match. Damn him for forcing it on her. She glared daggers at his back as he hastily left the room. The door was left slightly ajar for propriety's sake, and it was on the tip of Vanessa's tongue to tell him not to bother.

Vanessa took great care in smoothing out her skirt so it fell just right along the edge of the sofa. Then she clasped her hands in her lap and sat very still.

"Lady Vanessa," Lord Wetherald finally said quietly. She flinched at the sound of his voice and he sighed. "I realize that we are virtual strangers, but surely you must know that your father would never approve my suit if he did not find me above reproach. You have nothing to fear from me."

That did make Vanessa raise her eyes to meet his gaze. "I am not afraid of you, sir, but rather…uneasy over the circumstances of this meeting."

He looked surprised by her calm response. "Uneasy? In what way?"

"As you said, we are strangers, and yet I presume you are here to reach the conclusive end of a non-existent suit."

He ran his hand contemplatively over his beard. "You presume correctly. I was led to believe by your father that you would welcome my proposal."

"I will, of course, do as my father wishes," she replied. It wasn't a lie, though it was far from an affirmation.

"Whether or not it is your wish as well?" he asked wryly. Before she could answer, he walked over and quietly closed the door. "Well," he continued, "that is too bad. I'm not sure I wish to marry a woman who cares so little about happiness."

Vanessa grew wary. She may not want the marriage, but her father would never tolerate it if she drove his chosen suitor away. She really didn't know what he'd do if Wetherald cried off. "You misunderstand me, my lord," she corrected him. "I will marry you if it comes to that." Though she dearly hoped it wouldn't come to that. "I do not know you well yet, but I am sure we shall suit if my father favors the match."

"Do I misunderstand? So you wish to marry me, above all things, even duty?"

Vanessa frowned. "Now you are playing games with me, my lord. I do not like games."

"This is no game, Lady Vanessa," Wetherald said quietly. "It is our future you toy with. Tell me now, what is your heart's desire?"

"My heart's desire, my lord? What an odd notion! As if my heart feels separately from my head. I assure you, my lord, I have felt no desire that I have not imagined first." Unbidden, memories of her night with Oliver and Nick came crashing through her composure and she quickly turned away, pressing her tightly fisted hand into her stomach as she tried to breathe through the ache in her chest.

"You did not answer my question." Wetherald was determined. He walked over and planted himself firmly in her line of sight. "Let me speak plainly. Do you desire me as a husband?"

"No!" The truth burst from her in rush of emotion, and Vanessa tried in vain to stem her tears. "But that hardly matters, does it? Many people marry without desire. We cannot always have what we desire, for oh so many reasons." Wetherald shoved a handkerchief into her hand and Vanessa noisily blew her nose. Her celebrated decorum was dissolving faster than sugar in the rain.

"Does your heart belong to another, Lady Vanessa?" he asked softly. She nodded, not willing to say it out loud for fear the hopelessness of it all would overwhelm her.

"Then why have you not told your father? Surely he would sympathize. He cares for you. I was not selected for you without a great deal of scrutiny."

Vanessa laughed bitterly. "I assure you, sir, the scrutiny was to protect the family name and not my sensibilities."

"He is unsuitable, then." Wetherald took a seat next to her, careful not to wrinkle his coat. Vanessa almost smiled. For some reason his precise mannerisms were endearing rather than annoying. "Does he return your feelings?"

Vanessa twisted the handkerchief in her hands as she thought about it. Did they? She believed so. No words of love had been exchanged, but it had been there in each word and touch during their night together and the following day. Hadn't she turned away from Nick's longing glances, and ignored the unspoken questions lying beneath Oliver's carefully chosen words? She'd tried to drive them away. Had she succeeded? It was for the best if she had. "I don't know," she mumbled finally, unable to bear Wetherald's patient silence any longer.

"Then marry me," he said simply. She didn't bother to try and hide her shock. He smiled wryly. "You are a very desirable match for me, Lady Vanessa," he explained. "You come from an influential family, have poise, breeding, intelligence and looks. You will be an asset in my political career, exactly what I need in a wife. Your confessions here today only confirm my impressions. It is one thing to love and be loved in return, but to throw away a happy future—and I do believe we could be happy—for an unrequited love is quite another."

"My feelings are returned," she said firmly, "though what good that does us is beyond me."

"I see." Wetherald stared hard at her for a minute, clearly weighing her words. She returned his look, determined he see the truth. Finally he nodded. "I am not ready to walk away from such an advantageous union," he said. Vanessa was about to protest when he added, "Yet."

Vanessa gathered her courage. "Then perhaps I should tell you, Lord Wetherald, that I am very likely with child." That was what had kept Vanessa awake all night. She hadn't thought about it when she was with Oliver and Nick. Not until her father confronted her with Wetherald had she realized there might be consequences from their illicit passion. She hoped she was. No matter what happened with her father or Wetherald, or Oliver and Nick, Vanessa wanted proof she'd lived her life to the fullest and experienced a kind of passion that came only once in a lifetime, and even then only to a lucky few. To bear Nick or Oliver's child would be the greatest joy to her.

"I know you told me that believing it would end any interest I have in a match with you," Wetherald said after moment of hesitation. He was frowning and suddenly rose from the sofa and began to pace in front of her. "On the contrary, it has only strengthened my resolve to marry you should marriage between you and your paramour turn out to be impossible."

"I could not ask that of you," Vanessa said, shocked at his uncommon chivalry. "Whatever my circumstances, they are not your responsibility. I am not your responsibility. We've only just met. You may walk away content with the knowledge that you offered your protection. I decline it, though I thank you."

When Wetherald turned to her, Vanessa could see the determination in his face. She was struck with the notion that he must be a formidable opponent in the political arena. "I must insist on the man's name, Lady Vanessa."

Vanessa rose on shaky legs. "I will not reveal it to you. You have no responsibility here, no right to interfere."

"I take the responsibility and my right is the right of a gentleman to protect and defend the weaker sex. I cannot in good conscience walk out that door and leave you defenseless in your present circumstances. I could not do that and call myself a gentleman."

Just then there was a commotion outside and the door was thrown open. Vanessa jumped up with a gasp as Nick marched into the room, Oliver close behind him.

"Stop them!" she heard her father thunder from the hallway.

"You cannot marry him," Nick growled angrily. "You belong with us."

They'd worked it all out on the way over here. The last day without Vanessa, believing her lost forever to them, had been torture. Nick had been so angry at the world. But then Oliver had thought, why not? Why can't we have her? Nick had money and an estate, even if it was small. Surely her father would accept Nick's suit if it was what Vanessa wanted. They'd been slowly working up to it, anyway. It was as clear as day they were meant to be together. But they didn't have time to go slow. Circumstances were working against them. It wasn't that Nick or Oliver needed more time, but they were worried that Vanessa might. Marriage to Nick, and a commitment to both men, was a huge and rather scary step for a woman like Vanessa, who'd been shielded from the cruelty of society for most of her life.

Nick had grasped this chance with determination and they'd come without warning today to ask for her hand. Only to be greeted by her father, who had taken them to task for leading her astray during the frivolous Christmastide season. He'd firmly told them she was going to marry some baron and they were not to try to see her ever again. Without another word they'd stormed out of his study and begun searching for her. Luckily they found her before they were ejected from the house.

Oliver watched Vanessa as she went from shocked incredulity to a relieved smile. "Nick!" she exclaimed. As she began to run across the room to Nick she was stopped in her tracks by the man her father had chosen for her. He was unprepossessing to say the least, although the odd Van Dyke beard he wore gave him a rather dashing, romantic look, like a cavalier from another century. Oliver hated him on sight.

"Lady Vanessa," the baron said firmly. "You must let your father and me handle this."

Nick took a menacing step toward him. "Get your hands off her."

"Lord Wetherald," she said, trying to tug her arm free. "You must believe me when I tell you Nick would never harm me."

The stranger shook his head. "No. Not after what you've told me."

"Explain yourself," Nick demanded. It was one of the hardest things Oliver had ever done to stand there and say nothing. But they'd decided Nick must do all the talking. There must be no hint of an intimate relationship between Oliver and Vanessa. If they wanted her father to agree to Nick's proposal he must believe it was Nick and Nick alone that Vanessa was to be with.

"I am Lord Ambrose Wetherald and I promised Lady Vanessa that I would marry her, regardless of her past association with you." Nick took another step toward them and reached for Vanessa, but Wetherald knocked Nick's hand away in disgust. "As far as I'm concerned you don't deserve her. What were you thinking to drag an innocent young lady into debauchery and ruin? She may be carrying a child, thanks to you. Did you even think of that? What it would mean for her? Did you even care?"

"Get out," Lord Carlton-Smythe ordered the staff that had gathered in the doorway and were openly gaping at the scene. As one they turned and scurried off.

Oliver's head was spinning. A child. No, he hadn't thought of it. And if he had, he would have ignored the danger, would have embraced the idea of Vanessa round with their child. He glanced at Nick, who was staring at the floor.

"Yes, I thought of it," Nick said quietly to Oliver's surprise. He looked up and stared balefully at Wetherald. "And I wanted it."

Oliver grew hopeful. If she were pregnant with their child they would have to let Nick marry her.

"Have you no decency?" Wetherald angrily pounded his fist against his thigh. "Dammit! Didn't you think what this would mean for her? Is that what you want? Do you want to ruin her in the eyes of society? Turn her into nothing more than a whore?"

Nick growled and ran at Wetherald, ramming him up against the wall with his arm across the smaller man's throat. "Don't ever call her that again," he snarled. "Do you hear me?"

"It is not I who will say it," Wetherald gasped. "But society. You know it. Is that what you want for her?" Nick let him go abruptly and backed away, shaking his head. Wetherald rubbed his neck. "I will marry her, regardless of whether or not she's carrying a child." His voice was hoarse but sincere.

Vanessa was shaking her head. "No." She was growing more agitated by the second. Her head was pounding from her brief emotional outburst earlier. She really mustn't cry again. It was terribly distracting when one was trying to keep her wits about her. "This is all hypothetical, my lord. I don't know if I am indeed carrying, nor do I know if..." she paused, looking between Nick and Oliver, "Nick is able to offer for me at present."

"Perhaps it would have been wise to ascertain that before leaping into a liaison?" her father said sharply.

"I did not leap," Vanessa responded just as sharply. "I did not entertain the notion that the liaison would last longer than Christmastide."

Her father and Wetherald looked shocked. "You gave your innocence knowing that the connection was to be temporary? But why?" her father spluttered.

"You would not understand." Vanessa turned her back on him and stared beseechingly at Oliver. He could say nothing or he risked ruining their chances. Couldn't she see that?

"You presume," Wetherald said in a clipped tone. "I have offered to protect you should the need arise. Please show me the respect I believe justified by that action and reveal your reasons to us."

"Fine," she snapped, whipping around to face him. "I am suffocating in this life." She pounded her chest with her fist, letting her anger out for perhaps the first time in her life. Inside, Oliver was cheering her on. "I am trapped in here. I do not want this life. I do not want to be a Carlton-Smythe and all that the name requires and implies. I want to be Vanessa. I want to be free to come and go as I please, to marry or not marry as I please, to know that the man who takes me to bed wants *me* and not my family or my wealth or my connections. Just me. I want to laugh and dance and play with children and walk down the street with my lover without the censorious eyes of society condemning me. I cannot eat, breathe, blink or think without someone watching me for the tiniest little mistake, one slight variation from the path mapped out for me. I am dying inside. Or I was. Until I met Oliver and Nick I didn't even realize that slowly, insidiously, the real Vanessa was dying, becoming a marionette dancing on the strings everyone else was pulling." She slashed her hand through the air. "I'm tired of dancing on a string. I'm done." She sat down abruptly, breathing heavily, suddenly exhausted.

Wetherald stood there blinking at her in stunned astonishment. "Well," he said awkwardly.

"Yes," she agreed wearily, "well."

"I am able to offer for you," Nick said quietly. He went and kneeled in front of her. Then he reached into the pocket of his coat and pulled out a small bouquet.

"Mistletoe," she whispered as she took it. She grew teary-eyed. "Thank you." She looked behind him for Oliver, and he read the thank-you for him, too, in her face.

212

"I gladly offer for you," Nick told her. "I love you, Vanessa. Marry me. Walk down the street with me. Play with our children and dance every day. I don't care about your family. We will walk away from here right now with nothing but each other. Say yes."

Oliver felt the pain of not being able to speak cut through his chest. Vanessa turned tearful eyes to him and he nodded, trying to say without words that he felt the same. Her father intercepted the look.

"Who are you, sir?" he asked suspiciously.

"Oliver Gabriel, my lord, at your service," he said with a respectful bow of his head.

"Mr. Gabriel is a dear friend," Nick said as he stood up, still holding Vanessa's hand. "We served in the war together. He is here to support me."

Her father turned to her. "And these are the men we heard about? The ones you were carrying on with while we were in Kent?"

"We met Vanessa at the Shelbys' Christmas Eve dinner, sir," Nick answered, making an obvious effort to be respectful. "Perhaps it was wrong, but as soon as I saw her I began my pursuit without waiting for your return or permission. I beg your indulgence. My only excuse is that I fell in love with her soon after we met."

"My indulgence?" her father sputtered. "You blithely inform me that you have ruined my daughter, debauched her and left her carrying your child, and you have the effrontery to beg my *indulgence*?"

Oliver winced. Nick took a deep breath, his eyes narrowed in anger. "I did not leave her carrying my child. I am here to marry her. I want to marry her. I love her."

"Mr. Wilkes is far from an ill-advised match, sir," Oliver argued. Since Lord Carlton-Smythe had brought him into the conversation, he would say his piece. "He served valiantly at Waterloo, was injured in the line of duty and was decorated

213

for his service. He has an income of seven thousand pounds a year and a small estate in Oxford. More than enough to take care of Vanessa and a family."

"I need to know how Oliver feels," Vanessa said suddenly. She worried her lower lip for a moment, while Oliver's gaze clashed with the confused one of her father. Wetherald appeared stunned.

"Why?" her father demanded.

Wetherald cleared his throat. "Might I suggest that a simple explanation is preferable?"

"Yes," Oliver said. "A thousand times yes. This will work. Is it what you want? Say it is." He hadn't even considered that Vanessa would want a normal marriage to Nick, that she might reject the idea of the three of them together.

"It is," she said fervently, holding out her hand to him. He crossed the room quickly and took it, kissing her palm, not caring what her father or Wetherald thought of it.

Her father suddenly sank down in the nearest chair. He slumped over, his elbows resting on his knees. Wetherald rushed to cover the awkward silence. "Let us all remember that whatever happens in the privacy of the home is between a man and his wife and no one else."

"Yes," Nick agreed from Vanessa's other side. "Thank you."

"I did not choose Wetherald without thought for your wishes, Vanessa," Lord Carlton-Smythe said wearily. "Is he not in favor of expanding women's rights? My lord," he addressed Wetherald, beseeching him with a raised hand. "Did you not tell me you wanted a wife who would devote her energy to charitable causes?" He turned to Vanessa. "And isn't that orphanage the only thing that seems to make you happy?"

Vanessa looked at Oliver and then Nick, searching for guidance. By unspoken agreement, they remained silent. Whatever happened here would set the stage for Vanessa's future relationship with her family, and it was up to her to settle it. Finally she rose and went to her father.

"Thank you." She caught his attention, although his eyes met hers for only a second before focusing over her shoulder. "And you were correct. Wetherald was an excellent choice for me." Hope sprang to life in her father's expression but her next words killed it. "But that was before I met Nick and...and fell in love." She glanced at Oliver and he knew she'd almost said the one thing that her father might not forgive if it was spoken aloud. "Please, Father." She placed a hand over his on his knee. "Please understand. All those things are important to me. But I can have those and love if I marry Nick. Isn't that better? Isn't that what you want for me?"

He sat there for a moment, staring at her hand on his while Oliver held his breath. Then he briefly squeezed her hand, let go, sat back and looked at Nick. "I want assurances her dowry will be set aside for Vanessa's use. You're not to touch it. Any expenditures of that money will require prior approval from my man of business, who will manage the funds."

"Of course," Nick agreed immediately. "Whatever you wish."

"She must have adequate pin money," her father insisted. "I'll not have her looking shabby. She's a Carlton-Smythe."

"Absolutely," Nick agreed. "She may have as much as she needs."

"Come from trade, do you?" Her father stood up. "As long as you didn't crawl from the gutter, I can spin a tale that will keep the tongues from wagging too viciously."

"Hardly the gutter, sir," Nick replied stiffly. "Gloucester."

"Humph," her father grunted, making it clear he thought the two were located very near each other. "Let's have done with this, then," he ordered. He turned unexpectedly on Vanessa. "How far along are you?" he demanded, clearly shocking her.

215

"I am not at all sure I'm going to have a child," she confessed sheepishly. "I never should have mentioned it."

"Yes, you should have. If there is even a possibility, measures must be taken. You know this is true," her father said briskly. He turned to Wetherald. "I trust we can rely on your discretion in this matter, sir?"

Wetherald bowed. "Of course, my lord. Lady Vanessa," he said bowing to her as well. "As I told you, this would have been an advantageous match for me. And as you may have guessed, my heart is not engaged elsewhere." The smile he gave her was rueful. "The fact is, Lady Vanessa, that I'm fairly sure, given the chance, my heart would gladly have engaged itself to you."

Vanessa laughed a little tearfully while Nick put his arm around her shoulders. "Then I pity your heart. I would make a poor anchor for it, I think."

Wetherald smiled gently. "Nonsense. I don't think Mr. Wilkes is worried about his heart at all. Do you need any assistance in procuring a special license? I know someone in the bishop's employ."

"Thank you, no," Vanessa's father said. "I'm sure I shall have no trouble."

Wetherald saluted Nick and then, after a brief hesitation, turned to Oliver and inclined his head. "Good afternoon, gentlemen." From his expression it was clear Wetherald had a very good idea of what was going on.

After Wetherald left, her father sighed. "Good," he said, nodding. "The sooner we have the wedding the better, then. The timing will work. How long do you need to prepare?"

Vanessa quickly calculated in her head. "Two days," she told him. That would mean she would marry on Twelfth Night. She smiled at how fitting that was. This marriage was the greatest gift she would ever receive. To be Mrs. Nicholas

Wilkes by Epiphany was the perfect end to this magical holiday season.

She looked over at Nick and Oliver. They were looking back at her, and their expressions said they felt the same way.

"May we have a moment, sir?" Nick asked. Her father narrowed his eyes, looking at all three of them. "Please, sir," Nick said humbly, surprising Vanessa. "Just a moment."

Her father opened the door. "I'll be right outside. You may have a minute."

When the door closed she threw herself into Oliver's arms. "Oh, darling," she whispered. "Thank you. I know how hard that was for you." He didn't say anything, just kissed her passionately, letting his emotions loose in his kiss. When he finally let her go she was breathless and smiling. She loved the way they kissed her, as if there was nothing more important in the world.

"I would do anything for you, Vanessa," Oliver told her. "Do not doubt that, ever." He moved away from both her and Nick and faced them, his expression grim. "And that includes leaving you both. You know it would be better if you were two instead of three. You don't need me."

"Don't be an ass," Nick muttered. "Of course we need you. You can't go," he said quietly. "Not just because you will go mad without us, but because we would go mad without you." He reached out and palmed the back of Oliver's head, touching their foreheads together. "I got her for you, you know."

"What do you mean?" both Vanessa and Oliver asked.

"That night at Shelby's. Oliver talked about how lonely you were, and I saw the same sort of sadness in his eyes. I helped pursue you, Vanessa, because Oliver wanted you and I would do anything for him. Anything." Nick had let go of him and was pacing.

Vanessa felt a brief moment of panic before she remembered all the things they'd done and said the last few days. She knew he felt more than that now. "But you love her, Nick," Oliver said, voicing what Vanessa was thinking. "I know you do."

Nick nodded. "Yes. I didn't plan on it." He looked ruefully at Vanessa. "I'm sorry, love, but it's true. I didn't want to love you. But Oliver was right. Your eyes spoke to me as well. When we banished the loneliness from your eyes I knew that I'd do anything for you too." His hands fisted at his sides. "We were so caught up in the end of things. The end of the war, the end of our army careers. It just seemed like the end of everything. I didn't understand until you, Vanessa, that what we needed was a new beginning."

She grabbed Nick's hand and dragged him over to Oliver where she put her arms around both of them, forming a tight little circle of the three of them. "I like my mistletoe," she told them. They both looked confused by her change of topic. She smiled. "I've liked all the gifts you've given me. Look." She opened the gold locket she wore on a chain around her neck, the one they'd bought her yesterday, and showed them the small sprigs of rosemary and ivy inside. "But the gift of a life with the two of you is the greatest gift of all." She laughed. "And we shall be married on Twelfth Night! We should have a huge celebration."

Oliver nuzzled her ear. "Oh, it will be huge all right."

Nick laughed at his suggestive tone and nuzzled her neck on the other side. "Mmm-hmm," he agreed.

"Don't be silly," she said breathlessly, praying her father didn't walk in too soon. "I meant with all our friends."

"I meant with just the three of us," Oliver said, kissing her cheek.

"That too," she whispered. Both men kissed her then, taking turns at her lips and kissing each other, too.

"I love you. Merry Christmas," she said against the corner of Nick's mouth as he kissed Oliver. He smiled and they broke their kiss to hug her. "Merry Christmas, darling," Nick said as Oliver kissed her again.

Also by Samantha Kane

ℰ

eBooks:

A Lady in Waiting
Brothers in Arms 1: The Courage to Love
Brothers in Arms 2: Love Under Siege
Brothers in Arms 3: Love's Strategy
Brothers in Arms 4: At Love's Command
Brothers in Arms 5: Retreat From Love
Brothers in Arms 6: Love in Exile
Brothers in Arms 7: Love's Fortress
Brothers in Arms 8: Prisoner of Love
Brothers in Arms 9: Love's Surrender
Cougar Challenge 1: Play it Again, Sam
Ellora's Cavemen: Jewels of the Nile II *(anthology)*
Hunters for Hire: Tomorrow
Islands

Print Books:

Aged to Perfection *(anthology)*
Brothers in Arms 1: The Courage to Love
Brothers in Arms 2: Love Under Siege
Brothers in Arms 4: At Love's Command
Brothers in Arms 5: Retreat From Love
Brothers in Arms 6: Love in Exile
Brothers in Arms 7: Love's Fortress
Brothers in Arms 8: Prisoner of Love

Cougar Challenge: Tempt the Cougar *(anthology)*
Ellora's Cavemen: Jewels of the Nile II *(anthology)*
Hunters for Hire: Tomorrow

About the Author

ᔆᕍ

Samantha has a Master's Degree in History, and is a full time writer and mother. She lives in North Carolina with her husband and three children.

ᔆᕍ

The author welcomes comments from readers. You can find her website and email address on her author bio page at www.ellorascave.com.

Tell Us What You Think

We appreciate hearing reader opinions about our books. You can email us at Comments@EllorasCave.com.

Why an electronic book?

We live in the Information Age—an exciting time in the history of human civilization, in which technology rules supreme and continues to progress in leaps and bounds every minute of every day. For a multitude of reasons, more and more avid literary fans are opting to purchase e-books instead of paper books. The question from those not yet initiated into the world of electronic reading is simply: *Why?*

1. *Price.* An electronic title at Ellora's Cave Publishing runs anywhere from 40% to 75% less than the cover price of the exact same title in paperback format. Why? Basic mathematics and cost. It is less expensive to publish an e-book (no paper and printing, no warehousing and shipping) than it is to publish a paperback, so the savings are passed along to the consumer.

2. *Space.* Running out of room in your house for your books? That is one worry you will never have with electronic books. For a low one-time cost, you can purchase a handheld device specifically designed for e-reading. Many e-readers have large, convenient screens for viewing. Better yet, hundreds of titles can be stored within your new library—on a single microchip. There are a variety of e-readers from different manufacturers. You can also read e-books on your PC or laptop computer. (Please note that Ellora's Cave does not endorse any specific brands.

You can check our website at www.ellorascave.com for information we make available to new consumers.)

3. *Mobility.* Because your new e-library consists of only a microchip within a small, easily transportable e-reader, your entire cache of books can be taken with you wherever you go.

4. *Personal Viewing Preferences.* Are the words you are currently reading too small? Too large? Too… ANNOYING? Paperback books cannot be modified according to personal preferences, but e-books can.

5. *Instant Gratification.* Is it the middle of the night and all the bookstores near you are closed? Are you tired of waiting days, sometimes weeks, for bookstores to ship the novels you bought? Ellora's Cave Publishing sells instantaneous downloads twenty-four hours a day, seven days a week, every day of the year. Our webstore is never closed. Our e-book delivery system is 100% automated, meaning your order is filled as soon as you pay for it.

Those are a few of the top reasons why electronic books are replacing paperbacks for many avid readers.

As always, Ellora's Cave welcomes your questions and comments. We invite you to email us at Comments@ellorascave.com or write to us directly at Ellora's Cave Publishing Inc., 1056 Home Avenue, Akron, OH 44310-3502.

MAKE EACH DAY MORE *EXCITING* WITH OUR

ELLORA'S
CAVEMEN
CALENDAR

✝ WWW.ELLORASCAVE.COM ✝

ELLORA'S CAVE
Romanticon

Annual convention
for women who
refuse to behave